# MY FEET DON'T TOUCH THE GROUND

W. LEE BAKER

My Feet Don't Touch the Ground


ISBN: 978-1-7367318-6-4
Library of Congress Control Number: 2021943573

*To my wife Rebecca.*
*With your encouragement and support,*
*this book has come to life.*

# CHAPTER ONE
# HOME

I was born in the wrong house.

Mama's nagging could make anybody want to jump out a window. Outside, the trees in the woods whispered when I walked with them all around me, and they would bend over just enough to keep me out of the sun. They were real good friends.

When I had to be inside, it was like carryin' rocks around. Li'l sis Adele only stayed inside to play with her doll all day. Li'l brother Tom ran around making noise—and trouble, more often than not. Made me crazy when he stomped along, banging on things just to make noise. I suppose our place was like most, a fine-built log cabin that was cozy for us. Mama would sit out front in her chair anytime she could, lookin' out somewhere past the hills around our valley. The hills were covered with trees all the way up to where they met the sky. I'd sit beside her and watch the quiet look on her face. I'd wonder what she could be thinkin'. Whenever I asked her a plain enough question, she'd say something like, "The world is the way it is, and it don't matter what anyone thinks about it." I told myself that someday I might find out different. Here, there was just no way to tell, but I tried to not let it get me down.

I felt like something considerable was different in me. Something else besides my foot that's kinda twisted. I was born that way, so usually I get around just fine. It is turned some to one side so when I have shoes, that side wears out faster than the other one. When I was small it didn't bother me much because I didn't take notice. But when I got out and found other kids, they could be right mean sometimes. That made me want to hide my face. Had to walk around, didn't I? When I was walkin' along just fine for myself, I had to sway from side to side a bit, and that was too much for other kids to leave alone, so I got real good at spendin' my own time with my friends the trees. They would stand tall and proud, without makin' any fuss at all.

When I'd ask Mama something I was wondering about, she'd usually say something like, "I don't know, I guess you're just plain inside like some." That made me feel like mud, and still does even now, thinking back to it. Why would she say that, like it's a good way to explain anything? I liked to hold my hand up to the sunlight to try to see some of what was inside of me. I know Mama and Papa surely did really care 'cause when Mama thought I needed it, Papa would give me a whuppin' so I'd mind better.

Back then, seemed like every week I got taller. Papa said I ate more than just about anybody. Mama got a serious look on her and would say I was growing up fast as a weed. I was beginning to get some of those lumpy places like full-growed up women. At times I felt like I was in somebody else's body. My dark hair would get curly when it was making to rain. Folks would say my skin was lovely like a butterfly's cocoon, and glowed color like when all kinds of folks was mixed together. I liked when I could see how someone would be lookin' at my eyes, since they *are* full of wonderful colors, full of green and gold dancin' together. Grandma would tell me how fine I was. She was the sweetest kin to me. We had so many good times together while she lived with us, but then she caught something awful and died in the winter. It was crowded with us all together, but it was the best times I can remember at home.

But I've been gone from there so long now, ever since I turned fourteen. There was no way back then I could have guessed the huge changes that were going to happen. That was 1843. It still amazes me when I think of it.

Wrapped in my warm blanket, still sleepy, the sound of Papa at the stove would be the first thing I heard most mornings. He was right proud of our iron stove, the warmest spot in the mornings when it was cold. I could tell my little sister Adele was still asleep by the sound of her easy breathing right next to me. Papa would hum a tune and I'd know he was making a hot breakfast like he did just 'bout every morning. Mama was still in bed, of course.

Papa was the best papa anybody could have. He was funny, and his belly jiggled a little when he laughed. Sometimes I think he liked to laugh even more than he liked to eat. If he saw a dog wandering along, he'd get it to wag a happy tail wag with just a rub behind the ears and a kind word. He'd come up behind me when I wasn't paying attention and give me one of his best hugs while he whispered something nice in my ear, just for me. I can hear his voice like I'm back there again.

"The flapjack man is here," he says in his birdsong voice, just loud enough for me to hear.

I jump out of bed and pull my sweater over my nightshirt quick before I run to the front corner where he's at the stove.

"Good morning, sleepy head."

"It smells good, and I'm hungry, maybe more than usual."

"Well, you're in luck, the flapjack man left these for you." With a twinkle in his eye, he looks at me and does a quick little happy dance. This is how I love my day to start.

I plop down at the corner of the table closest to the stove to eat. The lamp is lit against the dull morning light and it shows the little rows of yarn in my sweater, all straight like the crops outside. He puts a plate down in front of me and I lean over so the steam warms my face. We both like this time, our quiet time, ours alone.

"Eat up before they get cold," he says as he puts on his coat and pulls the wooden door handle to leave.

With one last smile, he's gone like every other day, working somewhere 'til he comes home before dark, dirty and tired. I sit and enjoy bite after bite of the steamy cakes, until I'm warm and full. I hear footsteps and Mama appears, earlier than usual, sleepy as she gets to the stove to make her hot chicory drink.

"Mornin', Mama."

"Mornin', Crysalline. I heard the door close, so I'm up. There are things that have to get done today, so I need you to stay inside and help."

This is the last thing I want to hear. She's going to tell me what to do all day. She looks right at me, but I just keep quiet and stare at my plate.

"Chores don't get done by wanderin' outside."

***

For the whole morning, she keeps me busy, cleaning and sweeping. Sometime later in the morning, I stop to watch the dust swirl in the air. Thoughts of my big brother Jimmy fill my mind; it's the memory that won't leave me alone. He's gone, and I miss him so much. He always looked out for me. It's all I can do is stop the tears from getting full in my eyes so Mama won't see.

"Is that enough, can I go now?"

"No, there's more to do. You're the oldest and Adele is no help at all yet."

"I've been helpin' all morning. That could be enough for today. I really wanna go out."

Before she can say anything else, I grab a muffin and an apple and run out the door and down the single step, leaving a puff of dust when my feet hit the dry ground. I hurry to get out of sight as fast as I can. The wonderful outdoors is waiting for me.

"Crysalline, come back here, we aren't done!" The sharp sound of her calling gets softer as I get more space between me and chores.

I slow down when all I can hear is the happy sound of leaves and birds chattering together as a wind stirs. As I come over the next rise, I smell the change in the air from the grove of sweet- smelling trees that rolls on forever beyond our place. I don't rightly know the name for them, but calling them the sweet trees sounds right.

My arms swing out easy in these open places, the fields and woods where I'm in my own world. Out here for the day, I can eat the most tender leaves of some of the plants growing wild and pretend to be one of the people who lived here long before our kin came to settle the place. They're gone now. I don't know where they went. The damp scent of the blanket of trees rises up and into me. When it's raining, I like to sit by the open window where the moist air touches my face as it comes inside. Best of all is when the lightning crackles. That's like nothing else. The bumps on my arm stand up in a terrible excitement that flows through me.

I run all the way to the old wooden shed that sits in the shade of the biggest oak tree I have ever seen. I call it a Grandpa Tree 'cause it must be so old. It's a grandpa to me, the only one I have. Inside the shed, it's peaceful. I wonder about the people who made the place and then just left it with stuff still here. Rusty farm tools and a harness for a horse hang on wooden pegs in the walls. The cracks in the leather make it look like it might fall apart if I even touch it. No one has been here for a long time by the look of the dust on the spider webs that are everywhere. This is my own private place. After a bit, I leave to wander along the high ridge where I can look down on everything and Mama's nagging is far away.

The muffin and apple fill me so I can stay out all afternoon. While I walk, I think of things to say back to her someday. The slapping sound of my sandals keeps me in mind of how much I like being out here. Along the way, anthills get stepped on by accident 'cause my feet wander as much as my thinking. Those ants are working on their home so it's only right to leave 'em be. They work hard enough as it is.

Clouds cover the sun, and a wind begins to push at me. I wish I had my sweater. The tree branches waving outside this morning were trying to tell me it'd be windy today. Now I can only walk faster to keep warm before I have to think about getting back.

I wander wherever my steps take me, trying not to remember how Mama will be mad at me. Suddenly I notice that nothing looks familiar, so I stop. A fog is beginning to hang in the treetops. As I start walking, slowly now, it gets thicker and looks to be everywhere.

"Where am I?" I say out loud, wanting to hear an answer.

This is my woods, and I know it pretty well. Some spots look kinda familiar, so I set out to find something that might remind me of the way back. I know something will come clear to me sooner or later, but after walking a while more I see what looks like the same things again. Where is this? I haven't been everywhere, but I don't suppose anyone has. Around home, we walk where we need; don't keep a horse since they eat a lot and someone has to take care of them. Besides, I can walk just about as far as anybody.

A hard feeling begins to grab at my insides. I hear Mama's voice in my head.

"There's nothin' interesting out there, it's just mostly empty. What's so interesting 'bout empty?"

Part of me wants to hear her voice for real right now, so I can be home again.

I see her at home sitting out front, watching the hills. She doesn't do lazy talk like some folks do just to hear themselves. Sharp as a knife, she talks when she wants to tell you what's on her mind. She pulls sharp words out so easy. She can let some lazy wanderer know that there's no place for them 'round her. Sometimes I wish she was a little softer. Maybe she will be someday.

She can have such a peaceable look about her with her eyes closed, and a really nice smile, like there isn't a lick of worry in her. I'd sit to her side and drink in the good feeling of it. That chair outside is her favorite spot, like mine is my cozy bed in the morning.

Looking up at the cold gray sky sets me shivering. Turning to look at where I just walked doesn't help. Branches slap at my bare arms as I pass and the wind sounds strong in the treetops. Looking around, there's nothing I know.

Fog swirls in my head and I'm getting hungry again. My mouth is dry. An old fallen log is someplace to sit while I collect my wits. Rubbing the little wood figure I always keep in my pocket, my heart begins to slow some. That wood figure looks like a little bear. My fingers find a wrapped up dried fruit in the pocket that I forgot about. The dried fruit is good to keep for now, safe with the wooden bear.

The softness of the rotten log is comforting, but when I look around, there's a strangeness everywhere. A shiver runs through me as the dampness of the fog soaks into me. Everything is blurry as I fight back tears. I wish I could talk to Jimmy again. He always looked out for me. I wish I could have looked out for him that awful day, but that can't be undone.

I want to hear someone's voice, but I can only hear birds somewhere far from here. I see two ways to go. To the left it's straight and level and stays close to a rocky hillside. To the right it's out in the open. With the fog, darkness is coming early today.

My teeth are chattering as mixed-up thoughts swirl. I stand up, wanting to shake them off as I wipe away tears with my sleeve. I must find the way, but, after studying the place for any kind of help deciding, I'm not sure of anything.

"I'll make a pile of rocks where I've been," I say out loud, wanting to find something to do.

I make the pile point to where I have just come from. Standing over it, doubt pushes at me. Wiping my eyes again, I close them long enough to wish myself to be home again. Then I notice a tree branch bob up and down as a bird lands on it. The bird has bright colors and looks straight at me so he must be a papa bird, people would say. Maybe he'll show me a sign.

He takes off in a hurry and turns towards the open space. That's the way I'll go. The wind picks up again, wrapping my loose hair close to my neck. I'll walk fast to get warm.

I pass by several places, but nothing erases the doubt gnawing at my insides. The trees are dark and don't seem to care as I pass. A clearing opens where there's nothing but rolling, dark grassland as far as I can see below the gloomy, stained sky. It's colder here in the open. Fear grabs at me and my breathing comes faster. Nothing is helping. I shiver at the thought of being caught out here all night.

I remember a story about a little boy who hid in the hollow of a tree. Maybe I could hide for the night in a hollow tree. I've played in one, but that was daytime. Leaves could be a blanket. I guess I'm not completely lame-brained.

I think again about that piece of candy, knowing it's in my pocket with my little wooden bear. I wish I could find water. At least some dew might be on the leaves in the morning. I hope. Morning seems very far away.

"Howdy."

The voice comes from out of nowhere.

I jumped from shock, 'cause it must be talking to me. Now I see a man walking right to me, and, before he takes his pause, he's close enough that I get the smell of him. Tobacco and some kind of alcohol and he looks rough, his beard long and dirty. He is not so tall but kind of heavyset, maybe from a couple of layers of clothes.

"What're you doin' out here all by your lonely? Where's your folks?" he asks as a sly grin comes over his face.

"Just wandering 'round, I suppose, and it ain't nothin' to worry about."

"Well, ain't that just pretty fine and dandy," he adds.

Looks like he's kind of sizing me up. I'm doing it, too, to him. Don't know that I ever met anyone that looks like he hasn't been indoors for a while. He sure looks like he could be mean if he wanted to. Papa would keep this kind from coming onto our place whenever they would appear out of nowhere, smiling and looking like they were some kind of long lost relative. Wandering fools, he'd call them after they were gone again. I'd seen the hard bite of Papa's jaw soften after he knew they'd left.

I aim to keep a good distance. He keeps fingering his belt, like he's itchy or something.

"Well, we could just pull up and visit for a while, I suppose," he says.

"Don't know much of what there could be to visit about," I say.

"Oh, don't be unfriendly now. That wouldn't be polite. I think I know your folks. Yes, sir, I know it was your pappy that I came across one day not too long ago, and when he and I sat down for a spell, he told me all about how you was so nice. Now I see it for myself. That's right sure, I see it with my own eyes."

The words fall out of his mouth, almost like they mean nothing. That might be funny, but this is not the time to show anything of what I feel in front of him. Suddenly he steps closer, all easy-looking, and comes to my side, smiles, and puts his arm in a light grip 'round my shoulder.

"Your folks would be real happy to know that I've come across you and found you in fine shape. Yes, sir, they would."

He smells. Now my breathing is hard and I don't know how to make it go easy again. I turn to have his arm fall away and I take a couple of steps to get some air. I hope I look real casual. I can't tell what might be next.

"Well, don't get all cold on me now. I just want to be right friendly, don't ya know."

The smell of him lingers on me as I turn to show my nicest smile and keep edging slowly away.

"Well, sure now, I know that for sure," I throw back as casual as I can.

His arm comes at me again, this time like a claw, pulling me off balance and I feel my breathing get heavy and tight again. I want to yell out something, anything, but I can't. Nothing seems right inside of me.

"Aw, let's be friendly now, all right?"

The words fill my ear, and his hot breath is closer than I can take. I start moving my arms and legs any way I can, swinging wilder each time. *Please, someone stop whatever this is. Whatever it is, I don't want any more of it.* My wild swinging hits him a few times but nothing changes until somehow he loses some of his grip on me. He groans and kind of doubles over, yet lunges out again to grab hard onto my arm.

"You're hurting me," I yell at him as I swing around to get free.

He's trying to hold onto my arm but can't; all he can hold onto is my sleeve. Still I can't get free. I hear the sleeve tear and I'm loose. I start out as quick as possible, beginning to leap over fallen logs and branches to get to open ground and start uphill, hoping he isn't fast enough to catch me again. It's hard to get going as fast as I want. I hear him stumble behind me and fall down hard, hitting the ground.

"Ow, dang it! Now you've gone and made me twist somethin'. I hope nothin' ain't broke."

The words echo all around me and I begin to imagine that I may really be out of his reach. I don't slow down until I can't hear much but his grumbles, so I know he's farther away.

"Don't you worry none now. We'll be seeing each other again soon," he yells.

As I reach the top of the hill, I turn to see him lying against a log. Turning away, I run and run while branches slap at my bare arms until I don't know how long I've been running. I don't know how far I've gone, but I still wonder where he is now. Stopping to listen, I can't hear anything except my own heavy breathing until I hold my breath for a second trying to hear whatever I can, but there is no sign of him anymore.

"Papa bird, where are you? I need you." I plead to the sky above. All I can do is fall down in a heap and cry as the fear drains away but nothing safe comes to fill the emptiness inside me.

Looking up at the cold gray sky sets me shivering. Looking around, there's nothing I know.

Strange shapes begin to fill the spaces wherever I look. The sky is like dark smoke. There are no sounds of the birds that are somewhere close by all day. That bird I tried to follow before is nowhere to be seen. He's probably sitting with fluffed up feathers, almost asleep. At home I try to stay awake as long as I can, pretending I'm outside somewhere, but now I'm tired and I don't want to be out here. I turn around to study the loosely scattered trees. They are still and silent, reaching up as shadows against the darkening sky.

I spot a huge, old Grandpa tree with a hollow burned into the bottom. It's not far so I walk through the soft, thick mat of leaves for a better look. Round lips of smooth bark show the edges of the opening. I lean in closer, but the insides are black and silent, without a hint of what could be in there. Bending down, I make a squeaky noise to find out if anything might answer me. I grab a fallen branch and poke around to the corners. Suddenly several sets of wings are flying past my head. I fall over backwards, unable to make any sound at all. Finally, I can scream at the surprise. Bats. They don't hurt people, but I don't like them anyway. After a moment of the silence that has returned, I poke the stick inside again with my head turned to the side and my eyes closed. Then the stick hits something hard. It must be the far side. No more bats. The dark of night is gaining, so this is where I must hide for the night. As I crawl through the opening, the muffled insides pull me into its deep quiet. Bone weary, the quiet becomes comforting. The thick walls of the tree are my safe place against the endless black space outside. There are no other sounds now. I scoop up leaves from just outside to pull close to me. There's a musty smell as I pull them to me, opening the rich rot below the dry top layer. All of this mixes together, making it softer inside. This will be my safe place for tonight. Looking out the opening again, I see that darkness has buried everything. With another pull of leaves, I try to lay still until my shivering begins to stop. The only sound is my breathing as I lie there, unable to find real comfort for some time. I can only wonder how this night will pass. After a while, my eyes are too heavy to care much anymore and sleep comes, covering everything else.

***

Sometime in the night I'm startled awake. I'm almost sure there was a sound of something moving outside in the leaves. It isn't clear at all, but it might have been close. As I struggle to wake enough to know anything for real, only a ribbon of pale moonlight cuts through the darkness. Tall grass stands naked in the moonlight, all alone. Did something just move at one edge of the shadows? I hold myself still to look and listen as hard as I can, but I find out nothing. My heart is beginning to pound, pushing me wide awake. I dare not make any noise, trying to stay as still as my shaking will let me. Please, let it be just my imagination. Then there is a soft moaning sound, faint and different from anything I've known before.

Finally, after another awful, silent moment, I can't stand it any longer.

"Hello ... hellooo," I call kind of quiet like, and all I hear is how lonely my own voice sounds.

I'm not sure if the words even carried out beyond the opening. I strain to discover anything else but there is nothing. My breathing and the pounding in my ears are all I can hear. A whisper of air brushes against my face, and then it, too, is gone. Maybe, I hope, after all, there is really nothing to be scared of out there.

A deep hum from all around me fills the emptiness. Then again I hear that soft, deep moan. I decide it's from somewhere above me as the tree sways and rubs against another, swaying in some unseen breeze far above. Down here that sound is deep and soft. My clenched jaw and shoulders begin to soften as I realize that the sound is from the tree itself and how silly I've been afraid to move at all. In the daytime, the woods is a friend. Besides, there's nowhere to go for now. I must wait out this night, until the light and warmth of the morning sun comes back.

Drifting off, there's a heavy feeling at my feet but with a few twists and turns it's better again. It feels like Sam, our cat, who sleeps at the foot of my bed sometimes. But it's just a lump on the inside of the tree. Curled up in this small space, my feet are against the other side. My older brother Jimmy comes to me in the dark and it's like I'm that little girl again. I miss him. Why wasn't it me that drowned instead?

He was a lot bigger than me and three years older. His light-colored hair was easy to see as we walked along through the sprinkles of daylight in the woods to get to somewhere special for the day. He was always ready to make me laugh. When he laughed, his freckles got bigger and his forehead wrinkled up with happy lines. It hurts that nothing can bring him back, so I push it all away again.

A sad gray light of morning begins outside. Then I remember the sounds in the night. I push that thought away while I clear the leaves from around me and crawl out through the opening into the beginnings of the day. A lot of leaves are stuck in my hair and skirt, but with a lot of brushing, they mostly come loose. I have lost my sun bonnet somehow in the night. Mama will be mad. The musty smell of the early morning forest is all around me. I wish for the friendly, spiced smell of the sun-warmed forest floor, but it's too early. I could just enjoy that scent all day. But this is damp and cold. Tears are pushing at me again. Please let me be back home soon. How was I so stupid to get lost? I look around then sit back down again to sob until the wet ground pushes me back up to start moving. I need to get somewhere else.

I'm hungry, scratched, tired, and don't know which way to go. Walking fast, I warm up as best I can. My empty stomach is gnawing at me, and Mama and Papa must be worried sick by now. I wish I could take it all back.

It's hard to walk over the uneven ground in the dull morning light, but then I spot a blackberry thicket. With a sigh of relief, I reach through the thorny tangle for the berries the birds haven't gotten. I put them in my mouth as fast as I can grab them. I don't have to eat that piece of candy yet. There are berries enough to fill my hands while I start walking again to push back the chill. The berries feel good on my dry throat. Stumbling along until the light rises, I see no sign of anyone or anywhere I know. The scratches on my feet are burning. I don't know how they got there.

Midday comes and I'm hungry again. I keep moving, but only slowly, stopping to listen for any sounds of people. Doubt clouds the sunny day, making it hard to pick which way to go.

I want to stop and rest, but I keep moving until I see something. There is a movement ahead. It's mixed in with the shadows of the tree branches above. Is something out there or is it just the moving shadows? I don't want to play at imagining anything right now. After the sound of a grunt, I know it's not my imagination. The bumps stand up on my arms and neck. As quiet as I can, I strain to see through the bushes ahead.

The thumping of my heart is all I can hear. The rest of the world disappears as I wonder what or who is out there. I'm afraid it might be real this time.

# CHAPTER TWO
# THE WILDERNESS

The shakes have started. I can't stop them. I swallow hard and try to keep from being found first. A twig snaps under my foot and dark eyes swing to look directly through the brush at me. It grunts and I can clearly see its prickly, hairy snout, and long teeth. I can only wish to be somewhere far away and soon.

Creeping back as slowly as I can, I don't want to look directly at it again. It doesn't seem to be moving any closer. It looks away, then towards me again. What could it be thinking? My arms are like stone. It's all I can do to keep moving slowly while the pounding in me screams *run!* The space between us grows slowly, too slowly. It's hard to stay steady.

Maybe there's a tree limb behind me low enough to climb. While I'm wondering, a scraping sound starts deep in my throat. It's not clear to me if this is a good idea, but it's happening. I keep moving, glancing slowly backwards to each side to make sure I won't hit anything if I need to start running. This place is flat with small bushes and just one tree behind me.

The beast doesn't show me any sign of what's next. It's staying in the same spot, giving off mostly low grunts and an occasional snort. It lifts one hairy front paw and then puts it back down again, scratching at the dirt. This can't be good. In a shaky voice I say, "Nice piggy, nice piggy."

With a few more steps, more brush and that small tree are between us. *What will I do if he comes at me now?* I can't think, but that tree is closer to him now. *Could he be more scared than me?* I don't think so.

In a few more small steps, only the faint sounds of grunting and small movements through the brush are all that's left of him. My breathing is quick and hard, and I have to keep telling myself it's really over. There are beads of sweat on my forehead cooling in the breeze. I float off in a frozen stare at the sky through the leaves overhead. *You're not going to be hurt.* I tell myself that, but the pit in my stomach wants to swallow me. The heaving and wrenching come quickly but last only a short time since my stomach is empty anyway. Then something else comes. Like looking over the edge of a rocky hillside, excitement mixes with the relief.

I don't want to even imagine being out here wandering for another night. The sun is moving lower through the sky, so I must get moving again. That piece of dried fruit in my pocket is my treasure. It's been a long time since those berries this morning and no more have appeared. I spot some wild greens that look like something at home, so I rip them up and try eating a few. They're not too bad. There's a lot of it here, but soon the bitter taste doesn't let me eat any more.

Walking on, there seem to be endless valleys and rolling hills, and then more valleys and rolling hills. Finally, there's the sound of a small stream. I rush over and drop at the edge and take a long drink of the clear, cool water. There are paw prints in the soft mud at the edge, but I can't tell what animal made them. I splash water on my face and some of the weariness melts away. The bug bites on my bare arms are red and itchy. Cool water makes them a little better, but before I know it, darkness is beginning to grow all around me. I will be all alone again tonight.

There are probably things that wander around in the dark. Looking for another safe place, I see a pair of huge boulders at the side of a rocky wall. They make a tight spot between them that looks safe enough. I tear off a small tree limb that has lots of leaves to wedge between the rocks as some kind of protection from the cool night. It is only a little better than nothing. There are mostly pine needles for bedding, but they're dry. Getting into the close space between the two boulders, I pull on the top branch to wedge it tight and closer with the small branches around my feet. I don't want to be found by even the wind tonight.

I can't settle down. Every time I move, pine needles poke at me. The last colors of the day are gone, leaving only the dark color of slate in the sky. Maybe it's bats I see against the fading light, gone in an instant, quick and silent against the deep sky. From under my cover of branches, I can feel the world of the night begin, and I know that whatever loves the dark is out there. Now that I'm huddled as quietly as I can, there's only the sound of the insects of the night. Then I hear something else, and my shoulders tighten and my breath stops until all I hear is the insects again. I'm not sure which is worse, not hearing them or hearing them.

The world of the outdoors I love is gone. It is now a stranger to me while hunger clouds everything and mosquitoes keep me from any real rest. Imagining my bed at home is impossible because of the pine needles prickling me. My emptiness has me fighting for sleep, and this spot is not as comfortable as the hollow tree last night. The pine needles warm against me, and they begin to smell slightly sweet, but they're still prickly. I have quit trying to find anything softer for my bed tonight. I have to get through this night to find someone—anyone—out there tomorrow. As tiredness wears through me, the final sound I remember is an owl softly calling at a distance, and I drift off to sleep, away from any place at all.

***

The next thing I know, the sun is shining through the umbrella of leafy branches above me. In a breeze, the bright green leaves glow and wiggle against the clear blue sky. I start climbing this tree to see as far as I can. Looking from a perch above, the land beyond seems to go on forever. The sweet scent of sun-warmed earth reaches me as the tree sways, rocking me from side to side; my skirt flutters, then gets tangled for a time in the branches. In a stand of young trees far in the distance, something's moving. It's not easy to make out clearly at all through the leaves. Then there it is again. It's a man and he's walking. Then he's hidden again behind more trees.

"Hey!" I scream. "Hey! Over here, up in this tree!"

I catch sight of him again as he walks along slowly, looking to not have a care, and after a few more steps he stops and tilts his head like he's trying to hear something. He isn't looking my way, and I can't tell if he heard me.

Balancing on one foot and holding on with one arm, I wave frantically with my free arm through the leaves all around me.

"Hey, over here," I scream as loud as I can.

He stops and turns to look my way. When I see his face, I almost lose my balance. It's weirdly shaped and hard to look at. His long stringy hair is moving as wild as worms. Just as fast as he turned my way, he turns back to go on walking, and in another blink of the eye, he disappears, gone. I look down to see what's moving by my foot. A snake is winding around my leg and I scream. At the same time, the tree branches slap at me. Soon I realize that the branches are here, close to my face at my homemade bed. On the ground. In the dark. It was a bad dream.

After a moment, I feel a thickness beside my leg. A real snake has found my spot warm and inviting so it wants to spend the night with me. I scream for real this time, getting up from the ground and swinging my arms wildly at the tangled branches to get them away from my face in the black of the night. My feet dance wildly to keep away from what's down there. I get out of the tight space, but the dream still has hold of me. The horrid face, the dream snake and the real one, somewhere in the dark. I try to catch my breath while I rub my face to wake up, then stretch my arms out in front of me to find what's around me. I can barely make out anything. Step by step, I get to a place where the pale moonlight touches the ground, and I can see some of my surroundings. I plop down in the grass and sob.

The sun can't come back fast enough. I pace back and forth in the dark until it finally rises up over the line of hills. I move to a spot where it touches me with its warmth. That friendly glowing ball in the sky is comforting, but I ache in this lonely world. I desperately want to find something to eat. Remembering the berries of yesterday morning, I wander until I spot something that looks like it might be another large thicket of them. Getting closer, I see that the birds have already eaten the easy pickings on the edges, so I have to reach into the thorny tangles to get any at all. It doesn't matter much right now if I get a scratch. The berries are everything. As soon as I find one, I pop it in my mouth and struggle past the thorns to get another. I kept shifting my spot around the large thicket, and there are a few more berries for me with a little work.

"Thank you, thank you, thank you." I keep saying every time my hand finds a berry.

Finally, I sit down on a log, while the gnawing in my stomach settles a bit. Now I notice the new scratches on my arms." Oops." Even though I know better, I rub them, hoping to soothe them. Instead, they begin to hurt.

# CHAPTER THREE
# ANOTHER WORLD

The world has forgotten me. I'm hungry, dirty, and my foot hurts. My mouth is so dry I imagine the sound of a stream somewhere. Then I think it might be real. I pick myself up and wander around, looking for it. Beyond a small fold in a hill I find a tiny brook coming down the face of the hill, just big enough to get my hand full of water. The wonderful wetness brings me back to life. I sit down on a big boulder at the water's edge and notice the lush green all around. I drop down into it just to relax for a little while. My arms are tender and red, and my skirt is torn. I liked this dress; it's just like Mama's.

I would plead to any part of the world for help, but there looks to be no one to hear me. I'm as small as a bug that just travels in circles. *How can the world I thought I knew so well change so much? It doesn't care about me anymore.*

For a while I can do nothing but stare at the lush growth all around me. I don't want to start out again, but I can't just sit here forever. I begin with a sigh, plodding along all morning, looking for any sign of people. I find tiny paths in the grasses, but they're only small animal trails. The path I want to find must be as wide as a person's foot or horseshoe marks, but I can't find it.

It's cloudy but I'm sweaty from moving over many small rises and dips, up and down again. The stream is my only friend so I keep close to it, hoping that someone might be living somewhere alongside it. This is keeping me from completely falling apart. Sometimes I lose sight of the water, but I never get so far away that I can't hear its comforting sound. That's all I have. I find a tree with a few wild apples hanging within reach. I force myself to take several bites, but they are hard and bitter, and I feel worse than if I'd never seen them.

In the early afternoon, I reach into my pocket to find that piece of candy. There is no more waiting. Wrapped in the waxy paper is a piece of dried peach, sticky, sweet, and chewy. As I get the first taste, it's so good I have to slow down or I'd eat it in just one big bite. Even nibbling, pretty soon there's nothing left but the stickiness and smell on the wrapper. I stuff it back into my pocket, not wanting to lose any more of home than I already have.

"Please tell me, what should I do?" I beg the huge, open sky.

I stumble on rocks buried in the grass and keep trying to find easier places to walk. Once, sometime in the middle of the day, I think I hear a voice, maybe even more than one. Maybe it's something on the wind just to fool me.

"Hey, is anybody there? Help. Heellllp!" I yell louder each time time, but still no answer comes back. There is only the sound of the stream, birds, and the wind in the trees. Keep walking. You'll be all right. The small stream I have been following finally comes to a small pond, deep and full. Birds play without a care. I drop down in a heap on the soft, grassy slope. Grasses at the water's edge look good enough to eat so I tear at them and try some. They are so bitter that I have to spit them out, and then I have nothing but the bad taste.

This place is quiet and peaceful like a pond at home. Its deep spots were full of mystery where I could spend the whole afternoon watching for any fish to appear out of the depths and look up at me. The water would reflect the green trees and the blue sky above, moved by whatever passing winds or raindrops might make ripples. When a fish would come up and touch the air above, ripples would spread over the pond, if only even a little. Ripples could make the colors of the land and sky beyond wiggle. It was wonderful until the awful day I can't forget.

I learned to swim a little from Jimmy. That's when I first learned to respect the deep dark water. He showed me how to use a small rowboat that was always there, tied up and left by someone else. Knowing how to use the paddles out on the water helped me not be pushed around by the wind. A paddle can make a beautiful ripple on the surface when the water is still, too. I remember the slurpy sound it made as it dipped in and out of the water. I could pick a spot on the water and sit still in the boat for a long time. Looking into the depths, a fish would come gliding by and nibble at my fingertip touching the surface before disappearing back into their world. I'd watch them swim lazily just below the surface. Only Mama's call would make me come back home. That is, until that day.

I shared the spot with Jimmy. He was playing around trying to be like a fish, going underwater and then coming up to squirt water at me while I sat in the boat. Somehow, he choked, and then he could only thrash around trying to stop coughing, but that only made it worse. Then he went under, becoming only a hazy shadow. I sat frozen, waiting for him to come up again, thinking he was just playing, but he never came up.

I sat there, more alone than I have ever been. I began calling his name louder and louder against the silent water, until I was screaming.

"Jimmy, Jimmy! ... Jimmy!" I screamed until my voice quit.

The water only got smoother and quieter, like he hadn't been there at all. In that silence, the world collapsed, sucking me into it. I wanted to make it all disappear and go away.

After that day, I never went back there again.

Jolting awake, I'm surprised to find that I've fallen asleep here at this water's edge. My neck is sore. I stand up, wobbly at first, but I must move on. Passing around the edge of this quiet place, I pray for some path or cabin, or even just the smell of smoke in the air, that would lead to someone. Deer are everywhere and we eye each other before they move away with a cautious first step, then in leaps and bounds. It would be great if I could leap like that.

The scratches and mosquito bites on my arms itch. I think I see a cabin out in the trees, but as I walk faster to come close, it turns out there's nothing there at all. I'm haunted by being so alone. I would make any promise to find my way.

Mama's and Papa's worried faces drift across my mind. It's hard to remember how upset I was about Mama's nagging when I ran out. Now I can't see anything clearly through the tears. I need to find somewhere, anywhere.

My imagination is usually my friend but not anymore. I can't stop the swirling daydreams as I walk along, empty and worn down. Bushes and old dead trees take on strange shapes as I pass. The upturned roots of a fallen tree become the crown of some ancient king. Sunlight flickering through the swirling leaves overhead moves snake-like shapes on the ground. That makes it hard to move through the tall grass that twirls in the same breeze. As I trudge on, these imaginings come and fade. The smell of Papa's flapjacks is with me and I can't stop thinking about them covered with syrup. At home I could sit, still sleepy in the early morning until my flapjacks would appear, made on that cast iron stove that glowed and rumbled with the fire in its belly. Sitting there, I imagined seeing a face molded onto the firebox door.

I remember how Mama and I would walk to the village together, passing doorways along the road as we got nearer. At any open door, I liked to catch wind of whatever mystery or smell I could. When I was eight, one open door had a strange, painted symbol beside it that caught my eye. As I got closer, a strange odor came drifting out. I leaned into the dark insides where someone with only one eye under matted hair looked right at me and let out a sharp shriek. My foot slipped off the step and my head hit on the edge of the door with a thud.

I ran as fast as I could back to Mama's side and hid behind her skirt.

"What have you been doing to be acting so silly, Crysalline?"

"Someone inside that door scared me."

"Well, you silly girl, don't be so curious. That never helped anybody."

When I dared look back toward that doorway, the person with one eye was glaring directly at me across the distance. I felt like I'd fallen into hot soup. Then whoever it was disappeared back into the dark interior. It's still not clear to me what kind of man or woman it was. It's all I can do not to see that face again right now.

Hearing a grunt from just over the next ridge brings me out of my daydream. Stopping in my tracks, I don't know whether to be scared or not. The bumps on my arm stand up again as I begin climbing towards the top of the ridge. I get down on my knees and then crawl to the top to look over the edge, shivering against the cool ground. A cabin sits right there in plain sight, surrounded by a cluster of young trees. There's smoke coming out of the chimney. The grunt came from a pig in a pen at the side of the house. The sound of the front door closing is still in the air. That horrible face in the dream keeps me from moving. I want to run up to the door yelling "Help, please let me in; I'm lost and tired and hungry," but I don't know who'll be behind that door.

The wind pushes at me from behind. The ground ahead has large boulders spread out over the open space, so I move behind one to get closer and, when nothing else happens, on to another even closer. The pig sees me and grunts. Sparks fly from the chimney so I know that someone has just thrown a fresh log onto a warm fire.

After several more steps, I hear a squeal from behind the door. It sounds like a small child and I can't tell if they are hurt or scared or just want attention like my little brother Tom. Shaking all over, I force myself to step up to the door and knock on the rough wood. At first there's no sound from inside. My legs hardly keep me standing and my stomach is in knots.

Heavy footsteps sound on the floorboards inside, coming closer to the door. I'm frozen, wondering what's going to happen to me. The door handle moves, and as the door swings open, I see a large man standing in the opening. The lamp hanging in the center of the room puts him in shadow so all I can see is his full beard glowing around the edges. Surprised, he looks at me silently for several heartbeats.

Nothing can come out of my open mouth for a time until I finally get the words out.

"I'm lost."

I have found someone. and I pray he's not mean. I'm shaking badly. His eyes grow big.

"Uh, sure, come inside."

His nostrils might have whistled when he spoke.

My foot lifts and I take a step. One more and I'll be inside. I see a table with chairs in the center of the room. At the far end of the table is a small child strapped to a chair. Some kind of food is all over his face and he stops to watch me.

I see a woman's face.

That's the last thing I remember.

# CHAPTER FOUR
# FOUND

When I wake up, I find myself lying on a hard, wide bench along a wall. There's light coming through the shuttered window above my head. I hurt all over, but mostly my feet and legs. There are two voices somewhere so I stay as still as I can. I can't remember how I came to be on this bench. And that shadowy face at the door still has me scared.

Soft footsteps come from behind me and suddenly the same woman's face I saw last night is right over me. She looks to be quite a bit younger than Mama. She smiles and comes close to look at the bump on my forehead. She's close enough that I can feel her warm breath on my face.

"What happened last night? I don't remember much," I say, my voice weak and scratchy.

"We didn't talk after you passed out right inside the door and fell down. You just wanted to sleep, so we let you, covering you up for the night. We can sort it all out now that you're awake. Are you feeling better?"

My face is burning red with knowing that some stranger helped me to bed last night.

The bearded man appears carrying the little one on his hip. He stands quietly behind the woman while I try to figure this out.

I want to get away from being looked at. Sheepishly, I glance at the man's face. He's smiling but I don't know what to say so I close my eyes for a time. I'm startled into opening them when I hear the woman's voice again. It's soft and gentle.

"My name is Jenna, and this is my husband Darry, and our little boy Larans. He's about a year old now. You just relax and I'll go make a warm drink for you."

She gently touches my shoulder as she gets up.

I never heard these names before. *Just how far away from home am I?* The woman moves with an easy way about her. The man is tall and big around. He looks a little wild with that beard and he moves kind of slowly.

"Thank you for taking me in. I'm really lost."

My throat tightens and I can't say anything more. The sounds of a crackling fire fill the space.

The feel of her light touch on my shoulder lingers. After a time, she returns with a steaming hot mug. I sit up and notice that I still have most of my clothes on but not my sandals. They're on the floor right below me. The warmth of the mug gives me pause from my aches as I cradle it in both hands. It smells like some kind of soup. Sitting up straight, I'm light-headed and notice how starved I am with the first taste of the soup that tastes like a mix of many good things.

"It's broth with some herbs for good measure. Hope you like it."

"Thank you, it's fine." Actually, it's more wonderful than I can possibly find words to tell.

"Go ahead and warm your empty stomach," she says, nodding to the cup.

I take another sip, and then I can't stop and I drink the whole cup without stopping for a breath. Holding the empty cup for the warmth, I watch as they busy themselves with other things. As I look around, I see that it's less scary in the daylight. It's hard to look relaxed and just sit still, even if they are good people. I wonder if I'll ever have the comfort of a place again. Little Larans is on that same chair with a strap around his waist, ready to eat. He's sitting at the side of the table staring, probably wondering about me as much as I am about them. He stops staring at me and begins looking for food from his mother, who's fixing something with her back turned to the room.

The lingering taste of the broth makes me want more. It takes me away from remembering yesterday. Here in this stranger's place, I look around and see things I can't recognize, like at the back corner of the room where splashes of different colors are on a small, messy table. Looking up, I see the wooden beams of the roof have odd things painted on them. *What is that for?* But I'm too tired to wonder about all of that for now.

"Would you be better in a chair? You can bring the cover with you if you like."

Wanting to look calm is all I can think about. Maybe I'll feel less awkward there. I move to the chair she pointed to at the center table. From there I can see into the corner where she's busy mixing something in a wooden bowl.

The room is mostly quiet for a time, then little Larans lets out gurgling sounds. He's got one hand covered with what looks like oatmeal. Surely no one can know what he means, but Jenna smiles at him and puts a spoonful in his mouth after she blows on it to make sure it's cool enough.

These people look pretty much like anyone else, but they *are* strangers and I can't stop wondering what kind of folks they really are. They move around the room, pretending like this is a regular day, leaving me to cradle the mug that Darry has filled again with more broth. I drink it slower this time. It's as good as the first cupful.

I look around some when I see that they aren't checking on me as much. There's the worktable on one side where Jenna's making food, near the table that fills the center of the room. At the other end of the room is the splattered table at the back corner and the bench under the shuttered window where I woke up this morning. Around the edges of the room are the things that belong to these people. I can't imagine what some of them might be for. The shelf in the corner over the messy corner table holds mysterious jars and lumpy cloths that looked like they could be covering something. Even the shelf these things sit on is curious, with figures I've never seen before painted on the edge.

Darry moves to sit close to me, sitting backwards on a chair with his arms folded across the top. He only sits and smiles. He might be waiting for his breakfast, dressed in overalls like he might be going to work outside soon.

"Did you sleep all right?" he asks.

This time I'm not so shocked by his deep voice.

"Yes ... no ... uh, I don't know," I answer. I'm trying to get used to him being right in front of me.

I look to his wife who's stirring the pot over the fire in the fireplace. It smells like hot cereal and the wood smoke smells just like home.

Jenna turns and comes over to me to look at the bump on my forehead. She gently touches it around the edges. I can feel her breath as she hovers over me. I try to keep still and not pull back at her touch.

"Looks like you'll be fine. That isn't bad at all," she says.

"Last night as we were putting you to bed, I saw the ink drawings on the bottoms of your feet. I couldn't help but wonder."

I try not to squirm.

"Oh, yeah, I like to draw doodles on the bottoms of my feet sometimes. It's a way I make my own decorations and walk around without anyone else knowing about it. It's a little different, I know. I just like to do it anyway."

"What's your name, sweetie?"

"Crysalline. It's Crysalline," I repeat to be sure of myself.

"Well, that's a very interesting name, Crysalline," Jenna says, nodding her head. "When you want to get up, you can go clean up at the wash basin, which is on the left in the back." She points to the corner cut off from the front room by some wall planks.

Most of all, I want to escape them watching me for a time, so I cross the open space as quick and calm as I can, taking the cover wrapped around me.

The floorboards creak as I walk in the direction she pointed. It's darker and cooler back here. There is a wash bowel, and there are flowers and vines painted on the wall above it.

*This is different. What kind of place is this?*

A small pitcher of water sits beside the washbowl, so I pour some into it. The, I fill my hands with it and splash it on my face. The cold water helps clear my head. Raising my face again I see something shiny I didn't notice at first. It's a small glass mirror attached to the plank wall. I've heard of them, but this is the first time I've ever seen one. I glance back and see that no one's watching so I touch it gently at first to be sure it's real. I move slowly to see myself in it. There I am. I've only seen my wiggling reflection in the waters of the pond back home. I almost want to say something to myself in the mirror, it looks so real. My dark hair is a mess of tangles, and my skin is golden like clay in the sun. My eyes are big with surprise, showing the green and gold looking back at me. It's like I just met someone.

I make a face to be sure of who's looking back at me. Mama always tells that not everyone can be pretty, and I should get used to just being plain. I move away, back to the basin so no one can see that I was looking.

What else would this day bring? My hands are trembling with cold as I turn to go back to the front, to face these new people.

I take a deep breath as I step back into the room where everyone looks friendly enough. They're all looking my way, but the little one is mostly interested in the food in front of him which is also spread across his face and the table. An orange-color cat jumps from the floor onto a ledge to get a better view out the window shutters that are now partly open, then it, too, turns to look at me.

"Come and sit down. You must be hungry." Jenna's voice is gentle and friendly.

"Um, yes, I am." I'm starving.

I pull out the chair from the table and sit down carefully. I want to mind my manners. The table is smooth and shinier than ours at home. The wood shows the lines of the tree it came from and it glows with the smoothness. This is nicer than at home and I guess it must be waxed to make the shine so clear.

Jenna comes over and places a bowl of oatmeal and a mug of warm, clear brown drink that may be tea in front of me, then turns back to the pot in the fireplace.

"I hope you like this."

The bowl is thick pottery; there's a wooden spoon buried in the steamy oatmeal. I can see raisins and some other fruit cut up inside. I guess it might be apple. This is a different way to have oatmeal, but I don't let on. It smells like some kind of spices I don't know. The steam from the bowl warms my face, and with the first bite the tightness in my shoulders begins to relax. It tastes wonderful. I feel it going into a hollow ache in me I'd almost forgotten about.

"It has cinnamon with the apples and raisins," Jenna says simply, her back still to me.

I know I'm the center of attention but only care about eating. I'm even hungrier after the first bite. Everyone else in the room is pretending to be doing something else, except for the little one who now watches me curiously. Halfway through the bowl of oatmeal, I slow down to gulp the warm tea and look around again.

There are three worn but still good enough coats hanging on pegs beside the front door. Above the door is a round disc of wood with a drawing that looks like a bird that's flying. I can't tell why it's there, but it looks pretty anyway.

"Are you getting enough to eat?" Darry asks me. His voice sounds friendlier now.

While I was looking around, I'd forgotten he's still in the room.

"Yes, thanks," I say, looking down at the bowl.

"Do want some more? Or you can have more later if that would be better. We need to give you time to settle in." Jenna says without turning away from whatever she's doing.

I can't answer 'cause my throat is tightening again. What's to become of me? I sit looking at the bowl and remember the long days I was out there all alone. Pretty soon, I can't see clearly and a tear drops. I keep my head down, hoping no one will notice.

Darry silently offers me a piece of cloth. I wipe my eyes and start to breathe again.

"Where am I?" I ask.

Jenna comes to my side and, with a gentle touch on my shoulder, says, "You are here safe with us for now in this place we call Mihila. We made up that name since we're the only people close to here."

Just then I realize that I never thought much about the name of the place I come from.

"Do you know where Barrytown is?"

"I don't rightly know that name for sure, but we can try to find out where it could be," Darry says, trying to put me at ease.

The knot in my stomach tightens.

"We'll figure it out," Jenna says with a caring sound in her voice, and Darry nods his agreement with a smile. I'm not sure how they can be so cheerful.

"Well, today, we'll work on what there is to do. As soon as we can, we'll get you back home," she adds.

That home sits just over a ridge from our village, Barrytown. It was my world. I want more than anything to see that place again. Mama will be in her chair out front, worrying and wondering as she looks out over the open spaces beyond. Those were so many carefree places for me. Even if it was bad weather, I'd sit safe and dry by the open window and let the smells of the damp air come and sweep over my face. The sound of the raindrops on the leaves was music to me.

"Can you tell us some about your home place? Maybe we'll hear something that we'll know."

This doesn't help me feel any better. I just want to be there. But I must tell them what I can. These people are nice to me and I want them to find the way to get me back home.

"Don't worry too much, Crysalline. Please don't. It'll work out, I promise," Jenna offers, gently touching my arm again.

Mama would hug me sometimes, and I know I was loved and safe at home, but Jenna's touch is different somehow, of a way I haven't had before. Her hand is gentle, light on my arm.

"Crysalline, let's all gather over here," she says, pointing to the place beside the bench where I slept last night. "Let's all sit quietly for a while."

I don't understand but I follow her over to that spot. She sits down on the floor and pats the floor beside her. Darry comes over to join us. Larans stays at the table.

"What are we going to do?" I ask.

"We are going to sit here for a while, quietly together. Many times it helps us not be too worried and then a good idea can come right to us."

I don't see how sitting doing nothing could do anything. I fold my legs like she does and wonder what's going to happen next. As I settle down beside her, I keep looking for whatever I can see happening. Darry looks at me and smiles.

I figure this might be harmless enough. They close their eyes and sit peaceable and quiet. They begin to breathe deep and slow. Everything gets very quiet except for Larans who keeps fussing at his chair, but no one takes any notice of him. For a time I wait but nothing else looks to be happening. I'm right sitting here, but it doesn't show me anything about getting home. After a time, they both open their eyes and look at each other in a quiet way, like they know something I don't, how grownups do sometimes. They're sitting facing each other, relaxed and calm, awake in a way that I can't tell anything about. Not at all.

This is really a different day.

# CHAPTER FIVE
# CHANGING PLACES

The next two days pass in the blink of an eye. This morning I wake up in the dark with a fright and have to figure out where I am all over again. It's my third day here and I'm still wobbly. Most of the daytime is like a dream. I try to hide my face if it seems like I'm going to cry. Jenna will touch my shoulder as light as can be when I sit trying not to sob out loud. Her touch is helpful, but I can't tell exactly why. Jenna and Darry are different than any people I've seen before. They're happy in a quiet way. For me, it's like something's missing. Jenna sees my worried look, so she stops what she is doing and comes over to me.

"Crysalline, would you like to come along with me today while I do some chores outside?"

"Sure, that sounds good."

Maybe, somehow, this is going to work out. I take a deep breath. I glance around the room before we go out; it looks nice. Outside the sun is already high. It's a bright day. I follow her along a footpath that weaves pleasantly between small rises on both sides. Several birds swoop so close that I wonder if they might touch us. They make a small circle in the sky and then come back. Curious, I guess. Jenna turns around to look at me with a smile just as they land in a tree and begin to chatter away.

"Let's keep going. It's not far now," she says.

I follow her on the path through tall grasses where fuzzy seed heads wave in the breeze. I reach out with my fingertips now and then to touch them as we pass. Soon we are at a berry thicket, and I smile.

"We can pick the ones that are ripe and hope for more to pick later, if the birds leave enough." She opens a cloth sack, and we pick carefully. I don't need any new scratches.

"I like the walk to get here, and there's a different way back with a quiet spot you may enjoy," she says. A slight smile appears on her face as she looks up for any trace of what might be my reaction. I nod my interest in the idea, even though I'm not sure.

With the berry-stained cloth bag in her hand, we begin the walk back. The softness of morning is gone, and the sun is full and warm as we move across the open fields.

I don't say anything, since it doesn't seem like anything needs be said. Many times I only nod when she makes remarks. She turns, stepping off onto a narrower track through the tall grass.

Papa feels so far away. I wonder what he's doing today.

As we move along, more trees appear. We move down a small hill and soon I hear the sound of a stream. The sun gives way to a coolness under shade of the trees. It feels nice here.

"I come here sometimes," Jenna says as she lowers herself gently into the grassy slope. She looks relaxed as she settles down and her eyes move across the shady space.

"While Darry's watching Larans, I can do something I want just for myself. Sometimes I walk the slow way by longer trails and sit here while I listen to the water as it moves by. When it's hot out, it's sure to be cooler here."

I remember the times at home I crossed the fields to the old shed for my own time away from everything. It was mine, my secret place, just for me. I look at Jenna and see her peaceable look.

In the water I see a crawdad, as I call 'em, in the sandy bottom where the water pools before moving on. They are strange critters and I wonder if they are maybe a bit curious about us up above. I think we're watching each other. I pick a spot to sit close but not so it runs to hide in the shadows along the bank. Jenna goes closer, too, and puts her feet in the water very slow so as not to scare it.

Sitting here, I forget about any cares for a time. I watch the wanderings of the critters all around us. The bigger birds hop between the branches above. The smaller ones flit about, following each other from place to place and then disappear. Two squirrels run in circles around a tree trunk, their claws tearing at the bark, chasing each other 'round and 'round, shaking their tails and chattering at each other.

Jenna's voice brings me back to the ground. "We better get going now to get back home."

The word home takes me by surprise, and I feel lost again.

"Can we talk about how I'll get back home?" I look carefully at her, wondering if I can see anything in her thinking.

"Sure, of course. We'll talk with Darry, and see what we come to," she says in that same sweet calm tone that is always her way.

With that, I'm a little more settled again. As we get up to leave, I look back to remember how nice this is. Maybe I will want to come back here for myself.

We keep a steady pace, walking slightly uphill until we reach the end of the trees and are out in the open grass where the sun is full again. I keep up with Jenna; she turns her head now and again to see that I'm still close. Soon the cottage appears again with the poplar trees behind and the piglet at the side. Larans is playing under the skinny young trees. The sight of the place makes me smile and wonder what's going on inside what is my place for now.

Larans lets out a squeal when he sees us.

"Helloooo, my little Larans. Helloooo," Jenna calls across the short distance. Then she turns to one side and I spot a big garden behind a rail fence, at the side of where their cabin sits.

The garden with its even rows stands out from the soft, smooth-looking wild grasses beyond. A funny-looking scarecrow stands tall in the middle of it all with strips of faded straw coming out from the ends of his arms.

As we get closer, I see that there are many kinds of things planted here. There are wide, dark green leaves, frilly lacy leaves that would be carrot tops, tall stalks with corn ears that look fat enough to pick, and shiny red tomatoes. Many smaller plants have leaves too small to be any kind of vegetables that I know.

"What's all that small stuff that looks kinda like weeds?" I say, pointing to them.

"Those are herbs. They make everything taste better, and they make good medicine," she replies. "Rosemary, basil, thyme, oregano, parsley, mint, and catnip, for that old yellow cat you saw."

"What's his name?"

"Cellicot, but don't expect him to answer if you call him that."

I wouldn't believe that any cat would answer, but I let it go now that the garden was all around us.

"We'll take what we need for today. We use this almost every day now and will put a lot away for the winter, drying the beans, and salting and pickling some things for the cold months. We need a lot of dry beans to get us through, but I'm always glad to have the fresh greens when we can. Beans and potatoes get boring late in the winter."

"So you don't have anywhere else you go to get food," I say softly, almost to myself, looking around at all of it.

"Nope, there's no one close. When we get it, we have meat that we can dry. Darry's a good hunter, and we're thankful for having enough game close to us. The garden grows well and, of course, the wild animals take their share. We keep the scarecrow and those strips of cloth on stakes that wave in the wind to keep them away. We plant more than we need and then we have enough after the animals take theirs. We have deer, turkey, and rabbit and quail around here mostly. When they're here and Darry's ready, we get meat without much of a hunt. The quail have the sweetest calls to each other. We hear them even after we're inside in the evening."

I wonder what a quail is, but I don't want to let on that I don't know. We have scarecrows in the fields around our place, too. I'm still looking around wide-eyed at the plantings all around us.

"I notice you have a piglet. Is he for food, too?"

Jenna looks away for a minute and then says, "Yes, he will be for next winter. We traded some things to get him.

"What do you trade?"

Her face lights up as she answers." We traded a braid rug I made from old rags we saved up, a chair that Darry made, and a painted decoration on a board."

The painted board has me most interested, from what I could see about the small, colorful table in the corner of their place. This isn't quite like any house I know of.

"At home when I went to market with Mama, I remember the colorful fruits and vegetables. When one squashed on the cobblestones it would also make colorful stains that got on people's shoes. I was small so nobody big paid any attention to me, and while Mama shopped it was fun to watch the colorful spots moving around. If the shoes and sandals could talk somehow, they'd likely complain about the spots on 'em. I thought that was funny."

I didn't know that Jenna was watching me while I was talking. I look away, feeling a little silly for telling her this story. I do enjoy telling her something about my world. And at times, I like being here, too.

We pick corn, red ripe tomatoes, and spinach for today. The spinach is spotted with dirt from when it rained. That will have to be washed.

Just then Darry appears from around the back of the cottage, waving a pitchfork with one hand.

"Hello, you two! We can have our dinner soon."

It's strange, I think, calling it dinner in the middle of the day. Jenna picks up Larans and we all go in. She sits him on the edge of the kitchen bench to wipe him clean with a wet cloth while holding onto him with her other hand. The center table looks ready for a meal.

"What are we having?" Jenna asks, smiling as she finishes wiping Larans.

"The lentils that were soaking since yesterday have been cooking all morning with carrots, celery, and onions," he answers. "Oh, and with some fatback, of course."

We wash up and come to the table where Darry's serving the steaming lentils into the bowls that are sitting there, ready.

After a moment of just being quiet, almost like when I know people are praying, they look at each other in their own way and we begin to eat. Larans has a piece of bread already crushed in his fist as Jenna blows on a mushed-up spoonful of the stew for him. He watches with his mouth open, wiggling his feet in anticipation and forgetting about the bread still stuck to his hand.

Now I'm now seeing more of who these people are, and I like it.

# CHAPTER SIX
# THE MYSTERIOUS CORNER

Talk around the table is simple, mostly about the morning, while Larans makes whatever sounds he can to join in. I sit up straight to ask my question to both of them.

"I was wondering ...."

"Oh, yes, Crysalline," Jenna says, putting down her spoon.

"I'd be most grateful if we could talk about how I might get back home."

"I've been thinking about it and have some idea. Let's see how this looks as I tell it," Darry says.

He starts by telling what he knows about each of the four directions from here as far as he has been. He tells of those places, looking at me every so often to see if I take note of anything. Sometimes he looks thoughtful before he goes on, I guess to choose what he'll say next.

After some time he looks right at me and says, "Well, Crysalline, did you hear something that might help?"

I can't be sure at all, but some parts are certainly not right so they could be let go.

"The telling of some places sounds like it might be a way to go. To the south could be the right way, by the things you said," I offer.

Darry sits quietly for a moment, then glances at Jenna. She nods her encouragement, so he goes on.

"Well, then, we have the way to go. We'll gather up what we need for going out to find your folks."

He doesn't look quite sure as he finishes, but then adds a smile that brings a more settled look about him. Everyone sits quietly for a time, then Jenna breaks the silence.

"We have everything we need to go out, so we'll start getting it together right away."

This gives me relief but also some upset that they're doing all this for me. I can only sit quiet. At my house everyone talks around the table to fill all the quiet spaces. These people have a different way, a strong quietness about them.

Finally I find the words I want to say. "I'm most thankful for your help. Without you, I don't know what I'd do."

"Well, now, when I opened the door and saw you, I knew we could help. It couldn't be clearer. Now we know what we'll do."

Even though I'm looking down at the table, I can feel Darry looking at me with his usual big smile glowing all the way across his broad, bearded face.

"The day after tomorrow, we'll go." he declares, with Jenna nodding her approval as she puts her hand on my arm. My hands twist together in my lap, and a mixed-up happy feeling bubbles inside me.

The rest of the day things are moved into a pile close to the front door. Jenna gives me ways to help, but mostly I watch them, busy with it all. By late afternoon, I've had time to notice more of the small things inside this place. I also see that the ink doodles on the bottoms of my feet are worn down. Somehow now that feels a little silly.

There are bags of dried fruit slices, jerky, oatmeal, hard biscuits, potatoes, dry beans, onions, and fresh carrots to take along. There's a backpack carrier for Darry to tote little Larans. I have never seen so much going on, just for me. Late in the afternoon, the room is quiet again as they stop to check what's piled up by the door. There are hats, jackets, a blanket, hunting supplies, and even a cook pot.

"How long do you think it will take?"

Darry scrunches up his forehead and rubs his beard. "I don't really know. Since it took you three days to get here, it could be probably five or six. Maybe more. We'll take what we need for a while. I hope we find your place directly, but if we need to, we can find more to eat along the way when we need."

"What about the piglet outside? How will he get along?"

"He'll be fine. We'll give him plenty before we go, and as long as he has that and water, he'll do just fine for the time we're gone," Jenna answers, her back to the room as she's busy starting supper.

"We have the donkey that's pastured out back. He'll carry a lot," Darry adds.

I'd heard the sound of him, but only glanced around the back.

Hunger's beginning to gnaw at me, making me forget about what will start tomorrow, but I don't feel right asking what we're having for supper. I'm just glad to have it. Soon the sound of meat sizzling in the fry pan fills the air and the wonderful smells swirl through the room. A pot of steaming greens sits beside the fry pan.

"We'll eat soon. Everyone get to the table," Jenna announces loudly over the sizzle.

We all know something good is coming, at least judging by the smells that tug at me. I sit on the side of the table where I can see the corner of the room with those mysterious jars on the shelves above the paint spattered table.

"We're happy you're with us and we can help. This is an adventure for us too," Jenna says as we all settle down to eat.

"Thank you for everything," I say again. I can't quite look straight at her. It would be too much to show how relieved and happy I am to be here.

"You were asking about piglet," Darry says as a quiet look crosses his face.

"We put away the meat from a pig we raised earlier, and we keep the meat fresh by packing it in salt and keeping it cool in a root cellar we have under the house. With the coolness underground, it keeps for some time. We use it before it goes bad. A lot of it has been used up by now."

That the meat on my plate has come from somewhere like the cute pig at the side of the house makes me kind of sad inside. The face of the pig just outside keeps poke into my mind. I keep looking at the plate in front of me to keep from thinking about him anymore.

The first taste of the greens is a little bitter, not like anything I know. I push the pile around, hoping for some help to their taste.

"Those are collard greens," Jenna says. "They grow easy here, so we have a lot of them."

I smile, hoping she thinks I like them. I set myself to enjoy what there is. We all keep pretty quiet, except when little Larans shows how he can drop food on the floor easily from his chair. He looks at me when he holds out something to drop, watching me as he lets it fall. Jenna doesn't show any upset that I can tell, and I try not to let him know I think he's funny.

When everyone's finished and the dishes are washed, we all sit down again around the table. The warmth of the fire adds to the glow of my full stomach and the light from the lamp above makes everything cozy.

I feel kind of shy, but I'm curious, so I turn my head toward the covered jars on the corner shelf.

"I've been wondering about those things in the corner over there."

"Would you like to see them now?" Darry asks.

"Sure."

He moves from his seat and lights a lamp on the wall, chasing away the darkness at the corner. Pulling over a stool from under the dinner table, he sits down with a relaxed ease, like he's done it many times before. He pulls a piece of rough paper from under this table and lays it down under the flickering light. Taking the cloth cover from the jar on the shelf shows two brushes, one larger than the other. Opening a round tin at his side reveals a dry, dark lump of something inside. He dips the larger brush into a jar of water, against the dark lump, then onto a waiting small white dish after he wipes away blotches of dry, leftover colors with a rag. It sparkles, wet with the red brought by the brush. Opening another tin, he carries some of the second color to the same dish beside the first waiting wet red pool. The second pool is much darker.

The room is quiet except for the crackles of the fire and the lamps. I haven't seen them light two lamps at the same time before now. While I look over Darry's shoulder and Jenna moves closer and drapes her arm around me. Her touch makes me feel better every time. Mama doesn't touch anybody much, but I know she cares about me just the same.

With a light touch of the brush, Darry pushes a little bit of the bright red pool into the black one and they move, sliding into a darker color. He picks some of it up with the brush and makes a large, sweeping stroke that makes a slight hiss as the brush moves across the rough paper.

A deep red slash appears where the brush has passed, almost looking alive as it begins to sink into the paper. The wetness shines in the flicker of the lamp light. Where the brush has left the color, the paper swells, rising up to take it in, almost as if it has taken a breath. A tingle runs down my back seeing how the paper is moving as I watch.

Darry smiles as he turns to say, "Jenna or I sometimes do this. We call it work and play, something that is outside of words. We both like what happens here. Sometimes it isn't clear exactly what *will* happen, and that's when it's surprising. When traders come through, we trade what we've made for other things we need."

I smile and nod. I can't take my eyes off the wet color as it settles into the paper.

Jenna moves her arm and I glance up, noticing that beams of the ceiling have figures painted along them. Some of them look almost familiar like things in the world, and others I don't know at all. They seem like something from an older time. Then I see that Jenna is looking at me. I can feel that she cares about me. I look back to the sheet of paper; the red slash is now resting inside the paper. Darry rinses the brush and dips it in the bright red color on the dish. He moves the brush along beside the deep red already there and it makes the same sound again. The two strokes blend in a beautiful ribbon. The room is quiet as we all watch this beautiful slash of color glow. I think this is a wonder, for sure.

After a quiet moment, Darry turns toward us and says, "It's getting late, so we better turn in. Tomorrow will be a big day. With Donkey to carry supplies and with whatever we find along the way, we'll do fine." He looks a bit tired just thinking about it.

Jenna picks up Larans, who has fallen asleep on the floor, and takes him to their bed. I go to the wash basin, now a regular part of my day. As I glance at my reflection in the soft flickering light, there's something new and different. I smile. I feel like I'm looking at someone I want to know. Back at the bench that's my bed, I drift off as the last of the fire warms the quiet room, again looking at the designs painted on the beams of the roof above. The shadows of a footpath appear. It's in a meadow that leads to a forest, deep and unknown. With the comfort of the cover wrapped around me, sleep takes me away, far away.

# CHAPTER SEVEN
# FURTHER INTO A NEW WORLD

Someone is knocking on one of the several doors in this strange, sky-colored room. Where is the knocking sound coming from? All the doors are a deep red except for one that is lighter. I go to that one; a sound—not like knocking, but more of a tapping—is coming from the other side. There's something wrapped all around me. It's a cape in royal red—no, now it's deep purple. It's warm and comfortable as I move around.

The cape becomes a cover as I find myself waking on the bench, but the tapping is real and off to my left side. Light's coming in through my closed eyes, and I remember that the small, shuttered window is just above me. Raising myself up on one elbow, I push the shutter open a crack to see what might be making the sound. It creaks open and I see a shadow moving as the cool morning air streams in through the crack. A bird has been pecking on the outside, its sharp beak outlined in the early morning sun. In its quick escape, a wing slaps against the shutter as it flies off, leaving with a brassy squawk of complaint.

Rubbing my eyes, I'm amused at how the bird pecked its way into the dreamy beginning of my day. I relax and lie down again, snuggling into the cozy warmth of the cover that is no longer deep purple.

Footsteps sound from the back as Darry appears and looks over the stacked piles beside the door. The day is now very real. To find home is now more than a dream. We begin today.

Jumping out of the covers so fast it surprises me, I run in three great big steps to the wash basin. Standing before the bowl and rubbing my eyes, I tingle with the thrill of today while I splash my face quickly with the cold water. Drying myself with the cloth that hangs on a wooden peg on the wall, I think about Mama and Papa. I don't remember thinking about them yesterday. My eyes cloud, wet again, only now I'm not so sure why. I have mixed-up feelings about leaving here. But there is no time for that this morning, so I wipe my eyes quickly and turn to go back to the front room.

As I return, the red slash on the paper catches my attention again. I can still see that wet color moving in the lamp light of last night. The paper is still on the table, wanting me to look again, now with soft, red, smiling lips.

*How strange. It's just a piece of paper. How can it smile at me this morning?*

Darry's voice breaks into my wondering. "We're just about ready to go, far as I can tell."

He sounds serious as he moves quickly around the room, so different from the calm of last night. Larans is finishing his warm cereal, and Jenna just put a bowl of hot oatmeal on the table in front of me with a glance and a quick smile. I eat fast 'cause I know all this is happening for me and I don't want them to think I'm an ungrateful slowpoke.

When Darry sees me get up from the table, he calls me over to make sure that I can carry the pack he has ready for me. As he checks the rope straps, I see that it's worn but sturdy. There are two other packs along the wall, one with a larger wooden frame that's made up to carry Larans. It's already filled with just as much as I have. Darry lifts it up and swings it onto his back with only a small grunt. Jenna then lifts Larans into the upper part, where he'll ride as high as the rest of us. His eyes get big as he grabs onto the frame, looks around, and gives Jenna a worried look. She puts on her pack and, before I can think any more about what is happening, the door is open and the morning air floods in. Darry glances behind him to see if all is in order as we leave.

I may never see this place again. I turn back for one more look. It feels so good here after only such a short time. I want to stay longer, but this day has started. Jenna drops a knit cap onto my head and I turn toward the bright daylight ahead.

The piglet at the side of the house lets out a grunt and then a short squeal as we walk away. As I look up, I see a big black bird perched on a high branch against the pale sky, like he's been waiting for us to come out.

"Now Crysalline, you said you came over that short hill and saw our place, didn't you?" Darry asks. Larans is looking over Darry's shoulder, not really awake, watching the movements of the packs and hats everyone is wearing.

"Yeah, that's the direction," I say, pointing to the small rise I came over not so long ago.

We start up the hillside, winding among the rocks, making a crooked line of our own. As we cross the top, I slow down and look back several times as the cabin disappears.

We find our speed easily with Darry in front, me in the middle, and Jenna behind, holding the reins of Donkey, who follows without any complaint. Sometimes Darry glances back, checking on both Larans and me. I guess he wants to see if I can keep up or if I show any sign to tell him the right way.

As I look ahead, the land flows on and on and the sky stands big over it all. We stand at the start of whatever is ahead. The rolling hills hold onto bunches of trees that break the large open spaces of grass and rocky outcroppings. They add interesting lumps of different trees that look all mixed up along the way. Standing alone on some open slopes are the thick trunks of Grandfather trees. They stand with heavy branches arching and twisting wide like shelters from the huge openness. We walk through the grasses and find light paths here and there made by the small animals who have gone the same way over and over. Sometimes we follow on their paths for a while.

All morning, it's easy to keep the pace Darry sets. No one says much, since there is just the wide-open space to be covered by walking and walking. At times we stop to check our straps and bearings. It's too early for anyone to be tired yet.

As we sit in the shade of one of the Grandfather trees, Darry and Jenna look to me, wanting to know my sense of the rightness of our direction. But I'm not clear about anything. It's strange moving along from place to place without knowing if it's right.

"I don't know, I don't know," I sob.

Jenna strokes my hair, and that helps calm me down. After a time, we start out again, and I hope for something useful to appear soon.

We move around hills instead of climbing up and down every one. There's no sound other than the packs as they sway with each footstep. I find it easy to follow Darry. Our single line moves along through grasses, animal paths, and around hills and rocks for what seems like a long time. We keep a smooth pace, with me worrying how to find what we don't know yet.

Larans has slumped into a nap in the carrier. He's lucky to have an easy ride. The sun is warm and a light sweat is trapping loose hairs on my face. A breeze comes up now and again to help. Each of us has a gourd of water to last until we find clear streams.

About midday, we stop to eat in the shade of a single large tree with grassland all 'round. It sits on a rise, so the breeze finds us. Darry and Jenna bring out hard cheese and bread from a cloth wrapper and fresh corn on the cob. Sitting down, I realize how hungry I am. We're all enjoying the food and the rest. Wanting to be helpful for the search is hard enough, but doubt still swirls in my head. The pull between home and this place with Darry and Jenna is confusing.

Larans wanders around with a piece of bread in his hand, studying the ground for bugs that scurry away from his footsteps. The carefully built ant mounds are his favorite to walk on, scattering the ants into crazy activity that he can watch. They spread the word of this giant and then collect themselves to start fixing things again. He stays in the shade. I like to watch him.

My eyes grow heavy after finishing the food. The breeze under this tree is just about perfect, bringing the scent of the warmed grasses up to us. This is like other places we've been, but there's also something different. The wind comes under me, holding me as it combs through my hair, taking away the dust.

As I float out from under the tree, the sun fills my eyes. Like being on a storybook magic carpet ride, I swirl above the tree. Its countless clean, shiny leaves twinkle in the sun, filling my eyes with their sparkles. In the distance, other trees stand like green, furry lumps dotting the rolling grasslands. Birds swirl, playing on the same wind that holds me. They don't seem to notice me at all. I wonder if they care that I'm up here. The sky is clear and blue with only an occasional cloud. I look directly up, wondering what might be above me, and see only wisps of white against the peaceful blue. I want to reach out to see if I can feel the wispy lightness, but I'm not sure if I'd lose my balance. I remember to look out into the distance for home. On the edge of the land, I can see a small line of smoke rising, maybe from a chimney, and make a note of the direction. It's from inside a group of trees far from here, and I'm excited that I found it, and forget how far up I am. Strands of hair blow across my face, reminding me to pay attention. When I dip to one side, everyone below looks quite peaceful, still sitting under the tree. I glance back to the horizon, looking for the line of smoke, but I can't find it again. Now I'm shaking and not floating smoothly at all. I'm not sure what's happening until I feel the hand on my shoulder.

"Crysalline, wake up. Nap time is over and it's time to move on," Jenna says, bringing me back to earth. I began to shake off the sleepy fog and see that they are on their feet, ready to go. I make my way to my feet and sling the backpack on. Whatever they packed isn't heavy. I came to their door with nothing, and now I'm glad to be doing whatever I can.

Darry and Jenna both look at me and Jenna says, "When you think you recognize anything, let us know right away, all right?"

"Sure, I will."

I've been trying to bring back any memory about those days I was wandering. After I knew that I was lost, I tried to notice what I could, but the hazy sense of direction from the gray shrouded sky didn't help.

"I think I was coming from the south, so I was walking north, seeing only a moment of the sun all day. I kind of turned more west so the sun that broke through just before sunset would warm my front as I walked."

Darry has a serious look on his face as he's rubbing his beard.

"Well, that's good enough. We know to go to the south, since we'd set out from the cottage first on the line you pointed and that's kind of east. Like you said, you'd come towards the west later in the day. We'll find more clues as we go along, don't you fret."

For a moment we stand quietly, like we're each making it real in our heads. We set out again and the whole afternoon is peaceful as we move along, hopefully to somewhere.

Tonight will be our first night sleeping outdoors. Jenna and Darry have been out before, so they know how to keep comfortable, but it will be new having Larans and me with them. I wonder how that will be. We stop for the night and build a fire with loose wood we find. It will be cool tonight but not bad, Darry says. He's put stones all around the fire, telling me how they give off some heat even after the fire has burned itself down.

Overhead, the leaves show the yellow and gold of the change early this year. They flutter, bright in the swirls of air, while the last beams of the sun spear through the smoke of the campfire. We will be sleeping close together tonight. It makes me a little nervous thinking about it.

"Tonight is our best night for food. We brought carrots, potatoes, and venison already cooked," Darry declares proudly, standing over the glowing flames of the fire.

"Everything'll heat up easy over the fire, and we'll eat like kings—if the king was traveling," he adds with a chuckle.

I'm hungry and worn down from the day. Supper is ready quick as can be. We finish all the food, down to scraping the bottom of the pot. After supper, I can think of nothing but lying down to rest. Jenna turns to me as we sit around the fire.

"We'll all be closer together tonight, so it won't be cold at all. We'll all cuddle, and, with a bit of luck, we'll sleep well."

I've never done this before, but I imagine we won't change clothes. I don't believe anyone brought any night clothes anyhow.

"We can do something called spooning, like when spoons fit together."

Jenna looks at me for any reaction. In the twilight and flicker of the campfire, it's hard to see anyone clearly so I guess I look agreeable. I can only guess what it's like, and of course I go along with the idea.

"It sounds like you've done this before."

"Yes, and I hope it's fine for you, too."

We collect ourselves under a Grandpa tree, so any wetness that might pass by during the night will fall at the edges of the sheltering branches. They brought a cloth to lie on, and another for cover. Darry will face one end, Larans behind him and Jenna behind Larans, then me right behind her, on the other end. We gather leafy branches to place around to block wind from our nest. We each lie down on our sides, so we can spoon for warmth. It's getting dark with the campfire burning to embers, and everyone is settling down except Larans, who's wiggly and noisy. We all giggle a little until he finally wears down and is quiet.

Jenna's warmth right in front of me is comforting. She reaches behind her neck to pull her hair forward so it won't be in my face. The cool air is creeping around my backside, so I push in closer to her. She reaches over to my back and pulls me even closer, just the encouragement I need to stay as tight against her as I can.

"Good night, Crysalline," she says over her shoulder.

"Good night, everyone," Darry calls softly from the other end.

"Good night," I add. I put my arm over her waist and gently pull to keep close. I shiver at the memory of just a few days ago sleeping outside alone. Her hand gently pats me again, and soon I hear Darry snoring and sense Jenna drifting off, asleep.

# CHAPTER EIGHT
# MYSTERIES ALONG THE WAY

Sleep finally came after a long time last night. I can still feel the night chill on the part of me that wasn't snuggled up to Jenna. I want my own bed again. Larans was fussy for a long time once we woke up, and Jenna was the only one who could comfort him. Daylight has come full so we're all up to start the day.

The hot tea and warmth of the fire this morning are wonderful after last night. I stand with my back to the heat eating today's breakfast of jerky and dried fruits. It looks like the sun is going to be our friend again today. Everyone's doing whatever needs to be done to get moving except Larans, who's flitting about like a bird. Yesterday we set a good pace and I hope it can be the same today. My legs are tired, but I guess everyone else feels pretty much the same.

I try to keep a happy face, but my stomach's hurting again this morning. I like these people and that keeps the worry from grabbing hold of me any more than it does. Out here in the open, I can't find much to say to find my home again. Darry has asked again what my home place looks like, what kind of trees I saw outside my window, and what the hills looked like. Mama will be sitting on her chair, looking out and not knowing what happened.

Darry's voice interrupts the tears that have started up again.

"Crysalline, fill your head with seeing your home. See everyone in your family sitting out front, smiling because they see you coming home, right in front of their eyes. Take a minute and see that inside of you."

I don't see how this could be of any use, but I have no other ideas, so I begin to do as he said. I sit on the ground and Jenna sits at my side, lightly touching my shoulder, and Darry sits on my other side, cutting the wind from that direction. Both of these people are helping me, so I sit here, close my eyes, and begin to see my home and family inside my head. I almost begin crying again but manage to hold it in. My stomach relaxes a little, sheltered by these two people out here, wherever we are. Every day with them, I am more relaxed.

The quiet inside me grows and I remember what Darry told me. As if from another world, I see everyone on the front porch, and they're watching as I come closer, step by step. I want to be there, but now something has changed. It surprises me like that smile when I saw myself in the mirror.

The breeze whispers lightly at my ear. It's a friend in the world I love, but its whispers don't let me know anything of what is ahead.

Opening my eyes, I look around. Jenna and Darry are smiling calmly. It's as if we're all having the same things happening together, right here in this open place. I wonder what more they might know, these people who are still new to me. I hope to learn more being out here with them. And still, the need to find my home keeps at me.

"So now what do we do?" I say, breaking the quiet.

"We'll go on, and find out what comes," Jenna answers calmly.

Her steady, simple answer kind of makes me crazy but I can't find anything else to say. It doesn't really tell me what's going to happen. Darry stands up first, and little Larans stirs from his blank stare, sitting in the carrier with three fingers stuck in his mouth. Jenna rises, and that gets me up, when just before I had been lost in thought. Jenna looks to her far side and gives Darry a glance. He nods, and they both start off in the direction she had looked.

"Come on Crysalline, here we go." She smiles as she adjusts her own pack and looks at mine to see if anything is loose. I can feel where the rope straps rubbed against my shoulders yesterday but it's not so bad.

I keep in step between the two of them. The touch of the sun on me is comforting. The land around us isn't any different that I can tell. It does look to be like places I'd come through when I was lost, but I can't say it's the same place. There are clusters of trees in open fields and hillsides and valleys, and then we walk through shade where the coolness is only broken by the sun winking at us through the leaves. I'm searching to find something familiar. My breathing is easy as the land is flat and the trees are really a pretty sight. Sometimes I forget that we're looking for my place. Birds fly by, looking down at us as we pass. Some let out a cheerful call, maybe to tell others of us arriving, or maybe just because they're happy we're passing through their world.

Back out in the open and direct sun, the little brown furry dirt diggers—that's what I call 'em—are everywhere, standing on their hind legs outside their underground homes to watch us come by. When they see these giants that have come stomping along, they let out a chirp of warning before some run safe underground.

The squirrels in the trees stay safely above. They use the tree branches to go from place to place. It's funny when they chase each other 'round a tree trunk as fast as they can, grabbing at the bark. One time I saw two of them screech at each other in some kind of argument.

Their tails would flick up and down while they screamed at each other. Then one lost his grip and fell to the ground with a thud, bouncing as he hit the soft, leafy ground before he scampered back up the tree. I wasn't sure which of us was more surprised. A live squirrel had never fallen close to me like that. Darry and Jenna wonder why I'm giggling, so I tell them the story and we all laugh about it.

"Okay, now that way is south, so let's keep going that way." Darry points towards the rolling hills.

In the dream, I saw a wisp of smoke in the distance, and I want that to be home. We move along in our single line, walking like we belong together. The sights and sounds pass as kind of a walking dream. As they appear, I search for anything familiar before they pass out of sight again, but nothing fills the holes in my memory. We only stop long enough to adjust our loads or get water.

A tall boulder appears on the horizon, growing bigger and bigger the closer we come. When we're right next to it, I'm sure it's the biggest thing I have ever seen. It looks like it reaches clear up to the sky. I recognize the speckles in the rock as what granite looks like from what Papa told me.

As we're moving around it to keep on our way, all at once Darry, who is in front, stops. Then I hear a clattering sound and the strangest person I've ever seen appears before us. The skinny figure of an old man is covered with animal furs that sway with the breeze. The clattering sound is from a bell hanging from his knapsack. His face is brown and full of deep lines.

"Howdy," he says, raising his gaze to look right at us. I don't know what to think, he's so strange looking.

"Well, howdy to you, too," Darry says.

Then he just squats as if to settle down for a rest and loosens his pack, letting it fall to the ground. He sighs and leans back, the pack behind him. Swinging his legs out, he sits so that the bottoms of his sandals face us with the toes pointing straight up. He settles down as if to plant himself right where he is, wearing a smile that's friendly and unworried.

We all stand looking down at this sight. Then we follow him, settling down to rest. He's small and bent forward, all fur and wrinkles, looking almost not a person at all.

His eyes are bright and filled with interest when he asks, "Where do you come from?"

"We're from about one day's walk over that way," Jenna answers, pointing loosely over her shoulder. It seems to be the kind of careful answer one would give strangers, especially one like this.

"I wander many paths much of the year, and we have not met before.

I travel where the will takes me, and today it brought me to this rock, such a beautiful strong stone," he says with an unconcerned look on his face.

To me this is strange talk, riddles.

"And you, young lady, where are you going?" he asks, tipping his head to the side to look at me.

Before I can begin to think of what to say, Darry answers, "We are looking for her home, a place called Barrytown. She was lost before coming to our door."

Everyone must be able to see that my face has turned bright red. They're talking about me like I'm not right here. I sit up tall, not wanting any stranger to think I'm so lost.

"That name is not one I know," he answers.

He glances back at me like he can look right into my insides. Then he turns away and says, "I should introduce myself. I am known as Raspartan." He gets an odd smile on his face and his eyes close for just a moment. I wonder if he finds this all quite amusing. He looks like he fell out of the kind of story told at home late in the evening.

"And where are you from?" Darry asks.

With a slow smile, his soft eyes are still almost closed as he answers, "I am from a place like this but not here. Far away, but easy to find when you look for it. All anyone has to do is to imagine where it is and they will know about it."

After a pause, he adds "I am a peddler of things that most folks don't know about. What I carry is found in questions."

I certainly can't figure what he's talking about. I ask a question to sort of poke at this bag of fur sitting right in front of us. "What do you mean by what you say? I can't tell anything by it."

"It is all found in whatever you do not already understand. I can only answer so you may want to know more and only then you may find out something more useful."

By now I imagine there's only an empty bottle sitting here wrapped in furs. Everyone else is quiet.

Raspartan seems to notice that we're uneasy with his answers so, with his bright green eyes open wide, he says, "I am a wanderer who finds many things in many places, and I wish to help you. I want nothing in return. Perhaps we might chat a while, if you have the time to be here with me."

He's clearly very relaxed and doesn't look like he cares at all what might happen next. With a small shrug of my shoulders, I decide he may really be quite harmless. Looking at Jenna and Darry, I see they both look puzzled.

"Tell us of some of your recent travels. What have you seen? We need to find the direction to go to find Crysalline's home," Darry asks.

He begins telling strange stories of other places that make me curious. "There are places where the trees bow and whisper to each other when they think no one is listening. There are flowers that change color, blushing when they are looked at closely, and waters that chuckle in amusement when someone puts their toes in. I have seen animals that speak in words like you and I."

I am quite caught by his talk.

Time passes as we all sit and talk in the warm sunshine of afternoon close to this mountain of a rock that gives back the warmth of the sun. Sometimes I look out and see distant places shimmering and wiggling in the distance. If I let myself drift off, I can see the trees dance.

Jenna and Darry tell of their home with pride, the work of building it, and the joy they have in the place they call Milhila. They tell how they like making things by their own hands. Larans, who is still in his carrier, drifts off into a nap in the warm afternoon.

I tell of my family and the place where I grew up. The words come out slowly as I keep my head down to keep from looking directly at anyone. I don't tell much about how I like being with Jenna and Darry. It makes me feel a little guilty, if I think about it. Shortly, I can't find anything else to say so Jenna speaks up.

"How do we get to this place we are seeking, Crysalline's home? None of us knows for sure which way to go from here."

Raspartan closes his eyes and tips his head to the side, like he's chewing on the question, for a while.

He looks at each of us carefully, then reaches into his furs. He pulls out a small, old-looking box that has several worn figures painted on the sides. He says, "If you are willing, with help you will be able to know the place you seek."

I don't like his riddles.

# CHAPTER NINE
# THE FALL

The box in his hands sparkles as it comes out into the sunlight. With a shy smile, he gently lowers it to his lap, then continues, "We have come here, each from our own direction, and you are seeking your way. The way to a place you have not been and do not yet know. I believe I can be of help to you. I know something of these things, but cannot say how. It is that I am here, you are here, and there is a way. That is how I see it."

Darry sits straight up, looking ready to pounce on this little man inside all the animal skins. "What are you saying? I've heard stories of such things. Are you telling me there's a way of knowing more than what we can plainly see?"

The bumps on my neck and arms are standing up.

I watch Jenna, who is watching Darry, who is watching Raspartan, who sits quietly with his eyes closed. Darry looks tense, but is trying to stay still. I wonder what he might do.

"Darry, let me ask you some questions. Do you respect the wisdom in the world all around you, the world out beyond yourself? That there is order in the nature of the world, yet it works mainly as a mystery? If that is your way, would you be willing for that nature to speak inside of you, letting you know more about what is true?"

Darry sits, frozen still, his eyes tight, considering what to say next. Only his beard moves slightly, pushed by the breeze.

"I know the natural world as it gives and holds my life. Are you saying that I can know deeper truth?"

Raspartan turns his head to one side and lowers his face, appearing even smaller than before. A voice speaks, but I can't tell where it might be.

"This is the way, if you believe. You must believe that you are a student, and the teacher is everywhere."

The voice was not Raspartan's and it didn't even seem to come from him. I'm shaking so hard I think everyone can see. Whatever is happening, I'm curious. Darry's eyes look wild with interest. Jenna's sitting wide-eyed, so I imagine she might not see me shaking. Darry is sitting tall, like he's ready to leap to his feet. His mouth opens to speak, but for a moment nothing comes out.

When he finds words, a deep, smooth, voice comes out. "I am here, willing to learn, even of things I do not know of yet, the things that are in my blindness but truly are my dreams." A look comes over his face, as if he didn't know what he was going to say before it came out. His face turns red, then he adds, "I am willing to find out."

Jenna looks at him with shock and curiosity. I think I'll faint. Raspartan sits peacefully with his eyes closed and his hands softly in his lap, cradling the box. I don't know what to think or do so I sit as still as I can. I keep my eyes on Darry and Jenna and see that they look calmer, so I start to breathe normally again. Maybe they understand something of this strange meeting.

I feel myself drifting off into a haze. As I do, the voice from Raspartan speaks, clear but soft. "There are many things changing in many places, and your travels may be long and with great effort. We cannot be merely content, for change will ask much of us that we may not easily know what to do. There will be difficulty and confusion that is not written yet, but be sure, this will come to pass. Much will depend upon the greater spirit of people, as they are all in the same questions, each one looking for their own way."

Despite the warmth of the huge, sun-drenched boulder, I'm cold. There's a throbbing quiet in the air, and no one in this circle moves at all. It almost hurts to breathe.

Again Raspartan's voice breaks the silence. "These things are in the winds that move far, where they may come into everyone's thoughts, whether they know the truth of it or not. No man or beast is truly separate from all men and beasts. We are all moving towards what has not yet been born. If the blind feel these winds and only look backwards, they would not have any choice of futures."

For a moment, there is only the silence of the rock before a sound begins from deep in Raspartan's throat. Not a hum or a growl, this sound moves through everyone as it dances wildly around us in the great outdoors.

On the inside of my closed eyelids, the brightness is almost blinding. From this breath on I do not want to look out for fear of breaking whatever's going on around and inside of me. So much is still unknown. What is ahead?

The next thing I know, something awakens in me, something from a place unknown, like from where my dreams are made. It grows real, becoming the sound of my own breathing, as if for the first time, moving in and out from deep inside me, moving in the spaces inside me. My heartbeat becomes clear, drumming its own rhythm. These two things continue, together.

The wind whispers in my ear, saying, "I will be everywhere you go, washing calm over you." I'm not moving at all, just listening. It's not long before I can see things of home and the places I've walked, with blossoms that open and fade as I pass. Those memories bring joy and tears and my body aches with loneliness. Next, I see myself crossing the grassy fields following Jenna. The grasses reach out to tickle me as we pass. I put my hand out to meet them with a touch. Within a breath, my wondering and questions fade.

Raspartin's voice rises into the space, bringing me back to the hard ground where I've been all this time.

"Now it is time for the winds to take us in different directions."

I open my eyes to see Jenna and Darry beginning to stir. Raspartan is looking at us, and a gentle smile lingers as he studies each one of us. Larans is wide-eyed, looking at some distant place from his seat in the backpack that's leaning against the granite. Jenna and Darry glance at each other, and Darry clears his throat as he gets up. Raspartan rises and begins to gather himself to leave.

"We must be on our way, too," Darry says, letting the words fall out.

As far as I can tell, everything is just as confused as before. Darry's forehead is lined, deep in thought, and he's moving like he's weighed down with Raspartan's words. Jenna and Darry move into the shade of a tree not far from where we've been sitting. They seem to be having private talk, so I wander away a bit.

After a little while ,Jenna looks up and catches my eye, so I go to join them under the tree.

"Hi, sweetie," Jenna offers with a weak smile. Her voice sounds tight.

"Hi," I answer while looking down to watch my foot move some loose dirt around.

"We haven't found out anything that will help us find your home. But we do have an idea of what to do next, so let's see if it helps. It's getting on into autumn, and we know that the coming season will be colder. We're thinking that we need to get ready for a longer search and wait until after winter to begin again. Do you think you can stay with us over the winter? We can begin again after winter turns into spring."

A buzzing sound fills my ears and the ground is wobbly under my feet. I sit down, kind of crashing into a pile. Jenna and Darry have unconvincing smiles on their faces as I look up at them briefly. I poke my finger in the dirt at my feet.

When I begin to talk, my voice is so soft that I almost can't hear myself. "I guess you know what's best."

Down deep inside, I think that being in their place over the winter won't be so bad. It was hard to leave but going back again will be different. I'll be at their place for the whole winter, an extra person.

"We'll all be fine for the winter, and then make another plan to get the job done next spring. You'll have so many stories to tell your family when you get home," Darry says, confident and cheery-sounding.

I raise my eyes enough to see their faces, and they both have smiles that show me they care. I smile in return, but the lump in my throat is still there. I don't know anything else. What more is going to change?

The sky is showing the coming of evening and Raspartan has been gone for hours. We find a group of trees to be our shelter for the night before moving on tomorrow, beginning our way back to Milhila.

After the night of the now-familiar, warm spooning, we have jerky and dried fruits with water from the nearby stream for breakfast. We gather everything and, with Darry pointing the way, we start back. This time we know where we're going, so I'm relaxed, even with the change of plans. We walk a while without saying much. There's a dullness to the day but my mind is spinning with so many thoughts about what it might be like for the winter. Along the way, they tell me how winter will not be bad with the food they have put away, just darker and colder. This winter I know I'll be another mouth to feed.

Darry pauses at times to look for the signs that we're going the right direction. I watched him make notches on trees along the way, and we're looking for one of those notches.

"I might have made a slight change of direction some time back. The trees are different here than I remember," he says softly, almost to himself. Darry's been making notes as he notices small things along the way and taking cuttings of plants he's never seen before to plant in their own valley. Every so often, we find a stream to add to our water.

As far as I can tell, this looks the same from where we'd been all along, with its rolling hills, valleys, and several kinds of trees here and there.

"So that we don't waste ourselves, why don't you all stay here, and I'll go up that hill and see what I can find out. I'd like to be sure we're going the right way," Darry says, glancing at each of us.

"We could stand the rest. Larans will stay here with us, and we'll be fresh when you come back," Jenna says cheerfully.

The sun is dancing in and out of clouds, so it's a mild day. Resting in the open here will be easy.

"Take a bit of jerky and dry fruit in case you need more time than you think," Jenna suggests.

He takes some and walks off uphill, past a rock outcropping, and is soon out of sight. Jenna turns to me and says, "We have some time to stretch out and rest our feet."

I nod agreement, so we put our packs down to rest against rocks.

"How long do you think Darry will be gone?" I ask as we settle in facing the clouds floating overhead.

"Only as long as it takes."

With that I drift off, listening to little Larans nearby, tied by his length of rope so he can't wander off. Soon I can hear Jenna's soft breathing, a sure sign that she's napping, and I drift off, too. I come awake suddenly when Jenna bolts upright. Larans has come undone from his rope and has wandered off some distance, happily looking at whatever he might find.

"Hey, Larans. Come back here," she yells playfully.

She struggles to her feet and starts running to cover the uneven ground. I'm slightly amused as I watch her run. When she's about halfway to him, she makes a sidestep over some rough spot and her arms shoot out sideways, like she's lost her balance. In a blink, she disappears.

I can't believe my eyes. I get up and race across to where she disappeared, blinking away the fog of sleep and disbelief as I run along the same rough ground. Larans is standing still, eyes staring, in shock, I think. As I get closer to the rocky spot where she was last, I see the dark hole that opens up right in front of me. It's wider than a grown person can reach with both arms. Panic begins to race through me as I come up to the opening and kneel at the edge to look into the dark pit below. Jenna is about fifteen feet down, lying on her side and not moving. I look up again to see Larans still standing right where he was a minute ago. I run over to him, sweeping him up tightly, and run back and retie him to his rope. Hurrying back to the opening, I lean over the edge.

"Jenna," I yell, louder than I ever thought I could. "Jenna!" I try again but she doesn't move.

I can see bloody red scratches on the side of her hip and arm through torn spots in her clothes. Leaning my head as far down into the hole as I can, I see there is a rough, rocky outcropping, maybe a way to climb down to her. The bottom is sandy and shows how hard she landed, leaving marks in the sand.

"Jenna," I call again. She doesn't move.

Scared out of my wits, I wonder what to do. Going back to the packs, I grab a length of rope and rush back to the hole. I quickly begin looking for the best way to climb down. I have to be careful and not fall in, too. I look back at the hillside where Darry walked away and see no hint of him, so I turn to Larans, who is bawling, then back to the darkness of the hole right in front of me. It's soft and sandy at the top edge, and then quickly becomes rocky along the sides going down. I put one leg over the edge and feel for a foothold below but begin to slide on the sand. I catch hold of a tiny sapling growing at the edge and move my foot a little sideways to a different spot. I find a foothold, so I swing my other leg over and my weight is on the one foot under me. I slide more on the sandy edge and grab hold of a second scrubby piece of brush growing within reach, trying to keep my face out of the dirt as I begin to slide down, backwards.

The brush holds, and now I search madly for another spot to grab. I find a jagged rock edge with one hand and my fingers get a grip, so I start searching for a spot for my other foot. The brush feels like it's going to fail soon so I have to grab onto something else. I'm struggling to breathe with my face against the sandy edge as my other foot finds a spot that feels solid enough. I move my weight onto the side with the new foothold and start to let go of the brush to find a new way to balance. Breathing with sand in my face, I have no way to see below. I tilt my head to the right to try to see better. I can move one foot, feeling along the wall for another edge. The light in my eyes from above is also keeping me from seeing very much in the dark below. I find another foothold, going down a little farther. Now I blink and look down into the dark hollow space below. After a few breaths, I can see more of the rocks going down. My hand is weakening on the sharp rock above and I'm afraid I might fall trying to get to her. One more step down and I think I might be close enough to jump backwards to the sand and dirt below.

The cool dampness of the pit grows stronger. Looking to see what I can find out about Jenna, I see that she's still not moving. The rocks are slippery from the sand stuck to my feet so I need to keep moving so I don't fall. I go down one more step, then. with a look under my arm, I push off backwards, hoping for the best. It's soft where I land and my feet sink deep into the sand. My eyes adjust to the dim light around me while the sky above is blinding.

There's only a little bleeding in the scrapes on Jenna's side where her clothes are ripped. Her hip is scraped and coated with sand. Straightening her legs out, I begin stroking the side of her face and calling her name, hoping she'll come to. I nervously wave my arms around, not knowing what else to do. She begins to moan softly. I stroke her face again, and she opens her eyes. With a confused look, she smiles at me.

"What happened?" she asks weakly.

"You fell into a hole in the ground, and I came down to get you. Are you all right? Do you hurt anywhere?"

"Where is Larans?" she asks as she jerks herself alert, suddenly remembering.

“He’s fine. I tied him up again.”

We can hear Larans up above, screaming wildly.

Now I can study the pickle we’re in. I look ’round the rock walls and see that one side has more of a way to get up than the other. I came down the harder way. Jenna isn’t moving much yet.

“Can you move your arms and legs all right?”

She takes some time with the question, and I run my hands over her arms and legs to see if she’s hurt anywhere else. She moves to find out what she can, and winces at the scrapes on her side as she does.

“I’m not too bad.”

She begins to roll over on her side and raises herself up on one elbow.

“Oh, my, I’m woozy. I need a while before I can stand up.”

# CHAPTER TEN
# THE PIT

This is like being inside a giant mouth that smells, and I just want us to be out of here. The only thing on the sandy bottom is one big rock. That's all that's down here besides us. When I look up, the sky above looks so far away.

"Just rest a bit. I'm going to figure out how to get out us out of here," I say firmly, but not sure how.

Fear is gnawing me to pieces, but I pay it no mind. I've got to do something; there's no other way about it. I look for good places to climb up. It's not clear if Jenna will be able to help herself much very soon, and Larans is still crying up above. At least we know he's still there.

"How are you now?"

"I think I am somewhat better. I'm still lightheaded, and my arm is starting to hurt, but I'm some better," she says sheepishly.

I look at her arm, and it's showing an angry red from the scrapes but not bleeding much.

"When you can, try that rock over there for a first step up, and then we can find higher spots going up. You can stop and sit on that small ledge up on the left, and I can keep going up to the top and pull you up. What do you think?"

She nods to be agreeable, but she doesn't look all that sure. I wonder how this is going to go. Darry might not be back soon, and it seems like it's better to try now than later when we'll be cold and maybe worse off.

I tie the rope into a big loop and sling it 'round my neck and over one shoulder. After helping Jenna to her feet, she follows my words as we start up the rocky wall. She can't see much since she's face to face with the wall at places.

"Ohhh, I'm still lightheaded. I need to go slow."

"You can stop on that small ledge to your right side. Tell me when you feel good enough to start again."

I talk to her for a few minutes, hoping that I can keep her head clear enough that we can work our way out of here.

"I feel better enough now to go on. What's next?"

"I'll come up alongside you and find the best spot to get a hold on the top with the rope loop."

I come up past her, close enough to the top that I can see grasses out there. It takes me several tries before I can throw the rope loop over something. The rope groans but holds as I pull on it to see if this is going to work. With a new toehold, and my arm looped in the rope to pull, I struggle as hard as I can to get up and over the sandy edge. Over the top, I just lay there gasping for breath, but Jenna's still down there on that small ledge.

Turning around, I see her face smiling up at me. I lower the loop to her and she puts it under her armpits and reaches up to hold on. She pulls up with both hands as I pull from above.

"Slow down, I have to get my foot onto something so I can push up better." I stop and wait. "All right, now I'm ready," she calls.

The rope burns in my hands and my feet dig in, sliding toward the pit. We both strain as she moves from one step onto another, one hand on the loop and another grabbing at the rock wall. Finally, the top of her head appears over the top of the pit. She looks up and grabs onto my ankle with one hand while I keep my feet dug in. I grab her by that arm to pull her up over the top. Larans is at one side, flat on the ground, still screaming. Seeing him, we both break down, crying and laughing at the same time. I grab onto her hard in a long hug. We're all right.

We run to soothe Larans, who really doesn't know what happened. With the water gourds, I help her rinse the sand out of her scrapes, and we both drink until they're empty. She begins to shiver, shaking almost as hard as I was. I get close and put my arm around her, wrapping her tight.

"I don't want to do that ever again," she says.

"Me neither."

With that, we sit holding onto each other until Darry appears from the long shadows of the late day. The grin on his face turns to shock and then relief when he finds out what happened. The rest of the evening I try not to ask "How are you? Can I get you anything?" too often but I'm so happy that she looks to be not hurt too bad. I can't help but feel the hurt myself when I look at the scrapes. As we spoon our way to sleep, I'm careful to not touch her side. We're all bone weary but I don't relax until I hear her breathing soft. Only then can I fall asleep.

The next morning, she looks like her old self, bright and alert. After a breakfast of jerky, we fill our water gourds and collect ourselves for the way back. The walking is slower, as Darry and I know that Jenna would never complain but our normal pace would be trying for her. Darry uses his notes and only once wrinkles his forehead as he makes sure of our direction. He always seems pretty sure to me. Open grasslands roll past, with deer and other small animals that wander around us. I spot a fox who carefully watches us at a distance. The smaller animals mostly just scamper down into their burrows when we get close. Rocky places make me worry about Jenna, but she never loses her balance as we weave around those spots. I'm ready to be back.

The streams we find are weak, but we can still get some good water. I don't mind the time to stop. It gives me a chance to see how she is. Her face tightens when we sit down or get up, but she doesn't complain a bit. We eat biscuits while we walk, keeping a slow, agreeable pace. I begin to see things that look familiar, places we saw going out when I was excited and our spirits were high. Back here again and being with them for the winter is a new, unknown, kind of exciting.

While we walk through open grasslands side by side, Darry and Jenna begin to talk some about their life, I guess since I'm going to be here longer.

"Living in our valley is really pretty easy," Darry declares with some pride.

"Yes, we enjoy the place. It's so different from where we grew up, found each other, and married. People lived closer together there. We wanted to live with really open land around us, so we came here to start our own home. This is our joy. Darry's father came to help us start, but he's gone from this life now," Jenna adds.

I wonder about their other folks, but don't want to be too nosy so I keep quiet.

I do listen with more interest, since these people are my family for the winter. As we move along, Darry slows down at times like an animal on the hunt. Sometimes he makes a gentle sound at the sight of some landmark or a scent on the breeze. Seeing a particular tree, he runs his hand over the bark, finding the mark left earlier.

He turns to Jenna and me and then says with a grin, "We're close to home, and I know for sure we'll be home tonight."

My legs are tired, but stronger than ever before. I have deep, steady breathing, and have learned more about the differences in the air from place to place. Keeping pace with Jenna and Darry was harder at first, but not so much anymore.

The sun has dropped below the tree line, and shadows cover the way ahead. We're all keeping a faster pace, anxious to get home. The breeze is gone and sweat drips into my eyes if I don't wipe my forehead. We round a curve with Darry leading, and we hear a sound.

"Did you hear that?" Jenna asks.

We stop to listen. But the only sound now is of the slight rustling of the treetops. Darry shakes his head, and we look at each other, standing quiet to try to hear it again.

We go on again at a steady pace, and no one says anything. Then, there it is again, the sound. This time a little louder and clearer. We grin, and Darry lets out a loud whoop. Piglet's squeal tells us we're almost home.

We hurry the rest of the way, and in the gray twilight the cabin appears, dark and silent in the stand of trees. We smile at each other and cover the last steps quickly. Jenna pulls the latch and opens the front door, and the space fills with the sounds of our feet on the wooden floor. She lights a lamp, and the light flickers to fill the cold room. Everything looks just as it did when we left. For now, it's home. Inside, I'm happy.

I take off my backpack and drop onto a chair. Leaning against the hard chair back I feel at home even though Mama and Papa are still out there somewhere. I watch Jenna and Darry move about, busy with being back and settling in. All I want to do is get to my bench at the side of the room. It's good to be back and I don't want to do anything else, knowing that all winter I will be here in this place with the people I have come to like so easily.

***

Morning comes and I hardly remember going to sleep. The day is clear and bright, and I'm walking in the warm air in summer clothes. My legs are strong. Hills stretch out ahead, clusters of trees are sprinkled here and there, and an occasional animal trail shows the way to somewhere. Clouds float cheerfully overhead as birds sing, and squirrels scamper free, high in the treetops. I feel wonderfully alive, knowing I'm walking towards somewhere I want to be, humming as I move along. A sharp clanking noise from behind gets my attention. As I turn to see what it is, my foot catches on something. It's a blanket. I can smell the warm edge when I pick it up and hold it to my face, and I know where I am: back in Milhila.

"Good morning, sleepyhead!"

I open my eyes and turn to see what's going on, but I already know the voice. Jenna's across the room. The red scrapes on her arm are hard to look at, but they're not getting any worse. She's at the fire—with hot water for tea, I hope.

"How did you sleep? We slept very well being back home and in our own bed."

As soon as she says the words, she bites her lip. I turn my head to the side so I can see her more easily and pull the blanket up tighter.

"I slept good, thanks. And it's nice for me, too, being back here."

I'm ready to leave the comfort of my bed, so I jump up, going past the warmth of the fire as I move to the wash basin to begin the day. I'm back to the warm front room quickly, and into the kitchen corner where

I come up next to Jenna. It's easy being back with the memory of spooning so close to her. I want to reach around her waist and hug her from behind, but I settle for just standing close and putting my hand on her shoulder.

"Is there something I can do? Now that I'm here for longer, I can do more."

"Grab the bowls from the shelf," she says, taking my hand and touching it to her cheek.

The bowls sit stacked on the shelf, ready to use. They're thick and strong, heavy with the colors of the earth, and show the swirls of a hand on a potter's wheel. I know little of pottery, but had seen something like this back home in the marketplace, shopping with Mama.

By now I know where most things are in the day spaces here. I'm able to be useful without being embarrassed by making some silly mistake. Carefully, I pick up the bowls and wooden spoons, and set the table for breakfast.

"I don't hear Larans or Darry. Where are they?"

"They're outside, taking care of Piglet and Donkey, and checking on the garden."

Just as she finishes the words, we hear them coming across the front to the door, with Darry's muffled words making Larans laugh. When the door opens, Darry comes, in a little out of breath, holding Larans on his hip.

"It's colder out this morning, but everything looks just about like we left it, except the things that have grown a bit wild in the garden. Our animal neighbors have helped themselves, but nothing so bad."

Larans watches his dad's face as he speaks, but he doesn't let on if he understands much. He seems happy to be back at home and inside, wiggling his legs as the smell of breakfast fills the air.

Darry puts Larans down on the chair with the strap and wipes their hands with a wet cloth. Larans doesn't care much for the cleaning, I can tell, but he doesn't complain. He knows it means that food will be coming soon.

"We can eat," Jenna calls, so we all sit. I sit where I did before we left. Now everyone is in their regular place.

We hold hands around the table like we've been doing. After a moment of quiet and smiles, spoons are digging into the spiced oatmeal and dried fruits. For now, I think being here together is all anyone could want.

"That was a good try we made, but it's good to be back. Now we can get ready for winter. There's some digging to do to get the rest of the potatoes up before a hard frost comes."

Looking at me, Jenna explains, "They're important for us. They keep well for a long time. Cooked with some fat and salt makes them the best, I think. They really fill a lot of hungry spaces in the winter."

Frost will come, but it usually only lasts a short time, they tell me. I see how they live directly with the seasons. I guess there's less work in the winter when some of the outside world is asleep and people stay inside. Here it will be the four of us. Larans is growing like a weed, as Jenna says. I hope he doesn't get as noisy as my little brother was. I hope that maybe there'll be more time for the crafts.

For now, I have my own clothes that we patched and a sweater that Jenna let me use on the trip out. It fit loose on me for sure, but that might be fixable somehow when there's time. It seems like everything can be handled. I know the summer clothes that Jenna's been wearing. She's taller than me by a hand, being all grown up, and I'm still growing. I've seen her wear a sweater, and hope I can have one this winter. Just as I'm thinking such things, she comes up to me.

"We should look into what you can wear this winter, now that we're family for a while."

She knows how to say a thing so it carries no harshness. I can see a quiet beauty in her that fills the room around her. Her brown eyes are always warm. Her sandy brown hair is tied back most the time to keep it out of her way while she works. She moves smooth and sure, a natural part of the world where everything fits like nature wants. I never hear her complain, but she can be firm with Larans. With no more than her touch on the back of my hand, she draws me out of my thoughts. She knows how to make herself pretty with something simple. Her clothes are more colorful than what Mama would wear. I hear the yarn is colored with plants before it's woven into cloth. I sure hope I can be able to dress pretty some time while I'm here. Maybe today will be a start.

"We can go and look at something that might do for you."

I can't bear to look up directly as I work to find a regular-sounding answer. An excitement runs through me and I want to scream "Yes" but manage to say "That would be fine" with just a simple smile.

"How about right now?"

Without waiting for an answer, she takes my hand and leads me back to the far corner toward their bed. The bed sits in the middle of one wall with some drawers at the side. They look like something Darry's made. Jenna sits me down on the side of the bed, which is already straightened up for the day.

"You have a nice bed." That isn't something I would have thought I'd say, but after the words were out, I thought it was all right.

I can't take my mind off the idea of some clothes, and I guess she can tell.

"I've been thinking about you getting some clothes for winter, and I think I have something you might like," she says with her usual smile.

I think I might just bust wide open at the idea of getting to wear something of hers.

She reaches into a drawer and pulls out two things. "You can take these over to the wash basin to try on and see what you want for the winter. We have enough for the both of us."

With a soft, "Thanks," knowing that clothes didn't come easy, I look down, telling myself that wanting both would be wrong. I get up from the bed and try not to run as I go to try them on, almost tripping on myself. I need to try on each one several times before picking, just to see myself looking grown up in the reflection. I smile at my reflection. I like how her clothes feel and smell, even if they are too big on me.

Finally, I know I must decide and go back to where she's sitting at the center table with a cup of tea. As I take a few steps, I twirl around, looking to see her expression, then I study the sweater I have on and wiggle my toes.

In one huge move, I crash down on the chair across from her and say, "It was hard to decide, but I pretty much like this one best."

"Well, you might borrow the other one sometimes. We can share. Then, come springtime, we can choose something else when it gets warm again."

It's a better day than any birthday ever.

# CHAPTER ELEVEN
# CHANGING SEASONS

The tell of winter coming is on the air. The early morning air bites at my cheeks. Jenna and I wait for the morning sun to warm everything before we go out if we can. Darry's been digging up the last of the potatoes. He shows me how, with a turn of the soil, a bunch comes up out of the ground. If one gets cut in digging, it won't go to waste; we'll just eat it soon.

Darry and Jenna know the ways of keeping food. Dried or salted mostly, but some is pickled, too. I help as much as I can, trying to keep up with the work they already know so well.

Turnips, carrots, rutabagas, onions, and beets are the things to get in so we can eat well all winter, they tell me. I wake up in the mornings tired from the day before, and my hands hurt, but the work is for our own good. At home, it was easier 'cause someone else grew a lot of the food. Today I'm helping get the potatoes up after Darry turns the dirt.

"Crysalline, we'll have enough this year, but it can get pretty thin in the last of winter when there isn't much left. Of course, we'll have the fresh winter greens going on for a while, but I like to have more choices than them and the potatoes when we can."

There's so much to know about really taking care of yourself. So much is all connected. We get soap that's made from animal fat in trade. That sounds icky to me, but the soap makes everything cleaner and less stinky, but I don't like how it dries out my hands. When a trader comes, sometimes after several months, they take some of the small handicrafts as trade for things like soap and salt. While they're here, they tell stories of strange happenings in other places with a twinkle in their eye. Most of the time, I don't believe their stories exactly. Yet sometimes I wonder what's really out there.

This morning, a harsh wind is ready to nip at my cheeks and it's fine that I don't have to go out yet. As Darry opens the door, the cold rushes in and Larans, sitting in his seat, blinks his eyes and wiggles his legs after the door is closed again.

"What is there to do to get dinner today?" I ask.

Now I use their words, "dinner" for the mid-day meal and "supper" for the evening meal.

"It would help if you get an onion from the root cellar," Jenna says.

I go around the back to the root cellar that's dug into the hillside. I wouldn't miss the chance to do anything Jenna wants. I like it here now that I'm fitting in better. I feel like I'm a bit older, and I love having her clothes even though they are loose on me. That has me walking my own way to look like I want. I'm stronger from the work and feel more like a young woman. Sometimes I get tickled inside with it all.

The days get shorter and shorter, and I can feel the whole world around us slowing down. After supper, when the sun is long gone, we sit 'round the table, talking about the day and laughing about something or other. Many evenings, I tire out early and want to lie down right after supper's finished. That could be even earlier by the middle of winter, I'm guessing. I notice those books on the shelf near the painting corner, but they aren't as interesting as just watching everything Jenna does.

Darry comes in the door carrying two wide, flat pieces of wood.

"Crysalline, you could use a better place to sleep, and this wood has been drying for a while, waiting for a good use. I'll fix that bench to be wide enough so you won't fall off," he says with a chuckle.

"I haven't fallen off yet, but thanks. I was wondering if I might someday."

"This will make it almost wide as a bed and I'm making up more of a pad so those boards feel some softer on you."

As the afternoon passes, I watch him fix up the bench for me when I have time. There's even a cloth cover filled with fresh straw and dry grasses that smells as sweet as Autumn itself. I can hardly stand the wait to be on it tonight.

***

It's cozy when we let the days pass by inside the house. Larans mostly amuses himself with a little wooden figure that looks pretty much like a horse, and his face is bright and cheerful. Jenna and Darry both take time to play games with him on his fingers and toes. He's grown up in just the time I've been here. He can walk all the way across the room now without being wobbly at all. When he does fall down, he looks for around to see if someone has noticed, then he picks himself up and is all right again. Darry and Jenna like for him to help himself. Being able to take care of your own feelings and hurts is part of growing up, they tell me.

The shortest day of the year is coming. They've told me me that they always have a special meal for it, since after that the light begins to stay longer and longer every day into spring. I'm ready for the shortest day to be past.

"We always make a cake with dried fruits and nuts to celebrate. It's our way of being thankful for the return of spring each year," Jenna says.

"Tomorrow I'll be making the cake, and you can help," Jenna says in a whisper, like it's our special secret.

"Sure, that would be fine. I will."

Their way of marking the day sounds great. I'm still a bit shy being in the middle of all this attention, but being a part of their family doings is just wonderful. We didn't do this at home, and I wonder how tasty this cake will be. I've never even helped bake a cake before.

The quiet darkness of evening comes like a blanket and I'm sleepy. The ridge line of trees to the west cuts up into the sky so the sun has set fast. These days I'm back awake before daylight when Larans is wandering the house looking for a playmate. He comes over to my bed and puts a finger on my cheek to get my attention.

The early day air inside is chilly and lacy patterns of frost show at the edges of the window shutters where the cold air pushes to get in. Most mornings, wrapped in my warm cover and cozy stuffed mattress, I watch it melt away as the cabin warms. That's when I want to get up.

Today, Darry has come to the front carrying his boy on one hip. Larans has his thumb in his mouth and his sleepy eyes buried in his daddy's chest. I wish I could remember those sweet times from when I was small.

Darry puts Larans down into his chair, and stretches out with both arms, touching the wood beams of the ceiling. Then he begins building a fire again.

"This winter's different than most," he says casually to me across the room, rubbing his eyes with the back of his free hand. "But I guess they all are different," he adds with a chuckle.

"How is this year different?"

He stands still, thinking about an answer, and then turns to me. "I haven't heard the birds as much this year. Maybe they moved to warmer places earlier than usual. And," he adds, "the gardens didn't do so well this year, but I believe we had more turnips than ever before. That's different than I can remember."

Wearing a sleepy smile, Jenna appears to join us.

"It's true, things this year just aren't the same as before. But today, we have more important things to do. Today is cake day!"

Now it's impossible for me to stay in bed. It's a special day to mark the coming of more sunlight every day from now on.

"We have enough eggs, so let's have some for breakfast today, and the rest will go into the cake."

She starts moving about to organize the day. The room is warming from the rising fire and the frost has disappeared from inside. I jump up from my nest and rush to the hanging pegs on the wall. This special day is beginning. Seeing that no one's looking, I jump into my clothes, and hang the nightgown up.

Coming back to the front, the sound and smell of eggs in the frying pan fills the air. I put the plates on the table close to the pan so Jenna can serve them after they change from the runny, yucky mess into the yummy golden color when they're ready. We all sit down for the eggs with biscuits and steamy tea. It's a delicious start to the day. I can't wait to taste the cake tonight.

"We'll get the cake done by afternoon. There'll be a fine feast tonight," Jenna announces.

After breakfast, Jenna and I set to work cleaning up and getting everything together for the cake. She tells me what we need from the root cellar. I come back with my hands full.

"Did you find everything all right?" she asks, not raising her eyes from the yellowed recipe paper in front of her.

"I think so."

I put the heavy crockery bowl down on the table next to her with the other things all jumbled inside. I imagine it's big enough for two cakes.

"Yes, that's it." Jenna says as she checks everything gathered and touches her fingertips to the edge of the bowl.

I watch as she does lots of measuring with different spoons and an old looking tin cup with marks on the inside, and soon the bowl is holding everything in the recipe. The part I have never seen before is the chopped up dried fruits and nuts she adds to the raw cake batter. It takes quite a bit of work to stir the heavy batter all together to get it mixed. That's my job.

She gets the cast iron pot and I hold the heavy bowl tipped over it until all the batter is scraped into the pot. I've never seen such a big, heavy bowl before and I have trouble holding it up long enough while she scrapes all the batter out. At last it's empty and I let it back down, glad that nothing spilled. My arms are shaking a little, but I hope she doesn't notice.

"There we are, ready to bake. Into the fire for a while, and we'll have tonight's cake. We just have to watch it to know when it's baked all the way through."

She puts the pot on the bank of coals in the fireplace, shoving glowing embers against the sides and on top. Turning her face away from the heat, she stands back to look at me with a very satisfied look on her face.

"No regular work today, just celebrating. We have worked hard getting everything done, and tomorrow will be another day, but for this afternoon, let's just enjoy the smell of the baking cake."

"What's your favorite thing when you have nothing to do?" Jenna asks.

With my arms crossed, I think about it for a minute. I want to have a good answer. "I've always loved the open spaces outside. It's different now, since," I hesitate, "wandering lost and finding this place. Something changed in me. Now there's a difference to everything that I can't much lay a word to."

I don't like talking about being lost. I want that time to stay far away. Sometimes I wonder what it would be like if I'd found someplace different—or no place at all. It scares me to think about it, so I stop and look back at the fire.

"We're all doing pretty well with you as a member of the house for now. Today we are celebrating. I look forward to this day every year."

I see there's a kind of far off look in her eyes as we sit at the table doing nothing. The light of the day drifts in where it can, and then we step out into the chilly air for a quick minute to watch Darry cutting up fallen tree limbs in the distance. Before long, we go back inside to watch over the baking cake. It's a fine day to sit with her as the smell of the cake begins to fill the air. Larans is sitting quietly on the floor. Everything is just wonderful.

The only the sounds are of Darry chopping wood in the distance and the embers around the iron pot as they settle. Jenna gets up to add wood to the fire. Larans has fallen asleep on the floor next to the bench where I sleep. I can't imagine anything better than this moment.

"By the smell, I think it's close to done, so let's check."

She lifts the lid with a poker and reaches in, testing the cake with a knife point. Someday I'd like to be like Jenna. I'm finding out that I can do more than I thought I could by learning from her.

"Done," she declares, pulling the pot out of the fireplace and setting it to rest on top of the overturned iron fry pan to cool.

By now, the sun is low and hazy. It will be darkening soon enough. Footsteps sound on the front step and there's Darry, grinning as he comes through the door. The cold air swirls around inside as he closes it behind him, bringing me back from the dreamy feeling of the warm, peaceful day, and this moment, and this room. Darry looks at both of us with a twinkle in his eye and raises a corked bottle in his hand from behind his back. He puts it down on the table with a thud.

"Here's something to add to our supper. It's been waiting for some time, and I think it's ready. With a bit of luck, it'll be good."

Everything is set for tonight.

# CHAPTER TWELVE
# THE FOOT

Evening is coming closer and everyone fairly floats around doing their jobs. I chop, stir a pot, and mostly help move things to the table. Larans is happily playing at the side of my bed, so he's not underfoot around the cooking. This is a happy time that Darry and Jenna know well. Tonight's venison stew with potatoes, carrots, onions, and herbs happily bubbles on the fire.

The steamy scent fills the whole room. Finally, it's time for dinner and we all gather at the table, with a huge bowl of tasty-looking stew in the center and big chunks of home-baked bread in another bowl beside it. I mind my manners, as I want to look as grown up as I can. Tonight's meal begins as usual with everyone holding hands and a prayer.

"We give thanks for everything we have, our harvest of food from the bountiful earth, and the blessing of each other's company, with Crysalline as a gift of this season."

My eyes start to fill up and I keep my head bowed for a time. Only I know how good I feel in this wonderful place.

I'm offered a taste of the berry wine and I think it's all right. We all worked hard this Autumn to this darkest day of Winter, and now we're looking forward to the Spring that will be coming.

Larans waits impatiently for his chopped and mashed up dinner. He can handle a spoon pretty well, but still likes being tended to. Dinner is a feast, and without any trouble we are all pretty full. There's a nice quiet after everyone is done.

"It's time for the cake," Jenna says.

This is a special moment, one we've all been looking forward to. Baked bread is good, but this cake is special.

Jenna pauses before cutting it, looks right at me with a warm smile. "You are our welcome new family member. We are blessed to have you. You now have two families, and you can tell your other family about your time with us when you get home. When the season is right, we will get you there."

Darry nods his approval.

"Thank you so much again. I'm very happy to have found you."

Just saying that makes me squirm from being the center of attention, but I had to say it. I'm too happy to hold it in.

This is also a time when my insides are blooming. I know Jenna has noticed my changing shape. I am a little bit more like a grown up woman every day. She talks to me about what it is to be a woman. I can't look straight at her as she talks, but it makes me feel even closer to her.

As the days pass, nature shows signs of waking up with the light that grows longer and stronger. Our work of springtime chores is starting. There are more birds and bugs around starting to do their work again, too.

"We must get you fixed up with some more things of your own," Jenna declares playfully. I'm happy with just what I have of hers already. I don't mind that it's now kind of warm. She comes back from her bedroom with pieces of cloth I haven't seen.

"We've had this put away for the right time. Now's a good time to make something of it."

She drops three pieces of cloth on the table in front of me. "Which do you like best?"

At home, Mama would come back from the village with something she thought I would like. This is better than candy. These are colorful things, pieces that Jenna picked, and now I get one.

"I think I need something new myself, so I'll pick this one. If you want, we can make something from these and you can still keep what you already have," she says with her usual smile.

I touch one to see how it feels. I pick one like what she picked and can hardly put it down, it feels so nice.

We spend the rest of the day fitting it to be cut and sewn. By the end of the day, my fingers hurt but we have a lot done. When I see it taking shape, I can't help but be wiggly. With the other things, I'll have so much.

The next morning is a great show of the work we did yesterday, with Darry and Larans smiling their approval. I must be glowing all the time with the newness of me and the clothes. Nothing could possibly bother me for the rest of the day, not even the same old worn sandals. I imagine myself as the beginnings of someone just like Jenna.

***

Some days Darry's gone hunting or fishing all day. He's good with a bow and arrow, and most times brings something back when he goes. We do chores and I help watch Larans when Jenna's really busy. He's usually peaceable for a while but then gets bored. Darry generally gets back by late afternoon with his catch in hand, ready to be dressed out for supper the next day. Today, it's almost supper time and he's not home yet. Jenna steps outside often to look for him. I don't know how to help each time she notices another passing cloud or when the sun drops past the tree line.

"I hope Darry's back soon, darn it. He might think he should only come back after catching something. I hope he just comes in soon anyway," she says, facing the fire. She looks plenty worried. It's a look I haven't seen on her before.

Nothing's happening to start supper; it seems forgotten. She's biting her fingernails and staring blankly at the wall. Larans wraps around her leg to get attention.

"Maybe he wants something to eat. I'll feed him," I offer.

Jenna nods without saying anything, hardly hearing me at all. I give him a bowl of warmed mashed-up vegetables. He starts in on them and looks happy.

"I'm worried. Darry's almost never out this late."

We both run to the door in disbelief when we hear his distressed voice cutting through the gray dusk.

"Hello! Jenna! Crysalline! Come help me!"

We look at each other wondering what's going on and run out the front door to listen again to catch the direction. Larans is left in his chair.

"Helloooo, come help me!"

We can tell it's from off to the right and start running over the uneven ground in that direction. We find him leaning against a boulder.

"Darry, what's wrong?"

"I wrecked my ankle stepping in a burrow. It's pretty bad already," he says, looking sheepishly at Jenna.

He isn't a complainer by nature, and Jenna now has a serious look on her face. We get on either side of him to get him home. He's heavy, and the three of us hobble slowly toward the still-open door, moving unsteadily toward the light through the thickening darkness. It seems like forever before we make it. We get him to a chair and everyone collapses, exhausted.

"Let's see what you did to it." Jenna bends down to unlace his boot and he leans back with a grimace.

"I'm going to pull it off now," she says, holding the boot and watching his face.

She pulls firm and steady and the boot comes off. We all breathe a sigh of relief, and he slumps back in the chair. Jenna peels his sweaty sock down to look further. The ankle's red and fatter than it should be.

"Crysalline, run out front and bring in the washtub." She fairly spits out the words.

As I lug the wooden tub inside, she's coming back from their stored goods with a box of medicine salts, placing it on the floor next to his bare foot. She turns to the kettle for the hot water that's always at the fire. Pouring it into the tub with the medicine salts, she sticks her fingers in to check how hot it is, then adds some cool water. She gently lowers his foot into the water and he cringes, then relaxes.

"Are you hungry? I'll get you some supper."

"I'm not sure I want anything for now but some water." He looks at her with that sheepish look still on his face.

The three of us sit quietly making small talk for a time. There's nothing more to do for now, but we all know things will be different for a long while. After soaking until the water's too cool to be of any good, both of us help him to the bed. He fairly falls onto it with a thud and a groan.

"Thanks, Crysalline. I'll take it from here." Her voice is hard as she stands over the bed, looking at him.

I don't have a clear idea exactly how much will be different, just that it will be. I go back to the front of the room and check on Larans who's still in his chair, tired and a little worried-looking. I take him down and, as I wipe his face, he perks up and begins to walk around the room and back toward his parents' bed, stopping to listen at the corner post. I hear them continue to talk at times before Jenna comes to pick Larans up and get him to bed. After a while she comes back, stopping at the edge of my bed where I'm trying to put aside all the commotion. I'm worn down from all this. Her face is heavy and filled with worry.

"We'll know more in a few days. Probably nothing's broken and the foot might heal fine, but it will surely take a while. Good night, Crysalline." With her usual tenderness, she places her hand on my arm and squeezes gently as she turns to leave. She's always good at taking care of everyone and for sure even more so now.

"Good night, Jenna."

***

The next morning, I hear hard steps as they both get moving with Darry leaning heavily on Jenna's shoulder. It looks like quite a struggle. They smile thinly as they come to the front and Darry lands heavily on the chair by the tub of cold water. The room is chilly, and the fire has burnt down, so Jenna begins loading kindling to start it again. "I guess we'll just wait for this to heat up," she says. There is a worried, hard edge to her voice.

I stand up without another thought and say, "I'll go out and bring in more wood."

I'm out the door in a wink and come back with an armload of

firewood.

"Sorry I didn't think of it sooner," I say, glancing at her as she stands looking only at Darry who is oddly balanced on the chair.

"We'll get you soaking as soon as we can," she says to him. She grabs a pan and scoops the cold water to heat up at the fire, which is beginning to warm the room. "This will take a while," she adds.

"That's for sure. It'll be a long time for this to get over," he says.

Jenna lights both lamps for a good look at the foot this morning. It's swollen bigger than last night and laced with ugly red and blue marks. No one could be cheerful seeing this. They sit silently as the water heats. He keeps looking at the ankle. With one step into the burrow, so much is now on Jenna's shoulders. I want to figure out how I can help.

The water's now showing signs of being hot enough, so Jenna pours it in with the water still in the tub, and tests it.

"This will do for now. Come on, stick that foot in to soak some more," she tells him.

He lifts his leg over the edge of the tub, and gently lowers it into the water, careful as he lets his foot down. Then he slumps back in the chair, looking defeated.

No one talks. Jenna makes a hot chicory drink for us and I make the porridge with more of the raisins, nuts, and dried fruits.

"I can make a list of what must get done and can't be avoided, so we can figure out who does what," Jenna says.

Her face tightens as she thinks. Larans is banging his spoon on the edge of the table, spreading food everywhere. This morning, Jenna doesn't say anything to him about it; she silently takes the spoon out of his hand, still lost in thought.

"There's a pretty fair store of supplies, and we'll just have to do without hunting for now. Just tending to the garden and taking care of what we have to will do us fine," Darry says.

Jenna's quiet. Then she turns to me." Crysalline, this also means that we can't go out looking for your home place like we thought. Darry won't be up to it for I don't know how long. It may be a lot longer than this spring. I'm sorry."

I hadn't thought of that yet, but, as I do, it sends me into a whirl inside.

"Of course, I understand," I say softly, my voice shaking a little. The sound of it surprises me. I sit, beginning to understand how Jenna must now do a lot more, and I'll need to help as much as I can as the days grow into summer. The work must be done.

Darry has soaked a while, and the redness is wider and bright. "I don't think anything's broken," he says.

***

As days pass, he starts to learn to move around on one foot, bumping into everything, sometimes more like crashing. Jenna's always busy keeping up with the work, a large part being helping him move around without hurting himself more.

"I'll work on growing a third foot so I won't move around like a drunken frog," he jokes.

He spends a lot of time at the drawing corner, then out front carving wood when there's no more paper. I like sitting to watch what he's working on take form between chores. It tickles my insides seeing new things appear by his handiwork; it's like finding a new animal in the forest.

Helping with more chores, I feel more like a grown up. I'm hungry to grow up as fast as I can. Summer's coming out all over; there's so much aliveness all around. It's like being close to the lightning storms I liked to watch from inside when I was small. When it's been rainy, no one goes into the muddy garden any more than we need to.

"Crysalline, why don't you go out, but not any farther than you have to, and find a good sturdy branch that we can make into a crutch for Darry. Then maybe he'll be able to walk around more and not be so grumpy."

"Sure, I'll go now," I say, noticing the sun is high in the sky already.

I cover the open ground as far as I can and still be in sight of the cabin to look for just the right branch. I spot one that has a side piece where it grew out from another limb of the tree. It would fit and suit him, I imagine. I bring it back and everyone decides it will work, so he carves it down to a good shape.

"This will do quite fine," he says, putting it into his armpit to feel his balance and try to walk with it.

He takes a step, trips, and falls down with a thud, hitting and rolling over, then, with a hand, gets up and dusts himself off.

"Well, I'll just have to practice some more."

It helps his mood that he can get around to see what's going on and not have to just sit. He gives plenty of directions for the things we do now that were his jobs, so we don't have to waste a lot of energy figuring out how they should be done.

Jenna's busy and tired all the time. I'm learning to do more 'round the place, including more of the cooking. Working alongside Jenna is less like work. Little Larens wants attention, so Darry spends time amusing him. As things have changed, we're working well together, as well as can be expected under the circumstances.

There is very little time to spend alone with my imaginings like I did when I was younger. Larans, who's coming up to be two years old soon, likes to have me to play with when he can. He's mostly easy to make happy, but I don't have much time to play. Clothes washing is now my chore. I'm glad there's not more than two or three pieces of it to do at a time, and what there is is mostly on account of Larans. Hanging the heavy wet clothes up to dry after wringing them out with Darry's help is hard. My hands get red and raw from the soap, so I use some grease to soothe them afterward.

There is little meat since what was salted to keep is mostly used up. There are still dry beans in storage and lots of fresh vegetables. The chickens make eggs about as regular as the sun comes up, which is a real treat. Traders come every so often with their wagons full of stuff that's not easy to come by here like cloth, flour, salt, pepper, and soap.

Darry's made quite a lot of pretty things from wood. We're glad he's been busy that way. He makes things with decorations on them and toys for little ones. He made carved wooden animals and little people that stand up for Larans, who likes to throw them across the floor.

"Larans, look how I can make them stand up and walk them around. Then you don't have to throw them. They like to walk. You see how I'm doing it?" I show him.

Larans doesn't look like he cares much for the idea, but quietly sits down.

Darry's starting to stand lightly on the foot sometimes. He wants to try to keep it from stiffening up by using it some, and he uses the crutch, getting around pretty well.

"I can almost carry a plate of food with my free hand and not spill a thing. With the cane I've finished, I won't need this crutch much more, I hope."

The summer crops are full, and we eat well. It's coming to harvest season, so the days are beginning to shorten again into autumn. Later on, we'll be eating from the foods that are dried, salted, or pickled. With no hunting this summer, Piglet is now more on everyone's mind. I'm glad I don't have to decide if we're to turn him into food for the winter. It's going to be Darry and Jenna's decision, closer now that I'm another mouth to feed.

It's clearer to me how this is my time, becoming a young woman. I'm taller and my shape is filling out. I keep my dark hair off my shoulders and comb it every day to keep it nice. Mama told me that I have a good enough face, even if I don't show much of what's going on inside. I have dimples when I smile hard. If there's any free time, the path to the stream under the trees is my favorite place to go.

Today, I'm busy in the house when Darry comes in the front door.

"Hidey ho," he bellows as he sits down with a groan.

"Hello," Jenna fairly sings in reply. Her back it is still turned to us; she's tending to the pot on the fire. The place is hot from cooking, and the door and windows are open. Steam from the pot drifts and swirls toward the window at the front.

"Wow, I'm hungry," he says with a playful growl. Larans makes his own animal sound from where he's playing on the floor.

"Dinner won't be for a while, so you have time to get cleaned up," Jenna tells him.

Darry clomps with his cane towards the back to the wash basin, bumping against the wall as he turns the corner into the space.

"Crysalline, you can pick the biscuits up from the baking tin so they can be wrapped to keep warm. Dinner'll be ready pretty soon," she says, turning to me with a smile of approval.

I fill the bowls and we all sit down for the meal.

"I'm glad I got back as soon as I did. It was beginning to chill outside," Darry remarks. A piece of biscuit is showing at the corner of his mouth as he waves the hand that holds the rest of it.

"I have a surprise for tonight," Jenna says as we near the end of our meal. "Finish what you have, and we'll have a treat for dessert."

Darry and I look at each other and then to Jenna for any hint of what it might be.

She pushes back her chair, goes to the kitchen and opens a cupboard, bringing out a jar of blackberry jam.

"I've been saving this and tonight is as good a time as any, so we can enjoy it with another biscuit."

We all quietly savor the treat, together at the table. In this place, it's the end of a day and a season. I'm glad to be a part of it.

What's left unspoken for now is my other life. I don't think about it much since I can't do anything about it. By now, they might have given up hope of finding me, and the hurt might be easing a bit. I don't have any way to fix that. Here, I feel dear about each of these people. Darry is a kind and thoughtful man, who always wants to do the best for his family, including me. Jenna's how I want to grow up, just like her. Larans is happy and content, growing up right. I, too, am growing up in this place. It has become my whole world as the other one gets farther away, day by day.

# CHAPTER THIRTEEN
# THE SEARCH AGAIN

The weather is bad. The wind howls through the trees. We sit safe inside with all the windows shuttered tight, so it's dark. The rain pounds on the roof at times, and we find new leaks. The cold wind gets its fingers in through small cracks so we all dress as warm as we can. Darry has a pile of dried moss that we stuff in cracks that are letting in the chill. When it's windy like this, the wood smoke gets pushed back down the chimney. Larans rubs his eyes and coughs a lot. The cabin sure feels small in the winter.

Darry and Jenna stay in bed longer these dark mornings. Often, Larans wanders into the front room early. He comes to my side, puts his finger on my face and starts talking to me to wake me up. He climbs in bed with me until I stoke the stove.

Some mornings, I hear sounds through the divider Darry's put around their bed. At times it's like quiet talking, and other times sounds that aren't talking at all. It must be some kind of pleasant thing 'cause when they come out later there is a lovely, relaxed feeling about them. I like listening, for it brings up curiosity in me more than anything else I know. I like the way Jenna smells when we're close in the daytime. Darry has his own smell, and that's a curiousity for me, too. It's like I'm part animal, paying such close attention to scents.

On the days when we're stuck inside, Darry will tell stories that no one would ever believe, tales of long ago when people were different and big beasts roamed the land so men could prove how brave they were. Sometimes we play a card game. The cards are a set of thin wood pieces that he made with numbers carved into one side with a hot knife. The pieces of wood clatter as they mix together before the game. I like playing but I'm not so good at it. It's fun anyway.

Darry's foot is mending, so one afternoon as we are all sitting 'round, he begins to talk about that thing that's been put aside, the question of getting me back to my folks.

" Crysalline, have you been thinking about your family much?"

"Well, I wondered what would be the next thing to do, now that winter's passing. Time has really gone quickly," I say, glancing to see what I can find in their faces. The way I feel is confusing, like I'm two different people, but I don't want to seem mixed up in front of them.

"This time when we go out, it could be longer getting to the right place," he says.

There's a bit of a wrinkle moving across his forehead and he's following the wooden table's lines with his fingertip.

"We must find the right way to go, and see it clearly so we'll do the right thing," Jenna says with her usual quiet confidence.

"I've been pondering this for a while," Darry goes on, "and the weather is not yet right, but the time's coming. We should start out when we're likely to have good weather."

He sounds sure of what he's saying, and I'm surprised that this is really going to happen, maybe sooner than I thought.

Imagining that I might not be here for long, I'm afraid my knowing of this place will fade with time, becoming more like a far-away dream. I've grown up here, more than I ever could have imagined. I'm a young woman, but still partly a girl, too. When I think about leaving them, I get a knot in my stomach and have to keep myself busy to not think about it.

Since Darry's just about healed, I have more free time again and that makes it even harder. Working with Jenna on the big jobs has been really wonderful. We all know that I have a family back there. But Jenna and Darry don't know about the swirl of feelings in me, and I don't know what to do about them.

I spend my free time wandering to my favorite places. The shady spot in the spring grass is my favorite place to rest, listening to the gurgling of the lazy stream nearby. It's quiet and away from everything, where the sound of the water is better than anything else. As I lie on the ground with the tree branches and the sky overhead, I drift off while the stream plays on. It's my own private spot now, too. I couldn't dream of a better place. The day passes until it must be time to go back.

When I get back and open the door of the cabin, it's warm and familiar as always, but I know that soon this may not be my home anymore. I spend my time watching how Jenna moves through the day. I want to have more time here, and don't see any way to it. Wanting is a strange animal, like something caught in a cage. I don't see any way to change that, either.

I sit down at the table in a heap. After a time, Jenna sits beside me, wrapping her arm around me the way I love. I raise my face to see her looking directly at me and she takes my hand in hers. That always makes me feel better.

"Crysalline, this is hard on all of us, but mostly you, I must imagine. You're like a sister to me, something I never had before, and I'm happy to feel that way. It's going to be an adventure to find your home. You'll surprise everyone there with how much you've grown up. You're just about as tall as I am. When you find that home, then you can find out what will be next. There's really no way to understand these things before the right time, it seems."

It scares me to have to go away and not know how this all will work out. With Jenna and Darry, I feel safe. Out there somewhere beyond this place is my own home I hope to find. Some of Darry's stories from those wintery nights still stay with me. I don't know why such old foolish sounding stories would stick with me, but they do. I'm becoming less settled as the time to go out to search grows near.

One evening, talk about leaving begins after supper.

"The time's almost here for us to go out and find your place," Darry says.

"Yes, I guess it is—I mean, I know it is. I'm sorry you have to go out, too."

"We can look on it as our own great adventure, moving to places we haven't been and making memories of getting you to your people," Jenna says. "We'll all be fine."

"I have a cart for Donkey to pull along with us this time. It can carry a lot. Larans can ride on the cart, too. I can make him a seat, and we can all walk just fine without carrying as much as last time," Darry adds.

That night, I curl up in my corner, falling into only restless sleep. The light rain tapping on the roof reminds me of the pleasant stream where I like to spend time all alone. I float into a dream, looking off into the distance as I rise above the land, filled with the pleasure of it.

***

Larans' touch on my cheek brings me back into the soft, gray light peeking at me through the shutter at my side. The cabin is chilly, but the sun comes up strong most days now. Wrapped in the blanket, I get up to build the fire. While the cabin begins to warm, I stand close to soak up the heat and add water to the kettle for hot tea. There's a box of the dried leaves we have for our tea. As the bits of leaves lay in the bottom of the cup waiting for the water, I look around the edge of the shutter to the outdoors. It looks to be a beautiful day.

Soon everyone is up. Darry's at the table with some biscuits and berry jam. "Today I'm going to fix the cart for Donkey. Want to help?" he asks me.

"Sure. I don't know what to do, but I can help if you show me."

"Great. We'll start as soon as we're done here," he says cheerfully.

Suddenly leaving is very real.

Besides extra clothing, Jenna's gathering things like the jerky and dried fruits, and oats and corn meal to cook when we can. Two chickens will come along in a small cage to be dinner somewhere along the way. We'll have clothes, soap, salt, and salves that we might need. Darry's bow and arrows, fish line and hooks, good knife, hatchet, fire-making kit, extra straps for the cart, and feed for Donkey and the chickens will pretty much fill the whole cart. Darry says that we must keep everything as light as we can to help Donkey, who is old but dependable. He says we might gather some of our food along the way.

The day to leave is coming closer. The cabin will be left just as it is. Anyone wandering these parts will have to be trusted to be kind to the place. Getting myself ready, I notice how much I have learned and how good it feels. Moving out again is even more upsetting than last time. Making some new doodles on the bottom of my feet helps.

# CHAPTER FOURTEEN
# ANOTHER MYSTERY

For the next two days, the weather is not good. I've chewed my fingernails down waiting while Darry and Jenna have checked everything several times. We're as ready as we can be. On the third day, the sky is clear in all directions so, finally, we are on our way again.

Hearing the door close behind me, I am more certain to be leaving for the last time. We easily fall into a comfortable stride, only this time we have the donkey pulling the cart. Darry must pick a path wide enough for the cart to pass. It's almost as wide as two people side by side. We start out the same direction as before, at least for a while, with Darry looking at notes and tree markings from last time.

As the morning wears on, we stop to check the bindings on the cart and take our first rest. Jenna has taken Larans down from the cart and he's running around chasing a butterfly.

"We should gather together and sit. We must choose our direction."

Facing each other in a comfortable spot, we gather ourselves into that quiet place inside. I have a good sense of this now for myself, learned from my time with them. Air is flowing past, whispering in my ear, and the sweet smell of the warm grass rises, filling each breath. The sounds of birds nearby drift in. For the moment, I am quiet and content right here.

Darry is making a deep, throaty hum and Jenna a light one. These fade off and then we are all quiet. I'm comfortable now with these new ways, able to keep the swirls of fear and doubt further away.

Inside my closed eyes, I see my family and that home, the valley, and them coming and going during the day. They look to be all right. I don't seem to be there or see that they're missing me either. It's all soft and not exactly clear. I wonder where I am.

After a bit, we all open our eyes and are back together. Larans has been quietly playing, tied by his length of rope at the cart.

"Well, how are we doing?" Darry asks.

"There is certainly farther to go and then there will be more to know," Jenna offers.

"I did see the place where my family lives, but it wasn't any clearer how to get there."

Looking at each other and nodding, we begin again, moving forward in the same direction. We fall into the familiar rhythm for the afternoon, eating dry jerky and fruit as we go. The sunny day turns into long shadows and soon it's time to stop for the night.

We make our camp against a rock wall that feels cozier than just plain out in the open. Darry gets out his bow and arrow and quickly brings a rabbit back for dinner. Jenna has made a fire, and the evening begins with a warm meal. The meat is good after the long day of walking.

I no longer feel like a stranger in this family and appreciate everything they're doing for me. The crackling fire inside the circle of rocks is a home away from home. Its warmth is comforting against the dark of night. No one says much at supper. I imagine we're each thinking about what we might find tomorrow. We need to find some kind of marker to my place. It's out there, somewhere.

We spoon to sleep like on the last trip. It feels good to do it again. Larans is noisy, squirming in his spot between Jenna and Darry. Finally, he wears down and everything's quiet. Darry keeps his hunting knife close. I sleep on the other end behind Jenna like last time. She has no trouble settling down, curled toward Larans and Darry.

I turn to lie flat and look up at the starry sky with my arm just touching Jenna's back. I can feel her soft breathing by just barely touching her. Out here, there's nothing between us and the stars that spread across the whole sky. When the moon is hiding below the horizon, the sky is really dark, so there are more stars showing than blades of grass in the world. It's that clear tonight. The whole sky sparkles. The night noises out there somewhere are of no matter to me. As my eyes finally close, the sight of that beautiful sky plays on inside of me.

Larans is fussy part of the night. Jenna's the one to comfort him, and sometimes she talks in her sleep. Darry's the only one who probably sleeps all night, from the sound of his snoring. Maybe that'll keep the animals away.

Morning creeps in and the first color appears to replace the night sky, and finally everyone is stirring and up for the day. The glowing sunshine fills our camp, and we all pitch in to be ready. We have a sitting circle like the day before so we can better find our way.

"I feel like today is going to be a good adventure," Jenna offers.

I like this feeling myself when I have it. Sometimes it turns out to be right. We'll find out somewhere ahead.

The four of us and Donkey begin again. It's a pleasant morning, so the walking is easy. I'm looking around for anything that will help us. Sometimes they ask me if I remember a landmark they see, but I can't say for sure. Our path takes us to the edge of a woods at a slight dip of the land where there's the sound of running water. As we walk towards the sound, a strange animal-like figure appears at a distance from the thick part of the woods. Then it looks more like a man.

"Hey! Hi there," Darry yells at the top of his lungs. The figure stops and then sits, crouching.

"I think he heard us. Let's get closer and see if it's someone who can help." Darry's eyes sparkle with delight.

We all rush over the open space to see who it is. The crouched figure doesn't move at all as we come closer. A bit closer again and there's a shifting movement.

"Darry, be careful," Jenna pleads.

When we're within a stone's throw, the furry ball rises up and we recognize the face and eyes we've seen before. It's Raspartan.

We would be glad to see anyone and he's the one that we meet. Now maybe we can unravel more of his talk from the last time.

"Hello, Raspartan. It's good to see you again. Can we offer you something so we may sit a spell?" Darry begins, with an open hand and a welcoming sweep of his arm.

I watch him stand slowly, raising his face to show the sly smile that I remember. The fur on his cap sways softly as he moves his head.

Again we meet. You are ready for your long journey, I see."

The words are coming from his mouth, but I can't see his lips move much at all as they dance brightly in the air between us.

"We're looking for Crysalline's home again, and we'll keep at it until the job is done," Darry answers.

Jenna has walked to the front of the donkey cart, where she checks the ropes holding Larans in his seat.

She nods in agreement; Raspartan's head turns only slightly to see it.

"We may sit with this for a while, as here we are. It is the time that we would meet again."

My face kind of wrinkles up as I start to try to figure out what he means. By the looks on Darry and Jenna's faces, they don't get much either. It's clear that we'd like to have help, and he may be very wise, maybe more than we can know. This is an odd chance, meeting again.

"It is the time to be here now and see about these things," he says as he lowers himself to sit, again to look like a ball with a face wrapped in furs. His hands appear from under the furs, lightly touching the small box he has in one hand. It looks to be the same one as before.

We all sit down in a circle in front of him.

"You appear to be well. That is good," he says. His whole body sways gracefully, rocking slightly with his words.

"We are well, thank you," Jenna says, looking to discover what might be revealed.

"We have had fine seasons since we saw you last, and now we're on our way to find Crysalline's home. We would be most grateful for any help."

"Did you mention the place as Barryton?" Raspartan asks.

I am surprised that he remembers the name.

"Yes," Darry answers.

"This is a task, finding the way to go. We must consider what will be the right answer for her. Sometimes there is no way backwards," Raspartan muses.

His words hit me like a slap on the face. Darry looks pained as if he has just understood something he doesn't want to.

"This sounds like something new, and I ask you to explain, if you please," Darry says, keeping his head slightly bowed.

A soft smile grows on Raspartan's face, and he doen't say anything for a long time. No one is moving at all in this silence. His hands gently cradle the box.

Finally he continues, "I can only tell you that the future is not written as history. There is only the space ahead. That will be the guide for each of you."

Darry only looks more agitated. "Can you give us something more that will guide us?" he asks again.

"There are many ways that are unseen from here. All of these ways are possible, but only one will be this young woman's path. The only way is ahead. The places along the way where she goes will have choices, with swift movement so her feet will not touch the earth at times. Only she knows where her home will be. This land is large and wide. The way to go will be new for her. The way is forward, moving swiftly. Where that will lead no one can know now, as there are many things possible and only she can say how she will get to that place."

I begin to feel dizzy, as if the land is falling away from under me, angry at this lump of a figure with only riddles for answers. I want to know what to do so we can all get this done.

Raspartan looks directly at me and says, "You are to be living in the future. You will know what to do. Trust that. Your travel will be as if you move without effort, and you will find your place out there, ahead. You must go alone. That is your way forward. These others must give you over to the path ahead. There is no other way that will give you your life. You will part company at the edge of the land, moving into a divine life."

I start to shake and can't stop. That's the last thing I remember.

# CHAPTER FIFTEEN
# THE HORIZON

I come to and there's only the sky above me and grass tickling the side of my face. Jenna's hand appears to mop the sweat from my face. I look to the side where she's sitting, and she leans forward, her smile filling the sky.

"What happened?" I ask.

"You were really out. We're glad to see you back again." I hear worry in her voice. "Raspartan has gone on his way."

"Oh." I can't think of anything else to say. I wiggle my toes to feel the grass.

"Can you sit up and take a drink of water?"

As I start to sit up, I see Larans at her side holding bits of grass in his clenched hand and looking at us. Jenna's hand comes to my back to help me up, and I take a drink from the tin cup. I drink it all, filling the thirst I didn't know was there. Looking around, I see that we're still in the same place. I have no idea what we're going to do next.

Darry wanderers over and sits with us. "Well, that Raspartan character wasn't too helpful." The words drop out as if he can't hold onto them any longer.

We sit quietly and after a while I begin to feel like myself again.

"I'll start a fire for tonight. This is as good a place as any," Darry says, glancing around.

We're at the edge of the woods where we met Raspartan again, and there's the pleasant sound of running water nearby. I remember the babbling brook at Milhila, how it talked to me. The warmth of that summer memory is in my skin, but the smell of the fire brings me back to here. Evening is closing in. Overhead, the gentle whispers of the leaves rustle in the air while the gurgles of this brook give me that same comfort as Jenna's back in Milhila.

Many thoughts are swirling in my head, but there's no way to figure out anything for sure. It would be terrible to be wandering lost again, this time all of us. I lie back on the grass so that the treetops overhead fill my view. As the smell of dinner fills the air, I drift off with the trees and the brook into my own private world.

When Jenna gives me a gentle shake, I don't know how long it's been.

"Supper's ready. We should eat while there's still some light."

We gather 'round the cheerful fire, enjoying the hot meal. No one says much as we eat. It's enough for me that we're comfortable being together.

Then Darry speaks, breaking the quiet. "Raspartan certainly said more strange things today. No better than the last time. I almost wish we hadn't seen him. Do you have any sense of his meaning, Jenna?"

Jenna studies her supper for a moment and says, "I remember as clear as day what he said, but it doesn't give me anything to use right now."

"Crysalline, what did you get from this encounter with Raspartan?" Darry asks, staring straight out into the distance.

"I don't know anything, either," I say, shaking my head sadly.

We set out our sleeping blanket for the night. It promises to be pleasant and dry. At least that's not a worry. Maybe tomorrow Raspartan's words will seem different. As we all snuggle close, even Larans is quiet. I'm probably the last to fall asleep, hearing the sound of the brook that gently goes on and on.

The next thing I know, I'm gasping for breath, fighting to keep my head above water. The water is powerful and I'm weak against it 'til I let myself float, not fighting it anymore. Only then does the panic ease. Then I'm tipping over and a hand reaches out to me and I think it must be my grandma. Soon enough, I realize it's not her, it's Jenna shaking me and I'm where we went to sleep. It's still dark.

"Crysalline, you were yelling for help. What were you dreaming?" she whispers, groggy and a little upset.

"Um ... I ... oh yeah, I was in water, almost drowning, but then it was better. Then I was better," I whisper quietly since she is right beside me and I don't want to wake Larans. Darry's tossing and mumbling. We settle down to sleep again. Surrounded by the quiet darkness I try to push the dream away, but I can't.

Morning comes and we all shake off the stiffness from sleeping on the ground. After a simple, quick breakfast, we're ready for the day.

"We should sit now to see what comes," Jenna says in a firm tone.

Sitting together helps keep me steady, able to move on. Afterwards, we pack up and set out into the open spaces. A lightly worn path in the grass appears, a bit wide for animal tracks, but offering no clue as to who or what made it. We follow it for a while and it opens some, then fades away. I was hoping it would lead somewhere. We round the next hill and we're looking straight at the front of a cabin. We look at each other with relief and rush to the door and knock, calling, "Hello, is anyone here?"

I hear a sound somewhere that gives me an unsettled feeling and makes my legs wobbly. The door opens to an old man standing in the doorway, curiosity on his face as he looks us over before he breaks into a wide smile showingthat he's missing several teeth.

"Come in. You're welcome to be sure." he says, waving his hand to encourage us.

"I'm Gren, and glad to see anybody come by. What do you come here for?"

"Thank you. We are Darry, Jenna, and Crysalline, and we're looking for a place called Barryton. Ever heard of it?" Darry asks.

Gren scratches his head, shaking it from side to side. "No, I haven't, but come in and rest yourself while we sit for a spell."

The air inside is thick with smoke, so Jenna and I excuse ourselves and go back outside into the fresh air. As soon as we're outside, something comes over me, trying to get my attention.

"Let's go look around," I say to Jenna, who nods agreeably.

We round the corner of the cabin that sits halfway up a hill. I'm curious to see what's beyond the top, so we walk the rest of the way up the ridge. Before we get there, I hear a steady sound that keeps getting stronger. Six more steps and we both see what's been making the sound.

A river, wide and strong, is running along a ravine at the bottom of the hill. The sound of the rushing water is stronger than those small streams I enjoy on the lazy afternoons in the shady grass. This river is demanding. As mist from it wraps around me, I drop down into a heap.

Jenna sits beside me. "Is something wrong?"

"This river is so strong."

I shiver at the power of the water running down there, not far in front of us. A roar sounds from off to one side, the direction the river's coming from. More mist floats from that direction, and the hillside there is greener than anywhere else.

"Why is that sound so strong?" I ask.

"It's probably a rapids, where the river runs faster, more downhill, and maybe around and over rocks."

The river's demanding my attention and I sit, unable to speak, gripped by an excitement I don't know and fear, knowing how it can swallow a person whole. I shiver from inhaling the mist. Jenna pulls close and puts her arm around me. I'm lost in the powerful beauty of the place. The river is moving, always rushing on its path. Something's stirring deep inside, like there's another person inside of me. Sometimes I can feel a hunger that's rushing me along towards something I do not yet know. I keep fighting back tears.

"Now what Raspartan said is beginning to make some sense," I say.

Jenna's arm is keeping me close. I'm shaken by the force of the power surging along below where we sit.

"Why am I crying?" I wonder as if asking the whole world, not only Jenna.

"It's magnificent and a wonder for sure. It touches you somehow," she answers calmly.

Then she moves her arm from around my shoulder and we hold hands tightly. She gently rubs my hands between hers.

I turn to her to say, "I'm so glad that I found you and Darry. I love you like a big sister."

She looks at me with a smile and says, "It's a good thing that we met, and you know I, too, love you like a sister."

Just then Darry appears over the crest of the hill behind us. "Oh, here you are. I wondered where you'd wandered off to. Gren has offered for us to stay for a while. He's been telling me about how he's lived here his whole life as a few people come and go along their way. They take their boats out to get around the rapids just above here, then stop here for a while before they start out again. He has space enough, so we can rest here tonight."

"So of course he knows a lot about the river." I guess out loud.

"He must. We can have supper and maybe he'll tell us more then."

Darry sits down beside us to watch the misty, roaring river. Larans is keeping close, listening to the strange sounds. He amuses himself by pulling bits of grass. The river surges and swirls as it winds downhill as far as we can see, pushing against the land as it moves along to somewhere else. A thrill and fright run together in me.

"I better go back and let Gren know we're staying," Darry says, breaking the silence.

Jenna and I nod, and he rises to to disappear back over the crest of the hill. After a few minutes, both Jenna and I stir to go back inside. Standing, she hugs me and I hold onto her fiercely. I don't know how I could ever be any closer to anyone.

Once we're back, we open the door where both Gren and Darry turn to greet us from where they're sitting at the table that stands against one wall. Gren must have had the table for a long time, by the looks of it. Several stools are under it, waiting for us.

"I'm always glad to see anybody. I don't get many visitors, and some of them can hardly carry on a talk."

"What do you know about places down the river?" I ask.

I'm surprised at how clear my voice sounds and how it filled up the whole room. Darry and Jenna are surprised, too, judging by the looks on their faces. I can't help but wiggle a little bit, embarrassed.

Gren turns to me like he's giving considerable thought to what he will say next. His pale blue eyes are steady and bright and I can't look away.

"All kinds of people have told me many things, and I imagine some of it's tall tale. I haven't been down there to see for myself. I like it here very much, thank you, and so I've been in this spot for a long time, even after my Andra died five winters ago." His head lowers a bit and he suddenly looks lost in sadness. As he looks up again, a hint of a smile comes over his face and I wonder what he's thinking. Maybe he'll say.

"Well, we are sorry, and we're surely happy you're still here," Darry says, bringing the room back to life.

"Crysalline, what do you want to know about? Jenna asks.

"I ... I don't know. I just wondered, I guess. It seems like I'm wondering what's out there, and that's stuck in my head."

I blush at talking so plainly. Gren takes the moment to ask if we are hungry. I feel sorry that he has to cook on his own.

After supper, I can easily say that his meal is different. I hope his wife was a better cook.

As the light grows dim, I begin thinking about sleeping on a bed again tonight. He added an extra room onto the cabin for visitors. There are two bunk beds with lumpy pads that look to be well hollowed out where others have slept. We pull one onto the floor so Larans can sleep by Jenna where she'll be on a bottom bunk. Darry takes the other bottom bunk so I'll be in a top one. I choose the one above Jenna and climb up. I know we're all hoping for a good night's sleep.

With the candle blown out, the room is darker than black. I feel above my face to see if I can feel the top of the room, and my fingertips reach the wooden slats of the roof above. I have enough room to roll over and get out, but just enough. The sound of Gren's snoring comes through the walls along with the distant sound of the river.

I have a leg cramp and move to rub it. In the darkness, I catch a glimmer of light above me. I blink and reopen my eyes, and it's still there, like some kind of wiggling ribbon. Then it's gone again. I strain to see while, through the wall, I hear the muffled roar of the river off in the distance. Its dampness is everywhere. I keep wanting to know where the river goes, but I can't say why.

The door squeaks and I wonder who it might be, or if anybody's there at all.

Then Darry grumbles as he stubs his toe in the dark. Past the crack of the open door, I can see the pale light of the new day.

Twisting out of the bunk, I drop to the floor, searching in the dark until my hand finds my sandals tucked under the edge of the bed. Then I carefully move around Larans, who's sound asleep. Jenna's tossing and turning on the bottom bunk as I move out into the front room where

Darry stands at the window looking out into the rising light.

"Mornin'," I whisper.

He turns at the sound of my voice and smiles. There's heat coming from the fireplace, and he has a steaming cup in his hand. "There's hot water, if you like," he says, nodding to the pot close to the fire. A worn tin canister sits on the table next to mugs that look like they've been here forever.

"I guess I will."

I pick up one of the mugs and pour a cup of hot water, adding a pinch of the loose tea from the tin. It floats, drifting in circles, then gently sinks.

"What do you think of this place?" I ask him.

"Do you mean the place here, or this cabin?"

"I mean any of it, I guess."

Just then Gren comes out from his room, pulling up his suspenders and pushing his thin white hair back with one hand. "Mornin' to you all," he says sleepily.

His thin whiskers are not quite a beard. Just a lack of shaving by the look of it.

"Mornin' to you, too," I say cheerfully.

Gren gives me one of those sideways looks that people do when they want to study somebody, not thinking that I'm looking at him, too. He's still shaking off his sleepiness. He pours himself a cup of hot water and starts the tea as he probably does every day.

"Do you have many people come here?"

"Not many fer a while, then some. It's hard to say the count." Gren smiles as he thinks about what he just said. "That nephew of mine will be 'ere any day now, maybe only a few days, as he's comin' through. He's from upriver with my younger brother and his wife about a day up from here. Name's Taggler."

I perk up at hearing this. It could be another way to learn more about this place if we're still here when he comes. "He's comin' through, is he? Where does he go on to after here?"

"Oh, on further down a bit with that flat bottom thing he calls a boat, then startin' back home. Have to pull a boatload back up this way, ya know. He doesn't plan too much, just goes where there's trading to do. We have a chance to visit some when he comes, usually about once a month, so he's due here any day now."

Jenna appears, carrying Larans. She's rubbing her eye with her free hand and yawns while Larans, who is clinging tightly to her, studies Gren cautiously.

"Good mornin', sleepyheads," Darry says.

"Mornin' to you," Jenna says, taking hold of Darry's mug of tea.

Gren excuses himself to go to the outhouse. With just us here, Jenna and Darry look at me directly, wanting to see what I might say.

I take their look to mean it's time to say what I can.

"I know we're here in this place we didn't know we'd find. There's something else coming to me I can't put aside, even if I wanted to. I'm working to make more sense of it. So there it is, anyway."

"I can't get your meaning, Crysalline. What's that about?" Jenna.

My voice is thin and uneven, but I manage to push the words out. "I keep knowing the river is out there. There's always that sound of it, so powerful and moving, different than anything I've been around before. It keeps getting my attention even when I don't want, then I wonder 'bout where it goes. That's the most of it I can make out."

After a long stretch of quiet, Gren comes back in, and looks to us to see what might be our mood.

"This fine mornin' we may just go out for a bit, Gren. We'll sit on the crest of the hill, where we can see everything around, with that big river down there. We'll be back in a while, I guess," Darry says.

"I'll be here tidying up when you're ready to come back in," he says cheerfully.

The four of us go out and up to the green hilltop that overlooks all directions. Jenna puts Larans down and gives him a dry fruit. She calls us all into a circle and we gather ourselves into the quiet we each know. The air's filled with sound and mist that fairly coats me with a soothing feeling I feel in every breath.

This whole place wraps around where we sit. There's no escape from the demanding sound of the river in its endless pushing, writhing ahead, never pausing. My body's filled with some unknown ache. The sounds whisper in my ear, again and again. It's the river, somehow talking to me. I'm trembling. It's a little crazy.

After a time, we drift back from our quiet and rise from the damp ground to walk back inside. I can only put on a weak smile as we come to the door again.

"Hi-di-ho! We're back," Darry calls through the doorway.

"Ah, yes you are," Gren says as he turns to greet us. "Did you enjoy it out there? You haven't run into any snakes, I'd venture to say. They don't seem to like it up here at the top of the hill."

"It is surely wondrous out there. I've never seen such a sight. That river is big. How far does it go, do you think?" Darry asks.

"No one I know has been that far. Taggler says he always turns around to come back at Ulm, the next place downriver, but it goes on getting bigger and wider as far as he can see."

Gren smiles at me with a look I can't figure.

# CHAPTER SIXTEEN
# THE VISITOR

"How would anybody find out where it goes?" I ask.

"Taggler has told that he itches to go on sometimes. I heard him say it like that. But right now it's time to get fed, so let's all get to it. There's 'nough with the biscuits and pot roast for everybody," Gren offers cheerfully.

"We can offer some dry fruits for the meal if you like," Jenna offers.

"Well, then, that'll be plenty."

We sit at the table, telling the stories of where we came from and how it was to live in those places. Jenna pushes me to tell the story of the pit and how I got her out. She says it's one of the finest stories that could be told. It surprises Gren; he says you can't see it by looking at me. Then she tells about how I was lost and wandering for days before finding their place.

"I was wonderin' if these were your people. You're kinda close in age, so it don't fit so easy," Gren remarks.

"Darry and Jenna are like my family. I think of them like that."

As I say the words out loud, sweet tears fill my eyes, right here at the table where everyone can see.

The afternoon passes by easily with more story telling. Tea and biscuits that are almost tasteless keep coming out of Gren's stored goods long after the noon meal is past. Honey makes them all right. The day passes into soft twilight, and Gren lights the lamp. I think it's a good time, so I turn to Gren with a question I've been holding onto.

"Now, you know how Darry and Jenna have made me a place with them, and how we're out to find my home. It's pretty here, and I wonder how I—I mean, if we could stay here for a while to get to know this place and maybe go on the river sometime."

Darry sits upright at my words. I didn't expect that.

"Crysalline, this is a serious thing. I'm not sure you know what you are asking. You can't just up and ask Gren to stay here. This is something we need to talk about between ourselves first."

Darry's words pour out like water. By the look of him, I can see he might be more upset than his words show.

Gren lowers his head some which I take to show his agreement with Darry. I still have my wondering about what might be able to be done here, but keep it myself.

"I guess you're right," I murmur.

A quiet falls on the room, a quiet that I imagine is hard for everyone. Gren perks up at the faint sound of what might be footsteps somewhere close by. Then the door opens and a tall young man comes in, just as casual as can be. Surprised at seeing all of us, he stands in the doorway, looking confused.

"Hello there, Taggler. We have visitors. This 'ere is Darry, Jenna, Crysalline, and 'at little one is Larans. They be lookin' for a place called Barryton. Heared of it?" Gren asks.

Taggler looks to be full grown but probably not much older than me. He has sandy color hair and he looks like he's been outdoors a lot. His clothes are worn but seem to fit comfortable on him, not showing much of the long, lean muscles on him. He stands like a young man working to look full grown up.

Taggler twists himself up with a serious look as he works up what to say. "Nope, don't know of a place by that name." He shakes his head.

Now he looks around at the group of us to see what might happen next, and when he looks to me he almost smiles a little, then quickly hides it.

"Your Uncle Gren has told us that you've gone farther down the river from here several times," Jenna says.

"That's so. I go down a ways, but not far. Getting the boat back upstream is a lot harder than going down. Sometimes I can paddle it up when it's runnin' slow, but mostly it runs too fast for paddlin', so I have to haul it up on a line. Used a mule once but that has its own problems," he says with a chuckle.

Jenna and Darry don't look any better after hearing all this.

Since the day has faded into evening, we wander off into our own room. Darry sits on the bunk directly opposite to where I'm sitting.

"Crysalline, what are you wondering? What are you thinking about?"

I tell them what I have clear enough to say. How it's been itchin' in me and it's getting stronger. I can't get away from it. I tell about how the river is pulling at me and I want to see for myself more about it.

I watch how they sit and listen with serious looks on their faces, worried about me, I guess. They tell me about the time they started their lives together with a fresh place. But they say that was different.

On the other side of the cabin, Gren's spending his evening catching up with Taggler. It sounds like they have a lot to talk about. Sometimes I can hear them laughing.

My speaking up has lit up other's wonderings, it seems, and, once we catch Gren up on the conversation, we spend some time sharing our thoughts.

Gren says he remembers his own ideas when he was young, and how they were hard to understand 'til later. He'd been so full of questions. He remembers the time he met Andra, and what an adventure it was, and how they decided to live here. I can also see his pride in telling us how Taggler has become a solid river hand who can take care of himself.

Jenna and Darry aren't my parents, but they're trying to protect me like they are. I think this might be a time when I have different ideas for myself. After several days of talking, we all finally agree that it could a good time for Taggler to take me out on the river for just a short while so I can know what it's like. I'm squirming with the idea of it. What's it like out there, past where I can see?

Taggler and I have only talked directly a little, but some. Both of us have wanted to do something, something more. I didn't have an idea what more is until now.

We'll set out in another day or so, and I can't think of sleeping a wink before then.

It's agreed that we'll go only as far as to that place called Ulm and then come back. We would be back in about six days, all told. Darry, Jenna, and Larans will be here waiting.

Taggler knows his flat bottom boat well. He knows how to work through the currents and eddies of the river with oars. It's his world and I like seeing how at ease he is when he talks about it. I almost can't believe I'm daring to go out there with him as my guide. It sounds safe and a little scary at the same time. And exciting.

On the second morning after the decision is made, everything's ready. Jenna has a pinched up worried look on her face and can't say anything, but she gives me a giant hug. As we push off, I watch the group on shore get smaller until, with a last wave, they disappear as we round a bend in the river.

I turn towards Taggler where he sits in the back, watching the river ahead.

"This part of the river's strong but steady, so we won't have much to do for the morning except settle in," he says, looking very sure of himself.

I glance at him while he watches the waters ahead, and I wonder what he's thinking. When he looks at me, I make sure to show no concern at all.

We talk very little for a while as we get used to the idea of being all alone out here together for the next six days. I'm wondering how it will go.

"What's it like, back up the river where you live?"

"It's full of hills and rocks. It snows up past us in the winter some years. We keep goats. I like it down here where it's more open and the river's wide and more peaceful than the places upstream. Going downstream, in Ulm there are interesting folks. I like trading with them and that's where I always turn back."

"What's it like where you're from?" he asks, still watching the river.

"There are rolling hills, and valleys, and many, many trees. You can see far from a hilltop. But no big river like this."

I like remembering those open spaces where I could sit and feel the world breathing as the air moved around me.

After that, we both fall quiet, letting the river keep our attention. It's exciting to me when the river turns; I wonder what's ahead just about to come into sight.

"How long 'til we come to the other place?"

"We'll be there by mid-day tomorrow."

His tone sounds unconcerned. He might just be showing off a little.

The water is brown in places; cloudy with silt, he tells me. He throws a line over the side with a bit of hard biscuit as bait, and after a while we have two fish in the bottom of the boat for tonight's meal. They're shiny and slippery and flop 'round until they lay still. Looking at them all day doesn't matter 'til you're starting to get hungry.

Late in the day, we tie up on a bank and Taggler brings out two ground cloths from under a seat that will be the bedding tonight.

"Right up here's a grassy spot that'll be fine."

He looks a bit shy talking about both of us sleeping out here. He cleans the fish with the large knife he keeps in a sheath on his belt, and we sit at our fire not far from the shore. I watch the fish as they sizzle over the flames.

They're delicious. After we finish eating, we sit and talk about this and that, the look of the trees around here, or the sounds that come to us at times breaking through the stillness out there in the dark.

We spread out the ground cloths in separate spots but near enough to talk if we want, then quiet down to sleep without any more than a simple "good night". The sky's clear and there'll be no rain. I don't know if I'll sleep at all. It feels like the whole world here has invited me to come. It's different sleeping on my own under the stars I know so well. The trees form soft dark shadows at the edges of the star-filled sky. When the breeze whispers through the branches, a star will twinkle between the moving leaves. I lie here and watch the night sky grow bright and the world at my feet grow quiet, with only the sounds of the river that never sleeps.

Time slips away and my eyes close without me deciding. I wake again during the night, floating in the feeling of being a part of everything that's all around me. Finally the stars melt away as the sky starts to change into colors, and it becomes morning again.

We get going early after hot tea and biscuits. "Easier goin' in the mornings for some reason," Taggler says.

The water is like yesterday: smooth but unstoppable. A breeze teases us from different directions. The birds along the way fill the air with their cheerful morning chatter. I try to give them names as they appear and disappear but there's no way to keep up. The riverbank is quite plain, clay rising from the water's edge with young trees sprinkled in places close to the water's edge. The river runs straight for a stretch, and then wanders around many corners, turning different ways. The sun isn't high yet, but warm where its rays touch us.

I keep myself from showing much emotion or the excitement I'm holding inside. I want Taggler to see me as grown up. So, even though I want to, I don't ask many questions about things along the shore.

As we go around a bend, I hear sounds that might be people, but I can't see any.

"Did you hear someone out there?" I ask, turning to see if he heard it, too.

"I think so," he says slowly. "We're close to the village now."

He's busy watching the currents and making corrections. The sounds are louder now, and I'm watching for any movement on the shore. We're closer to the left side, so I guess that'll be the side where we'll be landing. Both my hands are on the top edges of the boat; my fingernails scratch at the rough wood. After one more bend, I see a boat dock. No people yet. There are a few buildings scattered around, all small and worn but well kept. Taggler moved to the bow and pulled a rope out from under the front seat just below me, brushing against me as he passes. Holding the rope in one hand, he crouches beside me, ready to grab onto the edge of the dock. I can see every pore of his skin and know how he smells up close.

"Here we are," he declares as the boat bumps against the dock.

I can't wait to see whatever's here.

# CHAPTER SEVENTEEN
# DISCOVERY

With that first bump against the dock, I know this is really happening. Taggler jumps out and holds the boat close, looking at me. I let out a breath, grab his hand, and he pulls me up onto the dock, letting go as soon as I'm standing on my own two feet. I'm grinning inside but will keep that to myself to look more grown up in this new place.

At first ,it looks as big as Barryton but on a river. There are several buildings close to the water, and others are scattered along the shoreline, farther apart as they get farther from the dock.

A man is walking our way. He's dressed in nice clothes and Taggler's smiling so I think they know each other.

"Hey, it's that fine lad Taggler. Come to trade, have you? An you're not alone this time," he says, turning to me.

"This here is Crysalline. Her people came to Uncle Gren's place looking for somewhere called Barryton."

"Hello, Crysalline. My name is Wamash and I'm pleased to meet you. Welcome to Ulm. I'm sure Taggler will show you around."

"Ulm, you call it. Do the people here like this place?" I ask.

Taggler shifts his feet some, and I wonder if it's because of what I said. Wamash has a kind smile on his face and says, "Well, most people here like it pretty well. We don't all agree how the name of the place came about, to tell you plainly. But now I must wish you both a good day."

With that, he bows and starts off.

"We can get a look around, and I'll check a few places I might want to trade with later. When that's all done and you're ready, we're free to start back," Taggler says. "It'll take a lot longer to get back upstream, and a lot more work, even if we used a mule to pull the boat along. That's less work, but has its own troubles."

We wander along several dusty walkways. People are going about, wearing clothes that are different than where I come from. There's a finer look about them. The shops have things I've never seen before. The shop keepers are nice enough and chat with me while I look over things that catch my eye. The carved figures of animals and pretty stones of different colors made into things to wear are my favorites. There's a store filled with the unusual smells of spices I don't recognize. Taggler says they could be for cooking or medicine. They smell so interesting.

People pass by who speak as different as bird's songs can be. They look cheerful and peaceful. Taggler tells me they're from other places. I like it here; there's so much new to see.

There are unusual pieces of cloth with interesting designs woven into them. As I stand admiring one, Taggler comes in from the shop next door where he's traded before. With a smile to the shopkeeper, I turn to leave, walking slowly, not wanting to miss anything on the way out.

"That place was wonderful," I say under my breath as we get back outside.

Taggler has a wrapped package in his hand.

"What's that?"

"I got us something to eat for the way back. It's a smoked duck. They're very tasty."

I nodded, not wanting to tell him I've never had any before.

"When you're ready, I guess we might start back," he says.

I don't want to go yet but agree, and we begin walking back in the direction of the dock. I try to walk as slowly as I can to not miss anything. Back in the boat again, we cast off. I settle back into my spot, my thoughts filled with so much that's new and different.

There are islands of gravel and sand in this slow-moving place on the river, Taggler begins rowing our way back against the current. After a while, he's tired-looking and the boat isn't moving much.

"I guess it's time to begin hauling this thing with a rope to get back," he declares with a sigh.

***

After four days of pulling the boat back upstream, I see how hard it really is. We have to fight against the current to keep the boat moving, hauled by hand while wading in the shallows or on shore by rope all the way back to Gren's. I help in places, but it is mostly Taggler's job. Every evening, he's soaking wet and tired, and eating is more of a chore than a pleasure.

Over the days, it's getting easier to talk since we both love the outdoors and to tell stories around the fire in the evening. I can't help wanting to talk until he falls asleep.

***

When we finally get back to Gren's place, Jenna and Darry are relieved to see me.

Jenna says, "We're excited and can't wait to hear about your time out on the river."

I'm tired and glad to be back and full of wonder at what I've seen. What more could there be to see, further along the river?

"There's so much to tell. I hope I don't leave anything out."

We sit on the hillside. Sometimes I can't get the words out fast enough. I can't believe how good I feel after those few days out there. But that hunger to fill hollow places I feel inside is now even stronger.

"Ulm is wonderful, full of things I've never seen before. There are beautiful wood carvings and stones made into jewelry. I saw colorful cloth they told me was made at home by hand with a loom. I didn't see a loom, but the cloth from it is beautiful. They said these things come mostly from other places beyond Ulm. Some of the designs on the cloth are like parts of plants and animals made into shapes, like a drawing of birds and flowers.

"And this was a place where there were people who have different sounds mixed in, almost like singing as talk."

Darry and Jenna listen, wide-eyed. Larans watches the river as it keeps moving on its way beyond here. Jenna's face shows her care and sometimes wrinkles in a worried look. She glances at Taggler a lot. When he gets the chance, Gren tells how his nephew has been taught well by his parents, who are decent people. I've seen for myself how he's liked by the people in Ulm. I make sure that comes through in my telling about our time away.

After a while, we move to do what needs done for supper. After the meal, I go back outside and lean against the side of the building and watch everything grow dark. Jenna comes to sit by me.

"It's nice out here. Everyone else has gone to bed." she says.

"I had to come out. I'm not sleepy yet."

Neither of us says a thing for a while, then I can't help but say, "Oh, Jenna, the time out there was so new and different. Taggler is a really good boatman. He doesn't talk much, but when he does, it isn't just lazy talk. I want to spend more time here at the river if I can. I wonder what it would be like to go on down more."

"Crysalline, there's so much that you don't know of these things. You have no one out there to be your family if you find trouble. What would you do? You don't even know if Taggler really wants to go out again."

Jenna means well, I'm sure, but I can't help thinking it's what I want.

"I don't know what trouble there might be to worry about. There's really no way to know what's out there without going. Mostly, I know

I want more. Taggler's so good with so many things, so we can figure them out when we need to. I've already asked him if he'd want to go, and he said he's been wanting to do something more than just the back and forth he's been doing for so long."

The daylight has disappeared, so it's easier to say things that are hard to say. I can tell Jenna's still being careful with her words.

"Crysalline, there is so much ahead that you'll discover for yourself that hadn't come yet. There's a time when a man and a woman come together and a baby comes. Being a woman has the responsibility of becoming a mother. That will come to you, and I'd like for you to know first how it is, so when it happens it's not a surprise."

With that, she goes on to tell me some of the more exact parts of this mystery. I'm glad it's dark, since my face is surely red. She explains in a way that has me remembering the sounds at their cabin that now make sense. She says that it is good when I find it for myself in a natural way, I'll know when it's the right time. I'm glad when this talk is over, even though it was good for us to have.

I wonder how it would be different if I was still back home with Mama on the porch and she was the one giving me this talk. But I'm here, not there. And all at once it's both scary and exciting.

"Jenna, I can't take any more for tonight."

"All right. Good night, Crysalline."

She rises and her soft touch lingers on my shoulder, leaving me rich with her kindness as she disappears back into the cabin.

I wander back around to the door and find Taggler sitting under a tree in the dark.

"Hi. I didn't expect to find you out here. Have you been thinking about what would happen if we just keep going on down the river?"

"I guess that's what there is to find out. Whatever there is, it'd be more interesting than here, I guess. Don't know how much longer I can stay here, just keep goin' back and forth."

There's a pause and I wish I could see his face in the dark, but then he says more.

"I've talked to Uncle Gren about the idea of going on farther. He says I should get back and talk to my folks if I'm going to go on down the river. Since he said it, I probably should."

I'm thrilled that he's thought this much through.

"When you can see yourself going, I'll be ready, too," I tell him.

"That settles it. I'll hike back upstream and be back as soon as I can."

In the morning, he leaves. Jenna looks like she might cry at times but she doesn't want me to see it. When I can, I wrap myself around her, wanting to smother her with affection. Gren is a good distraction for the several days Taggler's gone, and Jenna's started cooking to keep us all safe from what Gren might make. We walk and teach Gren how to play cards to pass the time.

Finally, Taggler's voice comes floating over the sound of the rapids just upstream.

"Hi, ho! I'm back, everybody!"

I almost knock over the table as I stand, looking at the door. He comes in, smiling, and says, "Well, my folks are agreeable if I want to go."

That decides it for me.

The next several days are a blur with Darry, Jenna, and Gren acting like parents, not sure if they can be happy about us deciding to go. They're so busy getting everything organized, knowing that we won't be coming back, at least not anytime soon. I'm sad, but I'm pulled by whatever's out there waiting for us.

Sleep is hard and in the daytime a fever of excitement comes over me. Taggler doesn't look as excited, but he spends all his time checking gear and working on the boat.

Gren has brought out all sorts of things for Taggler, including a smaller boat to take tied to ours to hold supplies. Gren gives Taggler four gold nuggets and several silver ones. Jenna and Darry give me all they can, as well, knowing they have more at home.

"Crysalline, I want you to take this bracelet I wove from flax strands for you to remember me," Jenna says as she works it over my hand and onto my arm. It has two colors woven together, golden yellow and red, and it fits me fine.

We grab onto each other with a strength that surprises me. I can feel her sobbing as she holds tight, her arms wrapped all the way around me.

"You can't know how much this means to me. I mean the bracelet."

Then it hits me. This is surely the last time I will ever see her. I can see in her eyes that she knows the river is pulling hard on me, on to somewhere else. I walk around the rest of the day bumping into everything as I'm fighting back tears.

***

The morning finally comes to leave. The last time to say our good-byes. Jenna's holding Larans close. Hugging tightly, neither one of us wants to let go. Sobbing, my heart is torn, knowing that I can't have both what's here and what's out there, as yet unknown.

Taggler helps me see through my tears to get into the boat. We shove off with the packed dingy behind us. I watch through the blur the four figures on shore as we come to the first bend in the river and, with a last frantic wave, they're out of sight. I let go of the breath I've been holding and let my fingers loosen from the edge of the boat. I swallow to push back the tears and hold onto that last blurry memory of Jenna and Darry standing and waving as we disappeared around the bend. Looking ahead, now there's just me, Taggler, and the river.

My eyes meet his, then I turn back to look out at the river.

"It's going to be a fine time," he says softly. I turn around to look at him again. He's intently watching the riverbank slip by. He smiles awkwardly as the familiar slips away. The boats are filled with so much more than the last time. They carry also all my yearnings for what's out there beyond today.

The morning is warm. The world all 'round our boats is alive and alert as we pass. Birds flit about, swooping low over the water, curious, I guess. Our boat sways in the ripples as I ride in the bow, looking ahead. Tree branches arch over the river with heavenly grace, and I remember when I was small I believed God must live up high in the trees where I couldn't quite see. Now I see God in every tree. Midday comes, and we tie up along a quiet stretch for our break. Taggler brings out food while I dig to get the apple and hard cheese I've been thinking about before I settle back against a tree.

"Well, we're doin' pretty fine so far," Taggler says with a smile I can't be quite sure of.

"Yes, this is fine."

"I'm pretty good at small game like rabbits and squirrels with a bow and arrow," he adds.

"As long as you're good at guttin' and skinnin', too."

"Yep. No problem."

After a short rest, we get underway again. I let my hand drag in the water as we glide along and cool my face with my wet fingers. All the while, the sun dances in the splashes of light that spill through the treetops as we pass.

This stretch of river is pleasant and relaxed, running slow and wide. We both settle in, watching the riverbank drift by. After we tie up for the evening at the same place as last time, we make our beds the same way, apart but close enough to talk. The night air is delightful, and we make small talk about the river and the day ahead. There's even some talk about what might be beyond Ulm. Finally, the night takes over, and sleep comes.

In my dream, the air smells of the recent rain as I fly free as a bird over the water. The sunlight dances on the surface while I sway easily from side to side.

Raindrops hit my face once, then again. I wonder how it can rain when it's so sunny. The leaves of the tree overhead rustle, and it's really raindrops hitting us here in our camp. We rush for the oiled cover we have, and I stay underneath, listening as the raindrops hit right above me. I try to drift back to sleep, but the sound of Taggler moving about taking care of our camp keeps me awake. Then the next thing I know it's morning, and I peek out to see him fixing tea over a smoky fire. I noticed that his shirt is stuck to him in places, but he doesn't seem to care.

"Want some tea?"

"Sure, I'll be right there."

I come over to the fire feeling damp but drier than he is. He hands me the only cup we have. The hot tea is good, warming me instantly.

"Thanks."

"Best thing there is on a cool, wet morning."

We pack up to leave, and I look around, thinking I'll probably never see this spot again. Ulm is ahead, the prize for the day. We're both in good spirits even if we *are* a bit damp. Ulm will be where we will find out what we can about the river beyond.

Before midday, Ulm comes into view. This time, though, the buildings look older and more worn down than I remember. We come to exactly the same spot and I leap out of the boat first, ready to explore. Taggler smiles as he throws me the line to tie up. My head's bursting with curiosity and questions as we walk toward the village.

I see a shop full of nice things I remember from last time. The shopkeeper is standing near the door and smiles.

"Hi! We're going on farther down the river. I wonder if you know what it's like ahead," I say.

He tilts his head with a quizzical look. "You are, huh? The prices down there aren't worth the trip. You won't save anything with the trouble of going all the way there and back again."

"Oh, no. I mean to say we're going farther anyway. I wasn't thinking about the prices."

"Oh, why didn't you say so?" he smiles at the change in the conversation. For quite a time, when no one else is in the store, he tells us what he's heard. We learn that the next place down river is about two days' travel from here, and it's on a hill a little bit away from the shore.

He continues to tell us stories, happy to find out that we're going beyond here and on our own.

As we ready to leave, he picks up something and, with a smile, hands it to me. "Here is something for good luck in your travels. Take it with my blessing."

In my hand is a flat stone disc on a rawhide string. It has these words cut into the stone: The time to live is now.

No one has ever given me a gift like this before, and now a stranger has done it. This must be the hand of goodness helping us.

"I really don't know what to say. Thank you so much."

"It's for your travels. Many times I've wished that I had done it myself."

Taggler takes it from my hand and puts it around my neck. I can feel the stone against my skin along with the memory of Jenna's warm embrace.

Wandering in and out of shops along the way, I'm filled with the newness of what's happened so far on this day. As I tire of looking everywhere, I turn to Taggler. "I'll wear this for today, but then tomorrow you can wear it if you like, and we'll change who wears it each day. It belongs to both of us, really."

This gift will go along with us, whatever is next.

# CHAPTER EIGHTEEN
# CHANGING COLORS

The boat is our new home. Moving along smoothly on the river is an unfinished dream, pulling me along. I drift away the time, my fingers touching the water's surface. A calm inside me grows, something bigger than me, and I remember a word Raspartan used: divine. I wonder if this is it.

Taggler and I talk about the new things that appear with each river bend that unfolds in front of us. At some places, the river is like a serpent, winding and not revealing anything that lies ahead. Then more unfolds for us.

"Did you think you'd ever really come this way?" I ask.

"Sometimes I'd wonder, but I could never see myself going alone. When you came along and brought it up, it fit together. I was tired of the same old places. I guess we could say this is your fault," he teases.

Hearing his easy way of telling it, I lean back, more relaxed. "Thank goodness I came along to save you."

I enjoy the play with words as much as he does while the boat takes us along, drifting and enjoying each day as it happens. The river has been very smooth so far, but he tells me that it will be rough sooner or later. Some places we pass attract my attention with their different sights or colors. I wish it would happen more often.

We usually shelter from the midday sun under an inviting, shady tree when we find one close to the water. The broad, leafy branches show shadow patterns all 'round us, moving as the leaves flutter with a passing breeze. We grow fond of this habit for our midday meal and sometimes nap before moving on through the afternoon. Finally, the fading light tells us it's time to stop for the day.

***

One morning, a harsh smell smothers any fresh air. I almost wish I could stop breathing to keep the sharp smell away. Then we see that it's coming out of the ground itself. A shiny black ooze is spreading, covering everything in its path. There's a shimmery colorful coating on the water, with rainbows that swirl in the eddy currents, as Taggler calls them. We fear we won't be able to get a drink or wash anywhere ahead if it keeps up. After we pass further on, the smell weakens, and the rainbows on the water fade into only a memory, except where the black sticks on the sides of the boats at the water line.

I know that water must move to be clean and good to drink. If it cannot move for a long time, it gets bad. There's something wonderful in hearing the sounds of the water chattering along. It talks without words, if I listen carefully enough, yet it seems to hold its own mysteries. Along our passageway that has been carved out by the water, there are secrets the water keeps. I want to know what it has touched or when it fell from the sky. Anywhere there's water, some kind of life blossoms. It babbles among the rocks and touches the bare roots of the trees that live at the river's edge. We are living and moving by its power and grace. How far could we get without it?

I wonder how I did not know this when I was younger, when the world was at my feet and I stayed home safe, listening to the rain that brings the water we must have to live.

The river carries life. Fish come to the surface, showing some interest in who or what we might be. They don't know they could become our dinner. Taggler's a good fisherman and I learn how he catches them.

I enjoy how calm he is as he easily guides our floating home. We work well together as I look out from the bow and signal him when I see rocks in our path. Sometimes a rock hiding below the surface surprises us with a thump, a reminder to keep alert and watch for the telltale ripples on the surface. The force of the river itself is holding and carrying us along, reminding us with those thumps of its unforgiving nature.

The river is moving as slowly as the day itself, taking us beyond our past. The sounds remind me of the babbling brook at Jenna and Darry's place. Every once in a while, with my fingertip in the water I feel a fish softly nibbling at it, like a kiss. As I drift along in this lazy sweetness, I am wildly happy and growing up, getting out into my life. It's mine to work for. Thank goodness I have the will and the gumption. A breeze comes, whispering to me, "Your body is the vessel that lets you taste life."

As I gaze over the side, my tears fall into the water below. This is certainly a divine moment, and it's mine.

Taggler is guiding our way with ease and I am free to be peaceful.

Sounds of the trees and chattering birds fill the warm scented air. Swaying above us, the branches seem almost crazy to escape the pull of the ground below. The leaves chatter, swirling in the breeze as they reach up to touch the sky. Then the scent on the air changes, telling me of other things and places.

The sun is low, darting through the landscape as we float along, so we find a spot along the shore for the night. It's a relief from the hard wooden form of the boat, reminding us that the world of land is part of us. We make a campsite in our usual, comfortable way of two sleeping spots.

I stop at the water's edge to wash off the dirt of the day. I love this time, feeling the water moving around me. At times when we need privacy, some boulder or bend in the river is usually enough. When the weather's warm, some of our clothing can be washed in the morning so there's time enough for it to dry in the sun.

Tonight, the campfire is sparkling, and I enjoy the warmth that pushes back the damp darkness. Dinner is fresh rabbit from Taggler's skill with the bow and arrow. Waiting sharpens my appetite as it cooks over the fire. When supper is done, we listen to the quiet sounds of the place as night arrives. Curious small animals move through the fallen leaves just out of sight in the dark. I wonder if we're going to have any nasty visitors, man or beast, that might not want to share this place with us.

The shy moon lights up the edges of the clouds, and a few stars dare to shine when it's dark enough.

"We've been out two days now since leaving Ulm. Do you think we might find the next village soon?" I ask.

"I saw a trail close to the water that looked wider than an animal trail. That may tell of somewhere coming very soon. Can't be sure, just maybe."

Taggler's answer echoes in me while I watch the moonlit cloudy sky. The campfire fades, giving off its last flames.

***

With the sunrise, I first notice only a few bug bites on my arms. Not bad. This is a welcome start to the day. There are the familiar sounds I enjoy while waking. Leaves drip the captured dew onto the roots below as birds begin to squawk and hop among the branches looking for their morning meal. The sun is spreading its warmth into the cool shadows where fallen soggy logs give off curls of steam where the sunlight can reach them. Tea, hard biscuits, and some of the rabbit from last night are good while we stand in the warm rays of the rising sun. Then we're on our way again.

Along this part of the river, colors are more beautiful than other places. I wonder if I'm seeing right. I can't be sure, but something strikes me as being unusual.

"Something's different here, don't you think?" I ask.

Taggler studies the shoreline for a minute before he answers. "Funny you should say that. I was having the same feeling. What is it?"

Not knowing, we fall quiet and watch to see if we can pick out anything. The morning hss now grown bright and warm. I see a bright shimmer that leaps forward from somewhere farther away from the shore. As soon as I try to look for it directly, it's not there anymore. Of course, we can't stop the boat from moving so I can take another look. Whatever caught my attention was brighter than anything else. Brighter than it should be, and then it was gone.

"Something caught my eye back there. It was shinier than anything else, but I didn't see it clear enough," I say to him, making sure he hears what I said.

We're now both watching and listening carefully. We sit in our usual places, each of us watching a side, as the shoreline passes, but nothing else new shows itself. I bite my lip, wondering what might be out there.

"Would you look at that," Taggler yells.

I spin around and see it, too. Coming alongside is a tall, bright purple plant with shiny, wide leaves. It's almost as bright as the sunshine itself. The river's moving fast enough that we can't get to shore to stop for a closer look. Soon it's faded into the distance and disappears from sight. We look at each other in disbelief.

"Did you see what I saw?"

"Yes, I did, but I can hardly believe my eyes."

We shift in the boat to be ready for anything, not knowing what might be next. It isn't long before another strange plant appears. This one is low to the ground with very frilly leaves that are as blue as the sky with purple stems. It, too, has brighter colors than anything possible. Taggler grabs the oars, furiously fighting the current to us slow down. We both stare until it disappears behind us. So far, they've been on the right side of the river, so Taggler comes a little closer to that shore. Just as he does, I spot a man on the other side, about thirty steps away from that shoreline. He sees us and darts behind some bushes. What's strange about him is that he, like the plants, is purple.

"Taggler, I just saw a purple man on the opposite side," I say as calmly and quietly as I can.

"What do you mean, a purple man? Are you sure you saw that right?"

"I mean his skin was purple all over, all the way to his eyes and his hands. I can't say if it was painted on, though."

Taggler guides the boat back to the middle of the river, not sure what else to do. He has his bow and arrow by his side, but I've never seen him use it from the moving boat—or on a person.

"All right, let's stay away from both shores and see what happens next," he whispers.

We begin seeing more and more strangely colored plants, and many are farther from the water's edge. I'm not sure which is stronger: my curiosity or my worry.

"Can we get close to the shore but not get out of the boat when we see another plant?"

Taggler doesn't answer for a time. He finally says, "If it looks like no one else is around, we can come closer, but I'll be ready to push off fast."

It isn't long before another bright plant appears. This one is different again. It changes color as it sways in the sun, from purple to bright yellow and then back again. At first, we can't be sure if it's because of our moving or if the plant is changing colors by itself. Taggler pulls alongside and grabs onto a sapling growing at the water's edge to stop the boat. Now we have a clear view of the bright plant which is easily within reach. Sparkling dust coats the leaves, and some falls onto the boat and my hand. The sparkles are bright purple, and my hand begins to turn a shade of purple where the dust touches it. I shake my hand quickly, sending the dust onto the wood of the boat, which turns a little purple. I looked back to my hand, which it is now fading back to its natural color.

"Yikes! My hand changed to the color of the dust and then back again when it fell off," I scream.

Taggler lets the boat move out into the current again, and we stare at each other, wondering what is going on. The edge of the boat still shows signs of purple moving along the edge, as if moving inside the wood fibers. We keep watching both shores for any more signs of people. There are foot trails along the right bank, so more people have been there for sure.

"Did he seem like he might be dangerous? Did he have any weapons?"

"I can't say for sure. He looked all right as far as I could tell."

"We could stop to find out more, if we see a good place to land."

I shiver as I stare wide-eyed directly at Taggler. We both smile cautiously, not sure if that's the right thing. I'm filled with excitement. Every moving leaf is now ripe for my imagination. My thoughts race, wanting to explain what I can't. The river keeps us moving as we watch for the next thing to show itself. Soon there looks to be a landing spot worn into the riverbank that's agreeable. Taggler pulls hard on the oars, brings us over, and jumps out. The only sound is the wet gravel crunch as he steps out and looks around to see what he can.

We tie our boats up to saplings and spy a trail that leads directly away from the river and up a lightly wooded slope. We share a look before we begin walking, staying close together in the middle of the trail so as to not touch any plants. Cut marks show that someone's been along this way to keep the path wide. We walk slowly for a while, then startle at a voice speaking clearly. We don't see anyone.

"Ha, so you are here. Two of you," a voice calls.

# CHAPTER NINETEEN
# AT THE EDGE

It's a woman's voice. We turn in that direction and see a middle-aged woman sitting on a boulder. The only thing I can tell for sure is that she's bright blue, right down to her fingernails. She's looking directly at us in a most pleasant and disarming way.

"You're very adventuresome, coming here. We don't get many people who are willing once they have seen one of us."

We both stand silent. I'm sure we're both seeing the same unbelievable sight right in front of us, and she's speaking our language clearly.

"You must have questions." She chuckles. "I will give you answers."

"We're curious about the strangely colored plants along the shore," Taggler begins. I can't manage to say anything.

The woman smiles again. "Would you want to sit for a while so we can talk some more?"

"Sure, we wouldn't mind," Taggler says with as casual a tone as he can.

With that, she puts two fingers to her lips and whistles a short sharp whistle, and a man and boy appear, each as blue as she is.

"We'll need some drink and a bit of food while we sit," she says without looking at either of them. They disappear and the boy returns with a bowl of blue fruits, a jug, and a cup, and places them on the ground in front of her, leaving just as smoothly as he had first arrived.

"My name is Asta. We live here where we've found these wondrous plants. We help them grow because they have wonderful, beneficial qualities when eaten. We have great health and mood, so we don't mind the other thing that happens, that we become the color of the plant."

I'd heard the word beneficial before, at home when someone was talking about something good happening.

"We don't go out to other places while we're blue, but after a while of not eating any more, the color fades away. Few others have ever stopped here to find out anything. Some of those who do stop already know one of us that they met in the outside world when we weren't blue."

Over the afternoon, she listens to our story with great attention, focused on every word.

"I'm delighted that you've come here with your curiosity. Because you are honestly curious and willing, I believe you will honor what I am going to say, this truth I am giving you." Then slowly and clearly she says these words in a deep voice: "Remember, your mind is the most fertile garden."

It's as if I could actually reach out and touch the words in the air. I sit shocked.

"Thank you," I say, barely whispering.

The afternoon comes to an end, and we get ready to leave.

"Thank you for everything," we each say to her as we turn to go.

"It has been a pleasure to chat with you. Have wonderful adventures in your travels."

On our way back to the river, we can't stop talking about her. This day is burned into me, to be cherished. We chuckle all the way back, each of us with a slight tinge of blue in our skin from our meal with her. She told us about a plant called Sperga that will be growing along the river ahead that is a wonderful food for us to enjoy on our journey. The stone necklace with the words etched into it bounces against me and I reach down, touch it, and smile even more.

For the night we stay close to here along the shore in this place we now call Astaland. We can't remember her calling this place by any name. The night is clear with only an occasional passing cloud. We lie on our bedrolls, talking and watching the night sky as time wraps around us. Our talks in the dark are something we both cherish.

"Sometimes I've wondered if we're doing the right thing, and then this happens and I wouldn't have it any other way," I say.

"We just have to be a good judge of places so we don't get into something we can't handle." Taggler adds, caution in his voice.

I keep repeating the name Asta in a hushed tone, as if I had met and now know someone who is quite impossible. I look up to find the brightest star and then watch the whole sky until a shooting star crosses. Then I let my eyes close, and sleep comes.

The next morning we laugh more at the pale blue that's still in our skin. The sound of the river is as comforting as always, but this morning there's something new and different that I hear.

"Do you hear anything different about the river this morning?

"I'll walk down a bit to see what I can and be back shortly," Taggler decides.

I think I see a more serious look on his face as he turns to go. I sit down to let myself enjoy the morning. When he comes back, I'll find out more.

He's back shortly with a quick stride and looks like he has a lot to say. "We've come to the first rapids to get around. There's no way to get the boats through it. We must unpack everything from the boats and carry it all past the rapids. We'll be here for a while."

After yesterday's glorious meeting, I don't mind doing anything. By the end of the day, though, I'm tired and sore from carrying everything through the forest of young trees we had to cut a path through. I hope we don't have many more rapids. We've moved everything just far enough past the bottom of the rapids so we can camp and won't get cold and wet from the mist in the air. With a warm campfire, we sit watching as the clear night sky begins to appear overhead.

"Crysalline, do you still like this the same after all that work?"

"Well, I'm sore all over tonight, but tomorrow I'd say it's not so bad, all considered. I'm still glad we're here."

He looks at my face closely. He can't know how at quiet moments I think of Jenna and get sad inside. I think my voice only tightened a little when I answered him. All the feelings swirl 'round together in me and I can't say anything else for a time. Missing Jenna is only a part of everything; there is so much more being in this place. I'm filled by being here and having Taggler as my guide on this, our river. He seems to know it's a good time to be quiet for the rest of the evening and we both settle in to drift off towards sleep. The mist of the rapids is close, and with every breath I slip off and away, into my own quiet world where the touch of the cool mist on my face is refreshing. I'm in the boat in my usual place, and the view moves by, along into the past. The air carries the scent of places that are soon to arrive. The boat sways as the water pushes and pulls at it, but that doesn't matter. I'm sitting at the bow with a hand on either side, feeling the movements. I feel the warm, fragrant air, then it's hot, dry, and dusty. It changes over and over, and through it all I'm in my seat, watching for what will appear next.

Whichever way I look, everything is alive and moving. The air and water give us what we need while the wind whispers in my ear. The boat knows what the water feels like and then so do I. With my eyes closed, I'm in my place, here in the middle of everything. The mist tickles at my nose as the boat sways, now more than before. Through the mist, Taggler calls my name.

"Crysalline, get up, the river's rising and we must get out of this camp."

By the softness of the light, I can tell it's still early and the sun hasn't come up. I want to keep my eyes closed and stay sleepy longer. I'm a little damp since the rapids are still close. Wrapped in my nest, these words come to me as the mist touches my face: "You are a part of all that is. Hold faith in yourself dearly."

***

When I hear the sound of the water closer than last night, I struggle to wake up. We move to higher ground and begin to relax again. The river is swollen and angry. For several days we must stay here, leaving the river alone while we stay safe and dry on the shore until the fury in the water passes.

We find an overhang along a rocky cliff when it rains, and we go out in the rain to be washed clean, refreshing our spirits and our bodies.

Today, I find myself wanting to know more about something else. "Taggler, I want to learn to use the bow and arrow. Maybe I won't be a great hunter, but can you teach me?"

"Sure. I 've seen you standing and pretending to be holding the bow, ready to shoot. Now's a good time while we're waiting here."

At first, it's hard to draw the bow and aim at the same time and I laugh at the results. With some patience, I get better at it over several days. My fingers hurt from pulling the bow string, but I'm glad to know how to do it.

We're living beyond the familiar world, moving along in this undiscovered life. We walk and find other people close by who are different and yet somehow the same as us, even though we speak different languages. It does take time to see more than the differences. We're treated as honored guests at some places, and gently we pass by others when it doesn't seem as friendly. When we can, we share our stories and they listen with a curiosity that seems to want to be fed. Then it's time to move along again; the river has quieted down.

We take the richness of meeting others along with us. We have no space for the burden of many things. We come to understand each other more. Taggler craves shade and slow breezes. He wanders along the shore looking at bugs in the shady places. When strong winds stir, he likes to tie up and be on land, where I playfully throw small stones at him when he belches out loud. It's a game we enjoy, belching and dodging pebbles. I always carry a small supply with me now.

Lying down for the evening by the fire, we make our beds closer than before.

We come to a place called Brevort where the people are skillful workers, so we stay to work alongside them in exchange for fresh clothes. It is most pleasant, so we stay longer than we'd thought to, for two full moons, replenishing ourselves and our supplies, and sharing our stories in the evenings. Then the river calls us again and, after a wonderful parting celebration, we're ready to be on our way, taking what we've learned from these people with us. Freshly outfitted, we're happy to be moving again.

"I will miss Brevort for sure," Taggler says.

"Me, too. It was lovely spending time there."

There's a quiver in my voice from being thankful that Taggler and I can talk about what we each like and understand each other. It makes our time together even better.

Leaving Brevort, we were told that the river will be stronger ahead, so we're anxious to find out when that will be. For now, the memories of Brevort linger as we move along this peaceful section for the morning. The river is wide and the day is mild, and being wrapped in the familiar comfort of our travels is bliss. The sunshine flickers over me as we pass under several trees. I close my eyes, and a new wonder comes to me: "Living larger than yourself, life can bloom wildly."

***

At our midday rest, when I tell Taggler, he gives me a quick hug. He usually keeps to himself, and his lean, strong arms give me something I've missed: it reminds me of Jenna's caring touch. I'm glad that he reached out to me.

Soon, the river channel narrows with rock walls on both sides and the water moves much faster. The excitement at first from pivoting and shifting in the strong currents changes to worry as the boats are thrown around like toys. We are at its mercy, now bound to it, as there is no way to slow down or beach anywhere. At times, a current will spin us so that our supply boat is in front of us and the rope between the two boats jerks hard. I'm afraid it will break. We're moving fast, too fast. I see the worry on Taggler's face, but the fury of the water drowns out any words as the world spins. We thump against the rocky walls. The water roars in the tight space between the tall canyon walls that tower over us. I'm quickly soaked. I must keep my hands inside the boat or they might get smashed. Taggler is braced against the tossing; there is no time for a prayer. Every muscle is fighting to stay safe.

Then it happens. I'm thrown out, and my face and shoulder scrape against the edge of the boat. I swing wildly with both arms to find the boat again. I can only see the wooden side rising and falling as the water thrashes in the small space between my face and the boat. My head thumps the side several times as I fight to find any kind of grip.

The water surges over me and I struggle to get air. I see Jimmy's face, scared and fighting for air through the water. This can't be. I'm spun around again and see a rock wall. The side of the boat thumps me from behind. I'm spinning, grabbing for anything, but the sides of the boat are slippery. Now I can't find Jimmy anymore.

Taggler is still up there somewhere, I hope. Oh, God, please let the water stop for just enough time for me to live. My arms swing, trying to find air and a handhold anywhere, when something or someone hits against my arm once, then again, and grabs my wrist. I can't see anything in the wild surge that wants to crush me against the side of the boat, but my arm is pulled hard upward. My face breaks the surface, and I know it's Taggler. I can only see his arm and part of his face over the side of the boat. Now his other arm is reaching out and catches hold of me, pulling me up against the side. My hand finds the top edge and grabs onto it, then the other hand, too, and we are both fighting to get me back. He drags me up out of the water and into the boat in spite of the thrashing water. I'm coughing, trying to get a clear breath from the water that's trying to swallow me. The fury of the river is still beating at us, but we're finally in a heap in the boat, clinging to each other.

I get a hand under me and lift up for enough space to cough. I grab him with a fearsome strength that surprises me. He pulls himself up to try to work the boat and keep from smashing into the rock walls while I cling to him. I can't let go.

# CHAPTER TWENTY
# BECOMING

The surging and bumping never seem to end. All I can do is hold onto Taggler as tight as I can. I'm shaking so much I think I might come apart. Eventually, the thrashing slows but I don't let up holding onto him. Soon, though, the boat feels like a refuge again, and he slides down to me. We stay tightly wound together with no space between us, our heads touching. We sway with the rhythms of the boat's slowing movements and my shaking lets up. His keeps us both steady against the occasional thumps that still happen right when I think they might be done.

My breathing begins to be regular and strong, stronger in being safe now with Taggler. His grip lightens and turns into holding me. I'm soaking wet and cold, so his warmth matters.

"That was terrible."

"Yes," is the only thing I can say, shivering with the wet and cold.

He guides the boat to shore as I move up to sit beside him, wrapping my arms around him. We hit a sandy shore and he puts his arm around me, and we get out to be on solid land.

"Let's get into the sun," he says as he points the way towards a welcoming sunny spot.

We both fall down, side by side in the warmth. I'm still holding him tightly. Still shivering from the wet clothes, I want all the warmth I can find. I'm warming slowly as we lie here, soaking in the sun, and the feeling that we are still swirling is mostly now nothing more than a bad memory. Our faces turn to meet and we kiss for the first time, then again and again.

"I almost lost you back there."

"'That was horrible. I'm glad it's over," I say quietly. My warmth is now like his, and wonderful.

Something new is awakening. Something more than I could have known to look for. My lips continue to taste his, sometimes lightly, sometimes more, leaving hesitation behind. I am now warm and wanting more, and I feel his wanting, too, if shyly.

"I want to dry out. I'm all wet."

I unbutton the wet, clinging clothes and take them off, throwing them into the open where the sun can dry them. He follows me, taking all his off. The warmth of the sun is wonderful, and, touching skin to skin, I'm trembling, wondering what's to become of this. A restlessness has me seeking something, and we began tasting each other's lips again. I remember Jenna's words from that awkward time. Now my body's telling me what her words meant. This is my time.

We touch, our fingertips shy, yet exploring. I'm warm all over. I gasp at the touch of his fully alert body and shiver again. I don't feel the ground under me anymore, only his skin on mine, and a wonderful heat that's building. We're both searching to find out what this is to be, discovering our nature together. Finally, any separation between us is gone as we find that secret place and join, and I am filled with awe. I'm all at once both a girl and a woman.

We spend the rest of the day exploring, melted in shared joy. There are few words as we let ourselves roam free. The sun glows and we glow in it. We move into the shade for the rest of the afternoon and get a blanket from the boat. Only the necessities of life force any parting, and then reluctantly. We bring food back from the boat and lounge in the glory of this day. Taggler's skin glistens and, as evening comes, we wrap ourselves into our cocoon and fall asleep in the dreaminess of our joining, now tasted.

The usual sounds of morning wake me into this new world. I am flooded with new happy feelings. We study each other all over again until hunger calls and I eat biscuits wildly. We spend the rest of the morning playing with our magic. We're now a different kind of partners, even though we're sometimes clumsy and impatient, finding our way.

Three more days pass in this place with us fully enjoying ourselves. The tree leaves are shinier, and the grasses sway in a dance, glowing in the sun. Taggler chases me and I pretend to not want to be caught, then enjoy him even more. The stars glow brighter now, just for us. It rains and we dance naked, thankful for the fresh delight. The small creatures watch at the edges of our celebration.

These are our blessings.

***

This morning we are tying things down tight, getting ready to leave again. From our camp I can hear Taggler by the river. He appears, wearing a smile and, with a soft touch, brushes his hand against my cheek. I hand him the cup of tea and we finish the wild berries we found.

"Are we ready to go?" he asks, seeing we have gathered almost everything.

"I guess. I don't want to leave anything behind," I answer with a smile.

"Me neither."

As we continue on, I look forward to so much more enjoyment together. My taste for this life has awakened much more than the taste of any simple apple could. If only I could tell Jenna how wonderful I feel now, knowing this for myself.

Life is as perfect as it can be. I stand at this meadow, imprinting it in my mind to remember what has come alive here, this new fire that was waiting to awaken in me. The morning is cool as we walk to the boats and shove off. I sit wrapped and cozy, filled with newfound joy as I watch Taggler guide our boat safely while the world flows around us. The blanket is warm with memories. He looks at me knowingly, for we both have received this blessing that had been waiting for the right time to be discovered.

With the sweet sense of being together, living as nature itself, we're bigger than only two people. We continue on, but now when we stop for a break from the boat, we eat, love, and sleep under some grand shady tree in the middle of the day, watching the branch tips touch as they pass in the wind, needles shaking against the cones heavy with sweetness, again giving me a wild love of each place, to remember forever.

We meet more new people. We laugh for the simplest things that are our memories made of these places and people.

A stand of huge, tall, stately trees appears as we round a bend.

"Oh, Taggler, we must stop here. Would that be all right?"

The trees stand tall and silent, majestic as I walk among them. They reach to the sky. It is a most peaceful place. Walking on the soft, moist forest floor, I wonder how long they've been quietly standing here. The softness keeps every footstep silent as the wind whispers up high in their tops. We relax, making love in their midst, feeling like part of forever.

I lie in awe with them all 'round us, for I feel they've been here long before I was born and probably will be here long after me. They're now part of me, like relatives I'll cherish even though I may be far from here. We stay for several days, embraced by their cool shelter. We finally decide to move on. I will never forget how they stand, silent and strong, becoming smaller and smaller as the living river takes us away.

***

Our next adventure is at very small place we almost pass without seeing, finding it only by our curiosity in following a small trail on a whim. We come upon it with a smile. A very crude, small hut is the first thing I see. Sitting on a low side branch of a small tree next to the hut is a boy whose eyes widen on seeing us.

"Hello," I say.

The boy says nothing.

"What's your name?"

He jumps down and his bare feet softly land on the dusty ground. He takes a few steps away, then turns to look back at us with a smile, and waves his hand, signaling for us to follow.

We follow as he walks quickly, his small steps making a crooked path between a few other huts. I see no one else and we keep following him past a stand of bushes. We pass two more huts that are oddly spaced. He turns back to make sure we're following.

We arrive at the back corner of a hut where we find a man sitting in a wooden chair held together with reeds, smoking a pipe. He shifts his gaze between the boy and us. He shows his surprise and delight with a ragged yellow smile and motions for us to sit, so we sit on the ground and nod our greeting. So far, we haven't spoken any words.

He speaks to the boy, then to us in words we can't understand. With a sweep of his arm, pipe in hand, he smiles and speaks again to the boy, sending him running off in a new direction. Waiting in silence, it's hard for me to relax. I'm trying to figure out his age, which is probably somewhere between a father and grandfather, while he sits smoking the pipe. The boy reappears, looking quite important. A young man and woman appear right behind him. They're dark skinned, wear simple clothes, have sandaled feet, and smile as they walk toward us holding hands. Their long, jet black hair is tied loosely behind them. Their lively eyes meet ours as they join us on the ground in a loose circle in front of the older man. He says a few words to the young man, who then looks to us, saying, "Naibira maramiba,"

"Hello," we both answer pleasantly.

"Oh, you speak in other way. I am Maiwan and she Siehtu. This is my people place. This older one is Taalana."

"I am Taggler and she is Crysalline," Taggler replies calmly, first placing his hand lightly on his chest then my arm.

"Well to you are now here."

He smiles as he speaks, then motions to the boy to go for something, sending him running off after nodding his understanding.

"You stay, we talk, yes?"

"Yes," we both answer at the same time.

The boy reappears with a pot that could be for some kind of tea, and several pottery cups in a wicker basket. He puts them down between

Maiwan and Siehtu.

"Yes, you want?" Maiwan says with a sweep of his open palm toward the teapot.

"Yes, please."

The strong, bitter taste surprises me, but I try to look pleasant with a smile on my face as I drink. Siehtu leans over to say something quietly to Maiwan, then he shakes his head from side to side. Taalana leans forward and says something to us that shows kindness in his face. I think maybe he is offering some kind of advice.

Then Maiwan speaks. "He says you be pleasant and now he happy for be this place."

Taalana then says something to Siehtu. It looks like he's wanting her to speak. She glances quickly at us with a shy smile and then looks back to the others, telling them something.

I'm a bit puzzled, not sure what's happening, but I stay calm and look pleasant, watching for what might be next.

"You can stay for eating? It must be for eating to be tree," Maiwan says with a huge smile that stretches across his whole face. He is waving his fingers as he smiles.

We quickly glance at each other, not sure what it all means, especially the word tree. There are more than three of us here. I am uncomfortable with the awkwardness in understanding each other and feel like it would be better to leave soon.

"Thank you. This is very good, and it is time for us to go," I say with as calm a voice as I can find. There is too much I don't understand.

With that, Siehtu rises and in one step crosses to my side. She sits next to me and places fingertips on my arm and her other hand lightly on my forehead. She takes her hand away from my forehead and looks directly at me. She says something that instantly melts into me, whatever it was. My body tingles with some mysterious beauty and wonder, and I am drenched in a deep, quiet joy. She softly lifts her fingertips from my arm and moves to hold my hand. It is at once gentle and perfect to be bathed in this moment beyond words. A whispered flood of love washes over my heart. It is as if she and I will always be moving through this life together, even if we are to be great distances apart.

She is still holding me in her eyes as Maiwan says, "You all go with the love you have, and be tree, coming to be tree, later, soon."

I say the only words I can find, still lost in the feelings flooding me. "Thank you. I feel your kindness. We go with your love in our hearts."

I turn to Taggler, who's looking very confused. We get up and excuse ourselves to begin our way back to the river.

As we walk, nothing is quite the same, and when a soft branch touched my cheek as we pass, this comes to me in a silent whisper: "Change is creation, unfolding with life."

There is so much I don't yet understand

# CHAPTER TWENTY-ONE
# BECOMING TREE

When we get back to the boat I can only sit, trying to figure out what's happened. Taggler still looks confused.

"I will remember her always, forever," I whisper.

He moves over and we sit quietly, side by side. Only the sounds of the trees in the light breeze and the river, moving as always, surround us.

"Taggler, are we going to have a baby?"

He has the strangest look on his face and doesn't say a thing, then glances sheepishly at me. Suddenly I am afraid of what is to be our future. Maybe we won't know what to do.

"Let's move on so we can find our spot earlier tonight. Then it will be just us with everything lovely all around us."

We push off, watching the rocky shore pass by. As the day eases into late afternoon, my ache find a good place for the night grows stronger. Finally, one appears. We are well practiced at making camp, a comfort that's more welcome tonight. I'm struggling to understand what will become of us, out here, on our own.

Supper is thin, since Taggler doesn't catch any fish or have any luck finding small game. We settle down side by side to watch the night sky awaken. From under the shelter of the tree, branches it sparkles. There must be more stars than ever.

"I don't know anything for sure about what Siehtu told us, that we're to be having a baby. I wish I could talk to Jenna again." I begin to sob softly and cradle myself closer to Taggler, who has his arm around me.

"My people didn't talk about this kind of thing with me, and the men are just happy when it happens, so I don't know how to help." He sounds a bit lost. "Somehow, we'll find out what to do," he adds.

In the dark, his voice is comforting. We *will* find out. I hope. I snuggle closer, and yet feel like I'm somehow alone again.

***

For the next two months, it's hard to eat anything at all in the mornings. I wake up sick to my stomach. Taggler encourages me to try. I tell him maybe I'll be able to eat enough later in the day. Moving on the river makes it worse, so we've stopped at a friendly place called Tunica. The people here are helpful, so we'll stay, but we're not sure for how long. Their language is somewhat different than ours, but we can figure out most of what's needed to understand each other, and in time we come to know more of their words. The universal language of a friendly smile and some hand gestures works wonders.

They've helped us make a simple hut to live in. It sits between the river and the village. I'm enjoying having a home on dry land for a change. I help others when I can while Taggler's out working with someone. We're learning how the food crops grow here, and there are handicrafts like Jenna and Darry made. Seeing these, I miss them both, but mostly a place missing Jenna pulls hard at me.

***

Without the tasks of being on the river, I can relax and take care of myself. It's morning, and Taggler is lying close enough for me to feel his breathing. I begin to feel a warm glow as he reaches over to hold me closer, and we begin touching and teasing, becoming one again, while the world outside falls away.

Life is blooming.

Memories of childhood rise. I'd sit at my window as the air brought a hint of what was out beyond. Running through the tall grasses of summer, the seed heads would tap at my arms and legs, and I'd play at what it was to be free and a little wild.

The magic carpet of memories goes on. I remember the pond where the fish and I met, and the old abandoned shed that was mine alone. The peaceful stream at Jenna's flows into this new bliss that Taggler and I treasure, that's all wrapped around me as I begin to weave the dreams to be born tonight.

The long vista of trees stretches as far as I can see from my treetop perch. I'm holding on as the branches around me sway. Out beyond, everything looks far away. Birds come to visit, and one lands and, after a quick look, flies away. Small animals wander on the ground below to feed on the ripeness of the season before returning to the deep stillness of their underground burrows where they are comfortable below where we can go. Down there, they are safe from the claws of the hunters that soar above.

The sun sparkles in my eyes through the moving leaves. Something is tickling my ear. I almost lose my balance as I shift to get away from it. It's Taggler, at my side with a grassy stalk, teasing me to wake up.

Opening my eyes, I see that the sunlight is playing through the thatch of our hut.

"You're beautiful to watch while you sleep. You should wake up, though, or you'll miss a beautiful morning. I'm going this morning to help someone in the village. Will you be all right?"

"Yes, I promise. I'm going to see Nisula this morning."

"You do need to eat enough for both of you. There's oatmeal made if you get hungry."

"Ugh. I don't want to hear about it. That sounds disgusting. Maybe later, but not now."

I have a new friend, Nisula, who lives alone in her home in the village. We spend time together almost every day. Nisula makes a special medicine drink for me. She watches to be sure I drink all of it, and then nods with approval. My worries have lessened a lot since I found her. Sitting in the morning sun at her comfortable, strong house is a delight until sometimes a sadness flickers across her face and a distant look comes into her eyes. Then she'll look at me and her smile comes alive again. I think it must be something about a husband or children that brings on her sadness, but I don't know yet.

Her touch is tender and caring, but her hands show that she's done hard work. Her other friends visit with us, too, and we have a good time, laughing a lot. They love to fuss over my growing fullness and enjoy making me blush.

Time passes easily here. I like being the center of attention, and Taggler walks around the village with a bit of swagger. He's worked to improve our hut with sturdier posts and a floor made of some local mixture that makes a good hard-packed floor. It's quite comfortable now with our frame bed that he built with soft layers of grasses, horsehair, and a sheep skin on top. We freshen the padding by adding to it as I get heavier. With the gifts of others, over these several months it has become our own sweet, cozy home.

Lying in bed, I listen to the sounds of the world outside. Small specks of sunlight peek through the thatch overhead, and I make note so they can be filled. The thatch chatters in the wind, and I feel the baby move inside me. Now in my eighth month, the baby will be here soon, making us three.

I weep when I imagine seeing Jenna again. Our talk would have the sweet understanding of the life I have growing in me. She has come to me in dreams, as caring and gentle as always and has told me: "Love is a rare bird, flying free with joy."

***

I hear the sound of footsteps coming closer. Taggler bursts through the doorway, stopping to stand tall and proud. "I come bearing fruit," he says, his arm high in the air holding it, as if he is a tree.

His smile lights up the whole room and I motion for him to join me in bed. He takes off his sandals and gently fits himself carefully around me. Waves of happiness pull us close, with the baby in the middle.

The season is fully ripe.

With Nisula as leader, the women of the village keep me occupied with their preparations for the delivery. It's quite notable, since I'm the first visitor in memory to have a baby born here. There are endless conversations to decide which salve is best for my stretching belly. Nisula's home will be the birthing place. We already have a cradle, passed down many times into a home where new life has arrived so it is smooth from many loving hands and newly cleaned and blessed by the village.

My life is rich beyond childhood imaginings. The flow of this life carries me along, finding the new of each day. My time will be soon, certainly within the month. I spend a lot of my day at Nisula's and now it's like another home to me. Our own hut has the sounds of the world around us that we know so well and love. We've been here longer than any other place and certainly will stay for some time after the baby is born.

Taggler walks with me every day. It's good for me and keeps me busy. It is also our own quiet time away from the helpful but sometimes smothering help in the village. We walk hand in hand on the easier trails to quiet places. Today, we're at an overlook at the edge of the lake closest to the village. From here we can look out over it all, at everything beyond as the wide earth beyond the lake arches up into the clear blue sky. The villagers call it a name we can't say well, laughing every time we try, so we just call it The Watching Waters and Sky Place. I love being here.

"We don't have any names for the baby yet," I say softly, breaking the quiet. We've been peacefully watching the movements of the water and sky.

"I don't have one in mind that fits right, either. Maybe we'll know better when the time is really here," he says.

"Ow, that hurt!"

Taggler jumps up and I almost lose my balance on the rock seat we've been resting on.

"What is it? What happened?"

"Settle down. I've been having small pains for several days now. Everyone tells me they're normal."

But now we're both worried and waiting for it to happen again. By the look on his face, it's more painful for him. Then it hits me: we're far from Nisula and her helpers. It was foolish to come this far, like it's some regular kind of day.

"We should start back."

I can see Taggler trying to figure out if it's more serious than I've let on. "We should. Let's go."

Another pain hits and I wonder how I'm going to make back, if only to the hut. I wonder why we came so far.

Taggler helps me to my feet. "Let's get going," he says seriously.

The path snakes between rocky places and young trees. Occasionally, one of us steps awkwardly on some small unforgiving rock or root. The saplings along the way are a nuisance when they slap at me as we pass, walking side by side holding onto each other. Taggler offers a curse at the distance to be covered and my pains that grow. At one point, we make a stupid mistake of direction, and then must go even farther.

Finally, we see our hut; it's the most wonderful sight I could imagine. As Taggler helps me onto the bed, the pains take me over. With each one, I see Taggler's smile tighten even more. All he can do is soothe me with a wet cloth because the day is hot and I'm miserable. I'd do anything to get this over with right now.

"Here, drink some water," he offers.

I don't want to try to make it to the village as planned. And our hut feels like the loneliest place there could be.

"I'll bring help back," he says, wiping my forehead again.

"Ow, ow, oooh!"

The whole hut seems to be moving around me. I look up at him, pleading for relief as sweat trickles into my eyes.

"I'll be back soon," he promises.

"Hurry, hurry."

He kisses me and turns, running out.

I can hear his footsteps digging into the dry sandy soil and fading away. I'm pretty sure he can still hear me.

"Ow, ow, ow, ooowww!"

In the distance I hear him screaming, "Nisula. Nisula, now!"

After a few long minutes, he reappears at the doorway wearing a sweaty, panicked look, then Nisula and one of her helpers appear, panting and out of breath, carrying their prepared bundles.

Now the only sound is me.

"Ohhh, ohhh, ow, ow!"

Rushing into the dark inside of the hut, Nisula bends over me, looking me in the eyes and giving me her usual smile colored with concern. I am desperate for relief. She pushes Taggler back out the door and he gives me one last worried look, then disappears from sight. He can only listen to my screams and the chorus of voices calmly pleading with me. Nisula and her helpers get to work, making hot water and setting up everything they brought.

People come and go, and they keep Taggler outside. Finally the baby is born, announcing his arrival as everyone inside gives joyful cheers of relief. One of the helpers goes rushing out with her finger wiggling to let him know we have a son. I hear him sobbing with relief.

While the sweet baby wiggles, making wonderful sounds at my side, I see concern on the faces all around me.

# CHAPTER TWENTY-TWO
# A NEW FACE

I hear Taggler begging to come in, but I can tell the answer was no, not yet.

Everyone's fussing over me and the baby for what seems like forever. I hear Nisula tell the helpers to let him come in. He falls on his knees to be face to face with me, careful as he puts his hands on the edge of the bed to lean in. I am holding the squirming, wrapped-up bundle. He kisses me softly and sweetly and leans over carefully for a closer look as he hears the sounds from our son.

I pull back the edge of the wrappings, and there is his wrinkled little pink face, a boy we will get to know. There is so much promise in that little bundle, the promise of a newly-born future. A tear falls onto my hand, and Taggler cups my cheek with his hand. Everything in this world is perfect at this moment. There is a deep quiet filled with love and awe as everyone quietly watches this miracle, a new life. I don't have any voice left but I am filled with joy.

Still, I see the concern on the faces around the room, while they smile through their tears in happiness. In the days after, Nisula comes every day from daybreak until after supper, fretting over the three of us. A wet nurse is found to add to the little milk I'm able to give in my weak condition. There is a quiet stream of comings and goings to bring special drinks for me and to keep baby well fed.

***

This morning, Taggler's still in bed A the light and sounds of the outside world begin to softly filter in while I nurse our little one.

"He's bigger already, isn't he."

"Yes, and you'll be getting stronger too. We need to get you fresh air and rest for some of the day."

"Nisula says that, too."

I roll over and give Taggler a kiss, filled with the glow of this magic. The baby needs a name, but we're in no hurry to choose one. Baby Dear is what we call him for now. Nisula radiates joy all the time. She's such a part of our growing family. Baby Dear's eyes move towards sounds he hears. We're glad he shows curiosity at the kind voices that shower him with attention and care. By his first month, he shakes his legs in delight when the canopy of leafy branches overhead dances in the wind, making the sky sparkle. He makes little sounds when he hears the birds sing.

When I was just a little girl, my world was small. That's the way it always begins, I guess. I found new places beyond home, and my life is now blooming in ways I couldn't have known then. Baby Dear's time to discover the world out there will come. Now that I look back, deciding to explore with Taggler was really bold, and I wouldn't trade it for anything. Nature has blessed us. I feel so much a part of everything, all that is, all the swirling mysteries and discoveries waiting to be found. Others will discover their own kind of happiness along the way. It has to be tried to be found out. It could be mighty amazing.

It would be perfect if I could share this with Jenna and Mama.

I am still weak from the birthing. The older women who know about such things give thanks that a mother and child both come through alive. It is not always so. Taggler spends most of his day close to the hut so he can hear if I call him.

***

Today is like many others. I have slept late and I'm waking up with the sun high in the morning sky.

"Taggler, where are you? Can you come in? I have something I want to tell you."

Taggler brushes himself off as he stands in the doorway. "Is everything all right?"

"Yes, yes. I want to tell you about my dream."

He slips off his sandals and gets back into bed with me. The baby is in his cradle alongside.

"I had the most wonderful dream. I saw him just as he is now and as a young man, and I heard the name he was called in the dream."

"What is it? Taggler says, surprised and excited.

"Proem," I say. "Proem. I don't think I've ever heard that name anywhere. Do you think it fits him?"

Taggler sounds it out for himself. "Proem." He looks back at me and there's a sparkle of delight between us.

"Proem it is." He then adds, "What is his other name? My people have always been called Stoekler."

I suddenly realize we've never talked about family names in all this time together. Somehow it just didn't matter. We've been living beyond the past with nothing to bend our future. On the river, I hadn't looked back often, as we uncovered our new world.

A playful grin comes to my face and I say, "Let's make up a new family name for us."

Taggler looks puzzled but gives a chuckle. Then we just sit quietly for a moment.

"Let's call ourselves Newly. We will be the Newly family. Taggler, Crysalline, and Proem Newly." With that, we both laugh, and Proem gurgles his agreement.

So it is decided. Everyone in the village begins to practice saying the name.

Taggler spends his time working on the comforts of our home. The floor in the hut has become packed by many footsteps and is hard and smooth. The thatch of the walls has been filled. We now cook on a charcoal fire in a stone chimney at the side of the front room that Taggler and helpers from the village built. It is our first home.

It has been several months since Proem was born and we're getting out for longer walks now. It's frustrating that my strength isn't coming back. Nursing Proem is my great joy, but by most afternoons I'm exhausted even if I'm in great spirits otherwise.

Today, as we walk to the lake overlook for the first time since Proem was born, the breeze around my face feels delightful, but the walk is tiring. When we get there, I sit, glad to relax. Concerns wash away in the warm air moving around us, melted by the sunshine. The warmth coming from the sunbaked rocks is comforting. Small creatures dart about, mostly not caring that we're here.

"Crysalline, you're looking better, and Proem is very happy today, isn't he."

"I'm feeling better, and in time I'll be fine. We're lucky to be in such a wonderful place. Nisula is so dear to me. I don't know how we could have gotten along without her."

Taggler looks upset just thinking about it.

"We were so carefree and we really didn't know how much things would change having a baby. We are lucky, " I say.

The silky lake stretches out into the distance. I sit with Proem on my lap and Taggler beside me and look out at the beauty of the place. Right here, right now, everything is right. Everything.

# CHAPTER TWENTY-THREE
# THE DIVINE LOSS

With a tap on Nisula's door, Proem and I burst in with huge smiles and a friendly "Good morning." In two steps, I'm planting a kiss on her cheek. She gives Proem one and he shyly buries his face. Nisula goes to the table for the cup of tea said to be good for nursing mothers. I expect it every time we get together. She pulls out a chair for me at the table and I settle down for our visit. Proem sits quietly on my lap, watching everything as usual.

I cherish every breath of time with her. This is what I need to grow into the woman and mother I am becoming. She watches over me, wise, and worried about my health but tries not to let it show. I wonder what joy and pain is hers alone that I can't see.

We hear familiar voices at the door and two of her friends come in smiling, carrying freshly baked bread that fills the air with its wonderful, warm smell. We sit around the table talking with great ease in the comfort and company of the day. Proem is amused and easily distracted by each wave of laughter. When he gets fussy, he gets my milk.

Soon it is late in the morning, so Proem and I leave to begin our morning stroll back to our hut. On the way, we are greeted with smiles and nods, with an occasional stop for pinching and cooing. I love all this attention. Taggler tells me it makes me glow even more. As I reach our hut, he's there, carrying charcoal inside and tidying up. He stops to greet us.

We share a huge kiss and I taste the moist saltiness on his lips. My hair dances around as the breeze takes it, wrapping our faces together. He ruffles the fuzz on Proem's head, and Proem giggles with delight. We are absolutely amused by our little creation. We are the Newlys.

After the midday meal, we settle into the quiet of the afternoon, watching him and happily teaching him all about fingers and toes. Proem gets tired and hungry, and after a feeding, falls asleep. Taggler and I join together in our bed, finding our delight in making love, then soon drifting off. There is nothing missing in this life.

The sound of Proem crying has me struggle through the cobweb of dreams. Taggler raises his head enough to see me getting up to comfort our son. I come back to bed, placing him in the space between us. Proem likes this, so he smiles as he looks at each of us.

"Nisula wants to make a celebration for Proem finishing his second season. He's now almost a half year old. She'd like it to be at her place in the village," I whisper to Taggler, who's only half awake.

He's quiet for a moment, thinking, and then he says, "That sounds wonderful. When would it be?"

"At the next full moon, in six days."

The day is set and everyone makes a fuss over every little thing. Everything is tidied up and freshly washed. Proem has new clothes made by the women of the village. There's more than enough for him to wear, and I must be sure he's seen wearing each piece.

***

The day finally comes that Proem is a half year old. It starts with us happily going about making ready for the celebration. Everyone is helping with food and drink for the occasion. Proem has caught some of the excitement and doesn't want to take his afternoon nap, so I nest with him in bed, and he finally goes to sleep. There's almost nothing better than being with this beautiful little person as I listen to the gentle sounds of his breathing.

We walk into the village late in the afternoon, greeted as the Newly family by so many of the people of this place, the people who live, love, work, and argue here. They *are* this village.

Nisula is grand in a flowing robe. Seeing us, she spreads her arms wide, trying to swallow us up in her embrace. Her soft strength is food for my soul. Proem wiggles in delight at being wrapped in so many loving arms.

He loves the torches that light up the evening. With so much food, drink, and music, the dancing continues long into the evening. Proem is held aloft before being taken off to bed by friends while we stay to enjoy more of the fine time. Finally, Taggler and I make our way back to the hut and we hug the woman who has been watching over Proem as she excuses herself to go.

***

Proem still demands feeding during the night, giving me less sleep than I want after the party. Morning comes with the sunlight pouring into our sleepy world, asking us to wake up like all of nature around us. Birds are squawking in the branches overhead and Proem is the first of us to wake up. We gather together in our bed for his morning feeding. It is a grand time for all of us to be quietly together.

"That was wonderful last night, wasn't it?"

"Mmm, yes it was," I remark softly, not wanting to change Proem's attention.

"Everything is so perfect. I love both of you," Taggler whispers.

The words glide without effort. I look up at him, my eyes full and brimming with gratitude and contentment.

***

Our world spins gracefully around this new star, Proem Newly. He is growing well and learning every day from what Taggler and I show him of the world we know and love. We take small walks out from the village to see what lies beyond. He wants to taste everything, no matter whether it is to eat or not. We show him things that move, and he watches with innocent curiosity. We teach him to listen.

Time moves easily while we're here, and soon Proem is almost one year old. He can walk on his own and has sandals to wear since he doesn't like walking on rocks or a crawling bug. He takes great interest in watching the small things that move around on the ground but doesn't want to ever step on them. It makes our every walk a slow one.

Today I'm at Nisula's for morning tea and we sit enjoying the peaceful day.

"Crysalline, Proem is to be one year soon. Another happy day, right?" I can see she is begging to have the celebration.

"Oh, my, the time goes so quickly. You're right. We will have a happy day, of course."

I have to look out the window as tears fill my eyes, and I wait to be able to say any more. Nisula is such a treasure, added to everything else I cherish. It has been a wondrous year for me, becoming a more equal member of the circle of women who gather at her house. Even though I don't understand all of what they say to each other, together we share enough words to have a grand time. They patiently listen and work to learn some of my words, too.

So Proem passes one year and we have that grand celebration. It's equal to the first one, and, as with any celebrations here, we feel like we're part of one big family.

***

As time passes, he grows, as do the other children of the village. He's healthy and curious, which is exhausting. He surprises me with his interest. It seems nothing misses his attention. Taggler takes him out to give me a break and they have their own adventures. Proem is less wobbly on his feet as he toddles along. He gets to be in a backpack carrier for longer distances simply so we can get there. It reminds me of Larans and the time out searching for my home.

We let years pass without a care. As Proem comes closer to being four years old, we go out often to the lake where we love to spend time. He's too heavy to carry for any distance so the lake is the furthest we'll go with him. Nisula's joining us for this outing, and we're all in great spirits for the day. It rained a little the day before and all the leaves are shiny clean. We walk slow so we won't tire her too quickly. We arrive at our spot overlooking the lake, and I breathe a sigh of relief at how easy the walk has been for me.

"Is a wonderful day today," Nisula declares, looking out over the lake.

"Yes, we love it here," Taggler adds as he wraps his arms over my shoulders from behind. I pull Proem closer to me while we all gaze at the wondrous view.

We don't get away from the village with Nisula often, so the day is a kind of celebration just being out here together. We know that Proem will tire first, so we start back early enough. Nisula is moving more slowly than on the way out, and Taggler playfully teases me to walk slower for his benefit since he's carrying Proem. I glance back and see that Nisula is wobbly and almost stumbles at times. When I put my arm in hers to help, she smiles and takes it, so we walk together. We finally get back to the village and, when I turn to wish her a pleasant evening at home, I'm shocked to see her pale and sweaty. I look at Taggler, who registers my shock. She gives me a tired smile and collapses in her chair.

"I'm going to make you a cup of tea before we go home. I think today has been very tiring, hasn't it?"

"Oh, I'm tired some, but no worry," she says.

"I'm going to check on you again after Proem's settled at home."

I'm sick with worry about her all the way back to our hut. As soon as Proem is down, I can't think of anything but getting back.

"She's an older lady, and I guess this comes with age. You should go back right away. I'll watch Proem, so go ahead. We'll be fine here," Taggler assures me.

I race back to her house and find her in bed, asleep, and looking all right. I fall asleep in a chair watching her. I wake up stiff and unclear about where I am for a moment. The house is dark, and the sky has faded. After I light a candle to see her face more clearly, I relax a bit. Only half awake, I blow it out and crawl into bed with her, falling asleep.

I wake up early in the morning and study her closely in the weak morning light, and she looks all right. I crawl out of bed carefully to go back home. I come into our hut as quietly as I can, and Taggler bolts upright in bed.

"How is she?" Even though our hut is dark inside, the worry in his words cuts across the room.

"She looks fine and is still asleep this morning. Sorry, I fell asleep and just woke up. Is everything all right here?"

"Well, yes, except I was worried. I fell asleep waiting for you to come in, and woke up with you still gone," he said, his voice softening but still tense.

"I"m sorry it was hard on you. I'm back now."

I take off my clothes and climb into bed. He lifts the covers, welcoming me, and wraps me in his arms. One small bit of me remains at Nisula's, wanting to watch her sleep. With Taggler's warmth filling the blankness of last night, making love comes to us as naturally as the sun rising.

After the morning light begins to pry inside, Proem wakes and we lie in bed listening to him begin to stir.

"Nisula was not well yesterday," I say.

"Yes, we have to remember she's older now."

My heart hurts thinking about her becoming frail. Proem climbs into the softness of our bed, kissing my face and putting his little arm around my neck.

"Mommy all right?"

"Mommy all right, Proem."

"Mommy all right," Proem repeats with his cheek against mine.

"We'll go see her this morning," Taggler offers.

We drift back into our own dreamy spaces while the sun fully blooms. Finally, the desire to check on Nisula gets us up.

"We're all ready. Let's go," Taggler announces.

I grab Proem in my arms and we start on our way.

We come quietly into her still-dark house, so I figure she's sleeping late, as she does sometimes. I move quietly across the open space I know by heart and sit at the edge of the bed to listen to her soft breathing. It's very quiet. I tell myself that we just came in, so I listen more carefully. Silence surrounds me, broken only by other sounds from outside and Proem's footsteps as he toddles around the room. I come closer to the side of her face, and still I can't hear anything. I start to tremble as the impossibly still air blankets the room.

"Taggler, come here, now."

My whisper is peppered with alarm. I touch her arm and she doesn't move at all. I shake her by the arm, pleading," Nisula, Nisula."

The emptiness in that place where life has been is a shock that can't be softened. I begin sobbing while Taggler's touch on the side of her face finds the same truth. Nisula is gone. Where there was joy and love, darkness now swallows me up whole.

This isn't the first time someone has left this life, but it is a first time for me.

Soon the whole village is mourning. Their love and care are heartfelt, but nothing can lessen my grief.

Nisula will be buried here, where her body will be taken back to nature, returning to the whole, delivered back to where everything comes from.

Her burial will be the next day, so there is a flurry of organizing by the elders of the village. I'm not able to do anything but cry. Proem quietly watches me, worried about what he cannot yet understand. He notices everything, stuffing it all inside, somewhere, with the blink of an eye.

That evening, I can do nothing but lie on the bed, and Taggler brings me a broth made by the women of the village.

"Here, drink this. I just warmed it for you. You need to drink it up, all of it, please."

I drink without noticing. Proem comes over to my side and looks to make me happy again, but this isn't anything he can understand. Understanding will have to come later.

He sleeps only after making a fuss.

A darkness of the heart has swallowed me. I live in its shadows where I'm far away. Still, Taggler climbs into bed, spooning behind me. I notice and let his warmth in. The coming of sleep is a welcome escape.

***

Daylight arrives like a cold wind and forces me to return. Today is Nisula's burial. There will be no escaping this day; there is only to plod through it. Others of the village wait outside for us to appear. When we do, we all walk to the burial place in silence. Nisula is wrapped in broad leaves and lowered into the earth. Leaves of all the plants of this place are to be her final bed, and I place my offering in with her remains. Howls and incantations in tongues not known to me fill the air, shrieking against the truth of the day. The air is fouled with grief, blotting out the sun. I stand blank until I see that those closest to me are waiting silently right behind me. Turning back to life seems like a long, hard road.

I spend the rest of the day at the river, watching it flow endlessly as it moves on, no matter what. Taggler stays with me, bringing anything he thinks I might want to eat or drink. Proem, who struggles with the pain he sees and does not understand, sits beside his father and watches. Then he comes to me and he gathers himself into my arms, wanting to find the hole that needs to be filled. It is a hole that may never be filled.

***

It was decided by the village that Nisula's cottage is to become our home if we want, but it's a full month's time before I can go through that door again. As I sit in grief, the leaves on the trees surrounding our hut change with the season. Time creeps painfully. The other women of our circle are some comfort, but also the reminder of who is missing. Several months pass before Taggler opens the conversation with me.

"What do you feel we should do about the cottage, Crysalline?"

It's our best time for conversation, in bed in the morning when most of the world is quiet. Proem is playing in the corner of the hut, as usual when he's not in bed with us in the morning.

I've avoided this moment as long as I can, almost never passing by the empty house.

"It may be time now for us to try. She'd want us to have it. Maybe in time we can remember her better from the wonderful times we had together there. That will be good for us, I think," he says, kissing me on the cheek.

I can see that Taggler is relieved at getting this out in the open. He gets up to make our morning tea, then comes back to bed.

"What's to be our future? Everything's different than when we started," I wonder aloud.

# CHAPTER TWENTY-FOUR
# BEYOND THE DARKNESS

"Can I get you anything this morning? Have you eaten that fruit I left out for you?"

Since Nisula's death, Taggler's been fretting over me as much as after Proem's birth, maybe even more. I know he means well. The emptiness of everyday life is hard. I know Proem wonders what he can do to help me be happy again. I wonder if I can ever be like before.

Her house stands empty, a monument to the loss. Maybe moving into it and being inside the village will be a good change. I want to hold onto the memories of her any way I can.

"We could go inside soon and see how it goes," he offers.

"Later today, I guess we could," I say, not really sure.

We get to the house in the afternoon, and, as I put my hand on the door handle, I wonder if this is a good idea. I push the latch and, with a small shove, the door opens. I can only stand there with Taggler and Proem silently watching. Others passing by pause, seeing me at the open door of this beloved place. I step inside and walk over to the table where we sat so many mornings. The woven bracelet that Jenna gave me slides down my wrist as my hand moves to touch the smooth wooden table, then the corner post of her bed. These are the places where Nisula has left her touch.

The sounds of life continuing drift in through the still-open door.

As I walk slowly around the quiet room, memories begin to flood through me, and I can feel my heart beating again. Behind me, Proem and Taggler smile as I turn and show the relief that's washing over me, and all of us.

"This isn't so bad after all."

"This would be a good home for us," Taggler says.

"Yes, you're right, it will be."

The next days are a whirlwind of activity as we move our belongings into the place we will now call our home. Moving here, we come into the welcoming arms of the village. But it's all different now. As I pass the spot inside where she made tea or touch the drawer where she kept her most treasured things, I weep a bit before I can carry on again. It's easier for Proem. He can toddle about just outside during the day with the various caretakers and distractions, human and animal, that keep him amused.

***

We mark Proem's sixth year of life with the village around us. They seem to enjoy seeing the little man he's becoming. His favorite toys are old pots, spoons, carved wooden animals, and a magic wand Taggler carved that he waves at everyone who passes.

Life with Proem is a joy I could not have imagined before he came into my life, our life. Every evening after supper, we make up stories while he's getting ready for bed. Listening, his eyes get large, then heavier as sleep comes, showing the way to the world of his own dreams. Tonight's story has a friendly dragon who doesn't know where to live and a boy who helps him find a good home. We sit at the side of his bed, taking turns making a new part of the story come to life out of thin air. This is my favorite time of day, guiding our little man into his life. I see his wonderings about the world out there, out beyond this place.

We look at each other as he falls asleep and into his dream world for the night.

"That was pretty good how you made the dragon smile in the story tonight," Taggler whispers as we move back to the center table.

"I thought that every dragon should smile once in a while."

We close the window shutters so we can stay warm during the night, then sit at the table, our hands wrapped around warm mugs of tea.

"When we were down at the river today checking on our boats, Proem was asking all kinds of questions about them. He wanted to know where we came from and why we have them."

Just talking about the boats brings fond memories to life. I look at Taggler with a smile. "I'm not surprised, since he's always asking questions about so many things." I move my cup from hand to hand, enjoying the warmth, and savoring the thoughts.

"We have such a good life here. Everything is lovely. But maybe someday we'll give him an idea of what that was like, being in the boats on the river," Taggler says.

We sit quietly with the idea turning over and over until it's time for bed .

I'm still mulling over Proem's interest in the boats as I drift off to sleep. I can see the boat in the water and hear the water lapping at the wooden sides. It rocks gently as the river pushes and pulls on it. The sound of the water mixes with the lingering damp smell of the soil along the shore. The shoreline's moving now, appearing and then disappearing into the past. I can feel the softness of the bed stuffing over the hard planks of the boat as we ride dry and peaceful on the water.

Beside me, Proem and Taggler smile as they look downriver, as a scent passes on the breeze to the front of us. The sun is spreading warmth everywhere. I turn my face up and it feels as if someone's hands are cradling my cheeks. Everything's glowing through my closed eyelids. The boat is swaying back and forth as we make our way. Proem's hand reaches out for me; when his little fingers touch my arm, bliss floods through me. We are all moving along, together.

Dawn comes to stir me awake for the day, and we belong to the movements of the village. Nisula's memory still lives everywhere in the cottage, especially where her hand rested on the wood, leaving part of her there, alive in what I touch every day. I have a window ledge filled with small things of hers, and Proem knows they aren't playthings. Small potted plants help decorate these treasures. Even though at moments it's still hard for me, I don't want to lose any memories of her.

The light of springtime is coming again and I realize we've been here for quite a while. The birds are returning and everyone's spirits are brighter. The river is running strong, and Taggler has had to tie the boats up higher along the shore. Proem is helping him tend to them. When they return, Taggler reports their conversation:

"When can we go out in the boat, Daddy?"

"I don't know, Proem".

"I want to go out in the boat, so can we?"

"We have to wait for the right time, Proem."

"I want the right time to come soon."

***

Proem is like a bottle full of spinning stars. He craves understanding, always hungry for more. He can recite the comings and goings of most of the villagers by heart. He has playmates around his age, yet sometimes I think he's a small size grownup. He notices the workings of the world all 'round us, from the bugs at his feet to the swirling clouds in the sky. He and I take slow walks in the afternoon to our spot by the lake. I love watching the lake's surface wiggle in the wind. That's so peaceful.

But lately, when I sit at the edge of the river that keeps moving, something churns in me.

I ache with living in two worlds, on land and on the flowing water. Tunica is where Nisula's alive in every place I touch that holds her. It's hard and sweet for me at the same time. When I hear the river, I have a wondering of what more there will be, what's waiting somewhere out there.

***

At the overlook today, Proem and I sit looking over the lake and the rolling hills covered with trees that go all the way out to the sky. He's amusing both of us by throwing rocks as far as his six-year-old arm can. There's no need for talk, and I'm enjoying it. He feels safe exploring his world, knowing I'm here.

"What's past the water, Mommy? What's out there?"

I wonder what sort of answer can satisfy both of us. "I really don't know. There are certainly many different things."

He's asking the questions that I had put away. I hope he doesn't see my yearning. The vast landscape was fine to watch while he was a baby. Nisula's protective wing comforted me as I found my way as a mother. The questions rise as I look out past the stillness of the lake, beyond, into the fullness of the future not yet found.

In the evening, I share all of this with Taggler after we put Proem to bed. His bed is in a corner, reminding me of mine at Jenna and Darry's.

Taggler pauses after hearing Proem's questions about what we'd both put aside for some time. "Well, I guess Tunica might not be able to hold us."

I look at him and see a smile creeping over his face. "I can't see how the three of us could fit into that boat."

"Me neither. We need more space than that. What would we do with this little wiggler who's asking so many questions?"

"I know we'd need a bigger boat, that's for certain. He'd have to have a seat where we can keep him safe, even after we teach him to swim at least some."

"I'll find out how hard it is to build a boat. The river's certainly wider here and probably more so moving on farther downriver, so a bigger boat could be a good thing for us anyway," Taggler says.

I can't hide my smile.

***

Taggler asks around the village and finds Aftler, an older man who's built boats before, and will help us. The wood will come from someone named Whistinger. I think that's an odd name, but no one knows him any other way. I think it may take a long time since it's different work than Taggler's ever done before, and I'm right. He finds out that it will take a year to let the wood fully season and dry enough, and then, after the boat is actually built, there will be the job of getting pitch firmly cured into the seams.

Taggler and Aftler spend long hours deciding how big to build it, knowing it will be our new home. Every time they talk about it, it changes size. They finally decide it will be fifteen foot measures long. It will be the same shape as the old one, just larger. Then the old one will become our boat for provisions, and the smallest one will stay here for the village.

The wood is cut and seasoned and the next spring Taggler begins, with Aftler's help. The work is slow because Taggler must learn everything. After several months, it's looking like it will be finished soon.

***

This afternoon, Proem is sitting in it while Taggler's putting in the waterproofing pitch to seal the seams.

"Daddy, when are we going to get in the water?".

"We might put it in the water in a few days, Proem," Taggler replies from the side of the hull where he's working.

"Yippee! Yippee!"

Proem's sitting in his seat built in the middle where he can see everything and be kept safe.

"Hello, boys. I see you're almost finished," I call cheerfully as I turn the corner behind the house where they're working.

These two mean the world to me. Taggler stops to smile at me, and I enjoy his attention, feeling more beautiful than ever. My health is still delicate, but that doesn't stop me from feeling good. He steps over to kiss me, holding the stick of hot pitch in his hand carefully pointed away. Proem wiggles down from his seat and I plant a big kiss on his cheek.

"It's time for supper. Can you quit soon?"

"Sure we can. That's plenty of reason to quit for today."

Taggler hoists Proem and they follow me inside.

We have a stew of root vegetables, leafy greens, and herbs that grow easily here. There's bread from the family that bakes it for the whole village. Everyone goes to them with other foods to trade.

After supper, Proem settles into his quiet playtime while Taggler and I sit at the table remembering the day, as we love to do most evenings.

"Proem's his usual happy self tonight. While I was washing him, he was tapping on the edge of the basin and singing. I couldn't help but remember Nisula's hands being there, too. I'm so glad we've had time here. It's our memory to keep wherever we go."

Life here is comfortable, like where I grew up. Then it hits me. We're leaving. Proem brought that yearning back to the surface. I can't imagine my life without having found Jenna and Darry, Taggler, and Nisula. Jenna and Nisula are part of me. They are my treasures. They're woven into the fabric of my life and so also into Proem.

***

The village is watching as the time draws near for the boat, and so our time here, to be finished. The circle of women gather to shower me with wishes for health and happiness ahead. The men of the village see to it that Taggler wants for nothing. Nisula's cottage, as it is still known, is to be passed on to a widow, Imasda, who will enjoy its comfort. Nisula's cottage is a central part of this place, and we have added our living and loving inside its walls. It is cherished as a place where people come together, and now is to be in Imasda's care.

There's a grand celebration before we leave, with plenty of food and drink, laughter and tears. Proem is the little prince who relishes every moment until, as little princes do, he must sleep and is tucked safely into bed. Taggler and I will remember this time as part of our becoming a family. The village has made new clothes as gifts for our journey ahead. Made from the best fibers and colors, there is so much love woven into them that we almost glow when we put them on.

We make a small outing onto the river to test the boat. We haul it upriver a bit to begin and travel the short distance and thencome back in. Proem's giddy the whole time we're out. The larger boat behaves well in the water, just as the old one did for the two of us. After that first outing, at supper there's excitement in the air.

"When can we go out on the river again?" Proem asks while rolling a piece of string bean between his finger and thumb.

We glance at each other with a twinge of concern, knowing it's going to be hard on him to be limited to his seat in the boat for a long stretches.

"It will be about a handful of days," I say, looking at him to see his reaction.

"How many is that?" he asks.

"How many fingers do you have?"

He drops the bean and holds up a wet, sticky hand, wiggling all his fingers at once.

"Five," he reports proudly.

Now he looks up into the ceiling and dangles his legs back and forth. "Are we going to take this house with us when we leave?"

My eyes fill as I follow his gaze up to the same rafters.

"No, sweetie, we're going to let Nisula's cottage stay here so someone else can use it. We'll will be going to new places, and finding new friends. There'll be camping under the big night sky and seeing new places and maybe some new animals."

"I don't want to leave Nisula's house. I don't want to leave my friends here," he bellows.

"It'll work out fine, Proem. It will, I promise."

I wonder if somehow we're making a mistake but convince myself that we, as parents, have to know our choices in order to be strong. We distract ourselves with the games of the evening and getting him ready for bed. I don't want the same doubts to rise again, so I let Taggler tuck him in; I only give him a quick kiss on the forehead.

Sitting at the table again, we look at each other with a delicate certainty. This place will be behind us, moving into our memories and later into the stories that we'll tell when the memories aren't so tender.

Finally, we drift into our shared private time. The joyful sounds that Taggler and I make together fill the cottage, this place where Proem dreams.

***

Cheerful sunlight breaks open the morning. Proem almost always wakes before us as the world gently begins to stir outside. This is when he notices more of the small things around him. This morning it is the wildflowers in a glass jar on the window ledge. He comes over to our bed and shakes me to tell me something as I struggle awake enough to understand.

"Momma, the flowers on the window ledge are smiling."

"Uh, mmm, that's good Proem.

"One of them winked at me."

I cannot imagine dampening his imagination, that place of great joy and revelation in a world that is more ordinary without it.

"Thank you, Proem. When we get up I'll look for a wink too."

He goes to stand in the middle of the room where a crack at the door lets the sunlight shine inside before he climbs in bed with us after he sees me watching him. We wrap up together, wiggling and snuggling. I pull him close and kiss the back of his neck. My hair tickles him as I press my face into him.

"Momma, get up, get up. It's today," he says.

"Mmmmm, yes, it is today," I say, pulling him closer.

"Momma, get up."

I throw the cover open and dust rises like stars swirling in the beam of sunlight that cuts across the room.

"Daddy, get up, get up, it's today," he says as he pokes at Taggler's back.

"Yes, Proem. Yes, Proem. You are right. Today is here again, and I will open my eyes again." He rolls over and gives our son a big hug. Proem is swallowed in the big arms holding him, and I fall back into bed to hug them both. Another swirl soars in the air, and another field of stars dances in the sunlight. I get up to load the fire and start the tea. Proem runs to wrap himself around me, causing me to almost lose my balance even though I slow down to let him.

"What are we going to do today, Daddy?"

"We're getting everything together for our boat trip," Taggler says with a sleepy grin.

So our day begins with dressing, eating, wiping, cleaning, and going out to see the new boat proudly sitting in the water just beyond where our old thatch hut still stands, now empty. It looks worn and wild, but it was home, where Proem came into this world.

"This is good; we have no leaks at all with the wood tightening up in the water," Taggler says, turning to me with a proud smile.

I smile right back at him. "It's beautiful. I'm sure it'll take us to wherever we want to go."

For three more days we're in a flurry of work, and then it's our final night here. Proem has been delighted every day we're readying the boats, of course. As he drifts off after storytelling time, I imagine his dreams will be about floating down the river soon. We'll wait until morning to tell him it's the day we leave, or none of us will sleep tonight.

Tomorrow we continue our dream.

# CHAPTER TWENTY-FIVE
# A WARNING

When I open the door, quite a few people are waiting to see us off. When Proem sees the crowd, he insists on being carried.

My heart is bursting with so many feelings. The path to our loaded boats is swept clean and lined with familiar faces full of smiles and tears. Hands reach out to give us a last touch or hug before we're gone, probably for good. Finally, we arrive at the boat, make sure Proem is safe in his special seat, and push off. The good wishes and sobs continue and then gently fade into the distance as the river takes us away. Soon there are only the echoes and the sounds and movements of the river all around us. This new boat seems to be working quite well as the river pushes and tugs at us. Taggler occasionally smiles at me as he watches ahead.

"Mama, today is exciting, isn't it? Daddy, are we going fast? Can I get out of my seat now? When will we eat? Is that an animal over there?"

"No, Proem, look at it again. It's a log in the water," I tell him. "Can you see that as we come closer? Look up at the beautiful trees above us and watch how the light changes through the leaves as we move along. Now sit still and listen to hear the sounds passing around us. Can you hear them?"

He's like a new star blazing clean and white in the sky. After a while, he settles down and the morning is soon behind us. We stop for our midday meal, and he's interested in picking up everything he sees while we're on shore. Keeping him clean and safe is becoming a big part of our day. I wait to wipe him clean until we get back into the boat.

"Proem, you have to leave all those things here where you found them. We can't take them with us or the boat will be too full soon. Pick just one to take today, all right?"

After some hesitation, he reluctantly decides on one stone in his hand, dropping the rest. With a final push of his sandal, he moves them away.

"All right," he says, turning toward the boat. We're ready to move on.

The afternoon drifts by quietly after he falls asleep. He's getting used to the boat as well as we'd hoped.

As the afternoon shadows deepen, we find a place to stop for the night. He runs about on the shore, so I must keep an eye on him while Taggler sorts out the evening's camp. I wonder how I'll keep up with him if every day's like today. After supper we have no wish to do anything. As the fog of sleep wraps around me, memories rise of the time with Jenna, and I am warm and comfortable.

***

Every evening, we snuggle together until Proem falls asleep. Then, when we are not too tired, we gently move aside to find that private time together.

After the silky dusk, the stars show themselves through the leafy branches above, winking if a breeze moves the leaves at all. Soon the sky is deep black, painted with stars from edge to edge. When it's cloudy or wet, we camp on a high spot if possible, under a dense tree or under a rock overhang to keep dry.

Tonight the sky is clear and the moon just past being full as it rises to take its place in the night, showing the patchwork of mysterious markings that dot its face.

I know my part in this moving life: as mothering shelter for Proem and his curiosity. Patience is my guide, with a touch of understanding.

Taggler does his part. He holds us with loving, sure security, moving among the things of this living world, moving us easily over smooth or rocky water.

Proem is filled with awe for what simple drops of water have done to change stone, to provide a home to fishes, and to give life to the simple seeds that find their place to rest.

One day, we stop at a thundering waterfall with fresh green surrounding it, soaking in the mist. As I breathe in, I feel it soothing me inside and out.

"Watch out. The rocks are slippery, Crysalline," Taggler yells.

"Yeah, Mama, watch out," Proem echoes.

I balance carefully on the slippery rocks, moving closer to the falling water. I raise my face to catch the mist and close my eyes to enjoy the fury of the sound as water crashes onto the rocks.

Taggler's hand reaches out to hold onto my arm. "Could you come back to a safer place, please?"

"All right. I've soaked in the mist long enough. It's wonderful that we can be here, isn't it?"

"Yes, it's wonderful—and slippery. I want to keep you for a while longer, so don't wish yourself into the water, please," Taggler says, teasing only a little.

We move on and sit on a sunny hillside where we can see the vast spaces spreading out in front of us. The tops of the trees are like a fluffy blanket over the land as they stand with their roots deep and holding firm. That giant blanket freshens the air and ripples with the wind at the meeting place of earth and sky. To watch it all wraps me in happiness. I'm a part of this, part of everything, part of all that is.

***

Every morning is another beginning. The river is our ribbon to follow, carrying us on with its twists and turns. We travel along, meeting different kinds of people, sharing stories of our adventures with those who are curious. With finding and sharing, giving and receiving, we are all richer.

Our life stories are our possessions. We live as simply as the very water itself that we must have for life and for how we glide along with little effort into new places. Our clothes keep us comfortable in all weather. The boat is where we live, sharing our lives. Proem's schooling is in the direct truth as much as can be. Truth is all around us yet does not always show itself plainly. It keeps its mysteries, demanding respect or we suffer from our misunderstandings.

We stay many times in places for simple relief from being in the boat so much and to be with others for a few months. We trade our labor for goods we need. We learn the local traditions. Our basic language is face to face, with words if we can find them. This give us an understanding of people who let themselves be known. The years seem to fly by.

Proem is as at home on the river as on land. I'm filled with pride watching him grow, seeing how he sees the variety in the world around him. He has a natural skill in the direct language of people without words. Sometimes I ask him questions in order to know more of what he understands.

"Isn't it wondrous out there, Proem? There's so much, and it can pass by so quickly."

"Yes, Mama. There's more going on than any one person could see."

Taggler listens and lets the boat wiggle on purpose. He only needs to share a smile before Proem continues.

"See how tiny seeds open and grow to make themselves into giant trees. Without things growing, we would have no food. We have medicines from plants. I'm glad for that. There's another thing, though. I've been wondering what someone means when they say there's a higher power. What do they mean by that?"

I am not surprised that he'd ask something like that. I'd watched his face wrinkle up when he heard others say it.

"I don't know exactly what they mean. I do know what I take it to be. It's about those wonderful things going on around us. What is the thing in life that lets a seed grow into such a strong tree, fed by nature to grow and thrive? Can you imagine such a wonderful thing? What gives that seed that power to change so much?

"We have the air, water, and sunlight for each seed. That's everything for the plants, other animals, and for us to be alive and enjoy while we are here. I'm really thankful for that."

I can see he is quietly absorbing my words, so I go on. "Every time you think about something, you're making a thought of your own. As we move into new places and times, you find things you didn't know about before, so you can have new thoughts. Every day we choose what we do by using our thoughts, and at times use the new thoughts for doing something different or finding a better way. This is what each of us does all the time, every day. This is learning. That's how the world grows, with this creating, both of the tree's seeds and our own thoughts, our new seeds to use wisely."

I stay quiet for a time, watching him think about it as a new thing, giving him time ponder the idea for himself.

Then I see that maybe he's ready for more talk, so I go on with my telling. "Each of us has a part in living, finding out, and choosing what to do. Together this makes up what I call 'All That Is'. You've been in places where people think and believe different things than others. That's also part of All That Is. Each of us has a part we add just by our living, 'cause in our living, we have thoughts and make ideas that we turn into the things we do. There's no place you can be outside of it, really. We're each a living creation of nature itself, not apart from it. That's what I know makes up this whole world that I cherish."

Proem looks into my face and smiles gently, letting me know that he's turning all this over for himself. "It's good that we're safe and happy. You and Daddy are happy and we're all safe. If we aren't safe, we can't be our own happy part of all that anymore," he declares, wondering.

"Yes, Proem, we're watching and careful. And when we find anything new and different, we make more thoughts, new thoughts. If those are from fear of what we see, it can protect us from real trouble, or it can stop us from seeing what's new to us, that part of all that is. So we're doing just fine and will find out more as it comes to us. Then we'll choose what we do with that."

The sunlight is playing across my face as I talk. I'm happy to see how our son is learning from our travels and the people we meet. I believe he sees the truth of it well enough for himself. He looks at me as he continues to think about it all. He turns to watch his dad's comforting stillness as Taggler steers us along the river.

There is a peaceful quiet in the boat as we glide on into the bigger world, where I love and am loved.

A new village appears as others have before. We land our boat and get out. The people look relaxed, happy, and friendly, so we're willing to stay for a while.

"Hello," Taggler and I both say to a man sitting in front of a home, our two voices in harmony. He looks at the three of us, squinting against the bright sky, with a smile that suggests his good nature.

"Hutsukla," he says.

"Hutsocla to you also," Taggler tries to copy.

The man holds a rough hand above his deeply lined face. He is asking us to wait. He walks toward a doorway leading to a darkened interior. He turns and signals again for us to wait. We look around, exchanging glances with others who pass by. I fidget, like I usually do in a new place. The man returns holding hands with a woman and they each offer a hand in welcome to us.

"Hello, Hutsocla," Taggler tries again.

Another woman appears in the doorway and smiles. She appears to be slightly younger than the others. "Hello, Hutsukla is our way of welcome," she says. Her voice strikes me as being like a songbird's, her words floating out, coloring the air as they appear. I don't know if I can believe my eyes; I'm trying to decide what's happening as the colors float slowly on the faint breeze.

"Hello, Hutsukla," the first woman says with the same softness. As the sound of her words disappears, a scent of flowers clearly wraps around us, as if we've been wrapped in a gift.

"I know your language enough to be helpful. I am called the name Wermera, and wish to add ease to your time here," she says as she tips her head in greeting. The scent of her words hangs in the air.

"We are Taggler, Crysalline, and Proem, and we are happy to come here and meet you," Taggler says, following her graceful manner.

I wonder if our words smell strange to them.

"What name do you call your place, your village?"

"We call this place Imbs." With these words, there's the scent of something like fragramt blossoms in the air.

They can see our surprise and Wermera smiles calmly in a way that tells us, yes, we can believe, it's not a mistake, I am showing you my heart.

Of so many different places, this is the hardest to comprehend, hardest to believe.

"Please, come into our home. You must spend more time with us, I wish. It will be easier with time," Wermera says.

We enjoy their hospitality as we've done with others so many times before, and they in turn enjoy hearing our adventures. They ask us to stay, saying that there are few babies born here, so several cottages stand empty.

This is such a strange request. I wonder what we don't know yet.

Taggler looks unconcerned so we accept their offer, staying for almost the time of two full moons, until, as before, we feel the river calling us again.

"Wermera, it has been wonderful staying here. We are friends and it is with some sadness we know it is time to go, so we will be leaving soon."

"Then I must tell you something I think you would call a warning," Wermera says.

My senses sharpen, waiting for her next words.

"In your travel on the river, there will be a place ahead where you should see what is in front of you as dangerous. It will not look that way. It will look like everything else. I do not know what form it will take, except that it is in the people that the danger lives."

I am speechless, wondering what I could possibly ask to learn more. The air is now carrying a scent that is harsh. Then Wermera gives me a wonderful hug and wishes us all well, and the scent changes again to the sweet one I recognize as hers. Her fingertips linger on my hand until finally her touch is gone and we turn to leave.

"Goodbye. I will remember you well, Wermera," I manage to say.

I notice that my hand is on my heart and it's beating strongly. Walking on to the boats, I'm still wondering what's ahead.

"What do you think that meant?" Taggler asks.

"I don't really know. Maybe it isn't so serious. Whatever it turns out to be, I'm sure we'll manage."

# CHAPTER TWENTY-SIX
# THE PROMISE

As we drift along, I look proudly at Proem as he sits watching what's passing by. He's as eager as some wild things to grow, becoming a wonderful young man. His life is starting so differently than mine.

"Mom, what do you make of that warning about something ahead?" he asks, interrupting my dreamy musings.

"I'm not so sure. We'll just have to see what comes along. I can't make anything of it right now."

The morning is so calm, I want to stay in the simple beauty of it. It seems so long ago when I was really lost and now I've found my place moving along and learning in this great big world. I look back at him, filled with lovely thoughts. But I'm still distracted by Wermera's warning. Watching the horizon far away, I keep turning her words over, looking for new meaning. I guess Proem has noticed my distraction. He gives a quick glance at his dad, but Taggler's busy watching the river ahead for rocks.

"Proem, there's something I must share with you. This is a simple rule that will help guide you. Treat others well, just as you would want them to treat you."

Proem listens carefully, leaning into the space between us. He notices more than most people. Today he's been looking toward me more often than usual. Like his father, he's concerned for my health. He watches my face like some people watch the sky for changes in the weather.

As the morning drifts along, the land passing by is pretty and interesting to watch. The shores are covered with lush, green growth to the waterline.

Soon we spot a landing, the promise of a village close by. It's quiet as we tie up. There's a wide, well-worn path that leads away from the shore. We're able to walk side by side and I let my hand rest lightly on Proem's shoulder. As we come to the village center, there are people moving about, but they don't pay much attention to us—or each other, for that matter. We've seen places like this before.

A man wandering apparently aimlessly takes notice of us with a cautious and questioning look. "Asooth, mishala, benangn," he offers. His hand, palm open, sweeps to the side, and he waits for our reaction.

"Hello. We are Taggler, Crysalline, and Proem. I fear we do not know your language," Taggler says with his usual charm while trying to display the same meaning in his body language.

The man looks to me with an unreadable expression on his face. He motions for us to come with him, so we follow, hopefully to a place where others might be more helpful. Along the twisting passageways, unknown smells reveal themselves as we pass by. We finally arrive at a courtyard where several people sit talking. As they notice us, they stop talking and turn our way. Our guide says something and several of them answer him. Then three of them speak to us in turn, but we can't understand anything they say, even though they each sound different.

A middle-aged woman speaks, and I hope to understand her somehow.

"Nertheen, wondor, may blee not."

I try next, using my hands a lot, hoping their faces will light up as I begin. "Hello, we come from far away. On the river. We come here friends, to know you and your place, if we may."

They speak among themselves and then the woman who I hoped we would understand speaks again. "Yesh, truthly, we and you here now days heres," she says with a tight smile. "Sits now, if you do," she adds casually.

Awkwardly, we all sit. Tea appears, brought from somewhere out of sight. Hand movements indicate offering, so we, as guests, drink some. Their talk continues without us understanding anything, so gestures and body language are the only way I can guess at how this is going. Now and then, someone leaves, and then someone else returns. The woman we can understand acts as translator and slowly we comprehend more.

Taggler and Proem both look uncomfortable, Proem more so. This meeting has a strangely disconnected feeling. At one point, the woman who has been translating looks to me with a sweet smile and moves to my side and sits.

"Hello, I Shilla, friend, right?"

She takes my hand and smiles at me. This is pleasant and I smile in return. We continue talking with some difficulty. There are comments about my beautiful skin and questions about my health. I've always been delicate-looking to some. By my answers, they understand that I'm all right.

Shilla gestures to someone who leaves the circle, returning with a glass vial that she places in her lap. Between gestures and soothing words I come to understand that the vial has something they know to bring color into my cheeks and build up my health. I take it to be a kind gesture. Shilla opens the stopper, places my fingertip over the opening, and tips it so my fingertip is moistened. She guides me to touch it to each cheek. A flurry of excited chatter ripples around the gathering and my cheeks begin to tingle.

She turns to me and gently puts a hand on my arm. "Crisollinn, please be this on you as you can take, and you good you strong later."

This somehow makes me suddenly uneasy. I shoot a quick look at Taggler's strangely quiet face to show that I want to leave. We gracefully thank everyone and gather ourselves to leave.

Shilla clasps my hands and gives me the glass vial when I stand up. She speaks to the man who brought us here and he gestures for us to follow him. We make our way back through the passageways and I breathe a sigh of relief when I see the shore again. We thank him and he nods, then turns away, disappearing from view. I notice I've been holding the vial tightly and relax my grip.

"Let's get going, I don't like this place," Proem blurts out.

We all laugh nervously as we climb into the familiar safety of our boat, casting off to return to the familiar movements of the river. The vial is still in my hand, so I put it into a safe corner and out of mind. Taggler gives a quizzical look and says, "You look blushed. Your cheeks have a rosy color. How do you feel?"

His question brings me back from being lost in thought.

"I feel fine, just a bit weary from this stop, I guess."

"This is the most color I've seen in you in a long time."

The stoppered bottle sits wedged where I put it with the clear liquid swaying to the movements of the boat.

"Could it be because of this?" I hold the glass bottle up to the light to see if the mysterious liquid might reveal something, but I can only shrug my shoulders, so that's the end of it for now.

I don't think to use any more over the next few days and my color returns to its usual softness. Taggler remarks at the change so I apply more of the mysterious drops, and again I have that rosy glow. We all laugh at this ability to change and I decide I like it. Applying the drops over several days, I don't feel any stronger, although Taggler and Proem see the color as a healthy thing, so I let it go at that.

Our days pass with the usual rhythms and enjoyment. We stop near a place called Ullin, seeing how beautiful the whole valley seems as we approach.

"Is it time for a hike up that hill I see ahead? We'll have a grand view of the river valley from there," Taggler says.

"Yeah, let's go," Proem cheerfully adds.

I'm not too excited about the idea but think it will probably be fine.

The hill is not steep and I don't want Taggler and Proem to worry so I keep up as well as I can. Taggler looks at me straggling behind them a step of two, and I smile weakly to show him know that I'm all right. The view from the top is grand, and we have our midday meal, relaxing. Everything is as it should be. At the end of the day, we start back downhill to the river. I'm exhausted by the time we make it. I stumble and our pendant from the very first village falls to the ground. A twinge of worry crosses Taggler's face as he picks it up.

"The time to live is now," he reads aloud as he puts it back in my hand.

We set up camp for the night. I feel rested now, so I apply more of the drops. As we settle down under the clear warm night and hear Proem's gentle breathing telling us he's fast asleep, we make love under the watchful, star-filled sky. I fall into a deep sleep, knowing that we all are safe and well.

# CHAPTER TWENTY-SEVEN
# THE WEATHER CHANGES

The warmth of the fire feels good against the morning chill. I sit with a mug of hot tea, enjoying its warmth on my cold hands. Proem is having a nightmare, judging by the sounds coming from where he's still asleep. I shiver a little.

"Son, you're safe. It's morning. You've been talking in your dreams," Taggler says as he gently shakes Proem, who begins pulling himself awake.

Tangler hovers over him, giving him another shake and a smile as Proem finally wakes.

"Oh, my, I'm glad to wake up," he says, rubbing his eyes. He seems to struggle to get out of the dream and understand what's real. It looks like he is trying not to weep.

"We couldn't help hearing you in your sleep. It didn't sound pretty," I say to him.

Getting up and rubbing his face for a minute, he then sits right in front of us and says,"It was bad. The wind was stabbing at me and I couldn't get away from it. My face was burning from the cold. I called into the howling wind for you, Mom, and for you, Dad, but my words were pushed back. I could tell that someone was out there, but I didn't know who. Raindrops were hitting my head like stinging needles. Then Dad's hand was on my shoulder to wake me."

I listen with sadness for my son, our son. He is to have his own life and I can't protect him from the hard parts that may become real. I see that he's still working to shake off the nightmare, glancing around and pulling closer to the warmth of the fire.

"It's just a nightmare and gone now. Thank goodness it's not a real part of our daytime," I say.

The fuzz on his chin shows the beginning of growing up, coming into his own. I love watching him, seeing the easy way he carries himself. His nature is to see the best in others.

He's always watched over me, looking out for my safety. It's been strange to me to see the glow in my cheeks on my reflection in the water and at the same time feel no stronger. Right now, I have my hand up, shielding my eyes from the rising sun. It looks brighter today than ever before.

"Crysalline, are you feeling any better? It looks like something different's going on," Taggler asks nervously.

"The sun does seem kind of bright to my eyes. I felt kind of poor yesterday, and today it may be a bit worse," I say in muffled tones as I sit bending forward to keep the light out of my eyes.

"Sit right there and I'll bring you more tea and a biscuit."

Proem follows his dad's movements and his troubled questions, this after just waking from his own nightmare.

"Mom, what's wrong?" His voice wavers as he pushes out the words.

"I don't know, Proem. It'll be all right in time, I trust."

Taggler's back with the tea and biscuit. "Here, let's see if this helps."

I drink the tea in sips, and the familiarity is comforting. I feel like we're holding our breath, hoping for the tea to make everything better.

"I want to lie down for a while. Everything is harsh, and I can't get comfortable."

Proem looks back and forth at each of us, watching for some bit of relief from the swirling discomfort. Nothing comes better all morning as Taggler hovers over me. I can only lie down for a while, then get up and pace, trying to relax again but never finding comfort. Usually when someone gets sick, they slow down, but this is different. I can't get quiet to rest.

At midday, Taggler helps me to my feet and wraps me warmly so we can get to the village we passed just before we stopped for the night. He looks about to see what he might need to take with us, grabs the vial of tonic, and we walk the short distance to look for help. Asking a passing stranger, we are pointed to a shop that has medicines for both people and animals. The young woman inside smiles as we enter. I can't offer much of a smile in return and she takes some measure of me with a serious look on her face.

"We need to find out what to do for my wife," Taggler says to her, trying to keep calm.

She goes into another room and returns with an older man who walks slowly. He has big bushy eyebrows and long, thinning hair that floats gently in the air as he moves. He fixes his gaze on me as soon as he enters the room. I try to stay still even though I'm agitated.

"Sit down here, girl," he commands with a pale smile and no further introduction. He glances warily at Taggler, then notices the vial in his hand.

"What is that?" he asks.

"I don't know. We—I mean she, my wife Crysalline, was given this in another village for her health, to use to bring her good color and health. She hasn't been strong for some time, we were told this would help."

Instantly the old man tensed, standing straighter than before as he inhaled and clenched his hands into fists. "Was this a place where the people seemed strange in a way that you could not understand?"

"I guess that's true. We felt very uncomfortable there, so we left soon," Taggler answers.

"Give me that vial," he commands. He raises it to the light, then opens it with a cloth he pulls from his pocket and sniffs the contents.

"Did you put this on your cheeks for color and vigor?" he asks, knowing the answer before the words leave his lips.

"Yes," Taggler and I both say at the same time.

Every muscle in the old man's face drops, and his eyes fall to the floor as he shakes his head, pausing to breathe deeply before speaking again. "I'm afraid there is bad news for you. This thing you have been given was for your look to be colorful, and you have used a lot of it, as I see the vial is now almost empty. The people of that place, as we know of them, are people who live twisted lives. They live making everything look better but ignore how bad things come out of it.

You have come here, sick from that ignorance of theirs. You have been badly harmed by this," he says, holding up the vial in the cloth, shaking it as if he is shaking a fist.

"What? This can't be true, can it? Are you sure?" Taggler demands.

"I'm afraid it is very clear. Sadly, I am quite sure of this."

I sit unable to take in any bit of air at all. It's as if nothing anywhere can ever move again. Even the dust floating in the stream of sunlight has stopped. I slump with my head in my hands and look down at the floor while everything inside me swirls with nauseous disbelief. My sweet, happy life is now soured by strangers' lack of concern for us.

"Why would anyone do such a thing? What can we do now? What medicine do you have to stop this illness?" Taggler is spitting out words, throbbing with rage and pain.

"I'm afraid there is no cure. This vial was filled with Belladonna. It's known as a way to color the cheeks and brighten the eyes to look better for a while. It's evil on the face of it if taken very much at all, taking away so much more than it gives. Keep your wife quiet and out of bright light; that will help give comfort. You must ask for her very nature to heal and preserve her. That is the only way we know to heal."

His words sweep over the three of us, pouring into the open wound that is me, leaving no place to breathe. I can barely resist flying away, out of this nightmare, out of this life. Barely. I begin to gasp for breath, sobbing. The air has stopped moving and time with it, maybe forever.

The old man stays close, giving us a chance to find a way to carry on. A darkness has lashed out, breaking everything into pieces. After what seems like an eternity, the young woman returns with a pungent tea, the smell of which makes me feel even worse.

"Drink this if you can. I know itsn't not a pleasant idea, but it can be helpful to you to drink it all." He places his hand gently on the bottom of the cup to encourage me and, after some struggle with the awful smell, I get it all down in several terrible gulps.

"You are travelers, not from here. You may wish to stay here for a time. There is a place close by where you can stay. It's a widow's home and she's a caring person whose family has gone. I know she would be happy to have you."

"I, uh, we thank you, sir. We are grateful for the offer," Taggler manages.

I can only sit without words. Every breath is a harsh struggle.

Taggler's crouched beside me, touching his forehead to my thigh. I put my hand on his back and he gets on his knees and grabs at both Proem and me, sobbing. I move one arm to include them both and we sit, clutching at our lives that are oozing away with every minute. The old man watches, closing each hand in a fist and then relaxing it again. He motions to the young woman, who disappears out the front door quietly. The only sound left in the room is that of the bell on the door as it stops ringing when the door has closed again.

We sit in silence, lost together. Then the door opens again, and the young woman enters with the widow, whose kind face shows that she knows much and understands.

"I would like for you to meet Heth. She would like to have you stay with her."

Heth stands quietly beside the old man, with her hands softly folded in front of her. "I'm glad to have you come and fill my empty house. What are your names?"

The sound of her kind voice brings me back into the room and I wonder how to speak. I look up from where I sit. I hear Taggler's voice, blank and dry. "My name is Taggler, my wife is Crysalline, and our son is Proem."

She steps next to Proem, placing her hand on his shoulder. He gasps, as if shocked by her touch. She touches me gently on the shoulder, too, and I am somehow calmed. The old man smiles as best he can under the circumstances and clears his throat to excuse himself as he turns to leave us in Heth's care.

"We should go so you can see where I live, and you can decide if it seems suitable for you," she offers.

I stand up without knowing if I can, stumbling towards the door and the blinding light of the day.

"Here, dear, you should borrow my sun hat and use this gauzy cloth over your eyes. It may help." With that she places the gauzy cloth around my head, covering my eyes so I can barely see through it, and I feel relief from the smashing discomfort of what a fellow man has wrought upon me. Someone puts the sun hat on my head, and we continue out the door and a short distance to another door that she opens, letting us inside.

"Here, let me help you take those things off now. First, we must get you comfortable and then later we can get to know each other. Take a look around. I have plenty of room for you."

The front room, as I can see it, is cozy and well kept. There are several chairs waiting for us.

"I'll get some water hot for tea, and we can all settle in."

With that same gentle manner she moves to the iron stove at the back of the room. The rest of the afternoon we sit and she distracts us as best she can while I continue to suffer as silently as possible. Taggler stays mostly quiet, and Proem fidgets while looking around, at times walking around the room like a nervous cat, looking at the things that fill the spaces. I can do no more than hold as still as possible against the storm raging inside me.

She surprises us when she suggests that we all sit quietly like I learned with Jenna and Darry. This brings back a flood of good memories for me, even if I can't really do it. Her her words lead us away from the rage of what's happening, and we share a small moment of calm.

Supper appears as if by unseen hands for Taggler and Proem as the daylight fades. Inside my closed eyes, I imagine that the stars are out filling the darkened sky.

"You must stay at least for a while and find your strength."

"Thank you. That is most kind," Taggler answers.

None of us could argue the comfort of this quiet place with real beds as a refuge. Proem is fascinated by the mysterious things tucked in corners and shelves everywhere in the house. He likes the shelf of old books, wondering what they may hold. Finally, weariness overtakes him ,too. Taggler is beside me in bed but awake while I struggle to find sleep until, after some time, I find that refuge at last.

With morning I wake up as early as the birds and have to figure out where I am before remembering yesterday. Taggler is still in bed, awake, lying next to me. Proem is on a smaller bed beside ours, propped up on one elbow.

"What's to become of us, Taggler?" I ask.

"I don't know. We'll have to find out with time, I guess. But don't you try to figure out everything this morning. Please just let Proem and me do the worrying for now."

We get up and dress and Taggler helps me into the front room. I'm wobbly and disoriented. Heth is waiting for us and gives me a warm smile as she points us to the table. I catch the scent of hot tea in the air, and see the bread and fruit waiting beside the tea.

"How were your beds? Could you rest?" she asks as I stumble to a chair.

"They are good. Thank you for your kindness," Taggler says.

I still can't believe how she took us in so easily.

"I'm able to share this space with those who want to stay as long as they need. It's my offer as part of the village. Many people here help support me, and I find myself blessed with the way to help," she says, almost as if she knew what we were wondering. " The old man's name is Gliffindish. He knows much about the plants that can help us with your comfort while you are here."

She's speaking as if she knows what will be ahead. She turns to me as I sit quietly, still in a fog. "Dear, I know of these things. You are not the first to suffer this way, and I will help as best I know to get you through this."

I can only pretend to smile.

# CHAPTER TWENTY-EIGHT
# HELP

Through the darkness, I hear a voice. I don't know if it's day or night, or how many days have passed. "Hello, Crysalline. I brought you a broth. How do you feel this afternoon?" It's Heth's voice, somewhere close by. I remove the damp cloth from my eyes and find her standing beside the bed. The light from outdoors is trying to pierce my dark, safe shelter.

"I can't tell you anything for sure."

"Well, that doesn't matter for now. You've been here for three days and you need only to think about how wonderful it will be when you recover. Proem has another young man in the village, Whiligress, to spend time with, so they are outside."

I'm glad that Proem can spend time with a boy his own age. He needs that.

"That'll keep Taggler busy looking into what they're doing for part of the day, which may help him forget about some of this for a while."

Taggler tries to spend as much time as he can beside me in the darkened bedroom where I stay. If I'm not too fidgety, we can pretend life is somehow regular again, but it's impossible for me to feel normal at all.

Proem appears at the doorway; I hear his footsteps and strong breathing. I motion him to the bed to sit with me.

"Proem, are you having a good time with that boy?" I can't remember his name yet.

"Yeah, he's different but we just kick things around like he wants to do. We have fun enough, I guess."

"When I was a little girl, I loved using my imagination and roam around in the woods where I lived more than playing with other kids. My brother and sister weren't any fun for me. They wanted to stay indoors too much. My mother would sit outside our front door for a long time and look out over the hills, I guess watching changes in the weather. I wondered how she could spend so much time at the same place doing the same thing. You certainly are growing up differently than any of that."

"Sometimes I wonder what it'd be like to stay in one place for long, but then I'd miss all of the good things we have done. I like our way better."

There is a silent moment and then he asks the question. "Mom, are you going to get better?"

"I hope so, but sometimes I don't know for sure sometimes what's real or not. I need you and your dad to hold on to while we sort this out. Right now I think I'll just rest."

The world of waking dreams is crowding out the real daytime world I love and I can't do anything about it, much as I try. The past is mixed up with what might be happening right now. There are times when I don't know for sure what's just outside the door.

Gliffindish comes with special drinks for me. As Heth warms them, the air of the house thickens with their heavy, pungent scent. I begin to look forward to his visits since they give me the idea that we're doing some good. I have no choice but to put my trust in their wise hands. This is my only refuge.

***

Today, I'm less foggy than I've been. It holds for a while before things get mixed up again, then I get clear for a little bit, and then everything repeats.

Taggler is burning with questions. "Why doesn't someone go back there and put out warnings before others come to harm? The bad ways of those few have spoiled everything for us."

Heth watches as he flings out the words, not waiting for an answer.

"Believe me, that's been done several times, and then it is undone by the blindness that lives inside those people. We've told them what's come from the things they do, and yet it does not change. It happens again. They hold onto whatever they believe, no matter what," she says, knowing that her answer can not possibly quench his rage and frustration.

He slumps back on the chair, spent and sad, his frustration filling the room. He raises his eyes to meet Heth's. She meets his gaze with silent acceptance of his pain and frustration, for that is all there is.

After a quiet moment, she rises and moves to the stove to make a tea, and comes back to deliver it to my darkened room. She knows to leave Taggler alone for now.

Proem comes in from outside and stands inside the closed door, aware of the tense quiet that fills the place. He moves quietly to his dad's side and wraps his arms around his neck.

"Is Mom going to be all right?"

After the eternity of several moments searching for the answer, Taggler finds his voice to answer, whispering so I may not hear, but I do. "I hope so; we must wait to see."

There is nowhere to hide the pain anymore. They both break down, sobbing. As they gather themselves, I hear Taggler's voice again. "We have a big job now, Proem. We need to be strong to help your mom. We must try to accept what we don't want but is true anyway and do the best we can imagine. We must."

Proem keeps his arms wrapped around his father. Life is continuing in the village outside, but for us, the world is no longer moving.

My coughing has them come into the bedroom.

"Hi, Mom," Proem says, his voice cracking.

"Hi, dear one. How are you today?" I'll be the same mother he's always known as best I can for as long as I can, although I doubt I'm hiding the trouble that throbs through me. He sits close and I find his arm, encouraging him to come even closer, so he curls up at my side, as gently as he can.

"I want to get outside later, after the sun's down. I need to get out, somewhere outside. You men will have to tell me when that is. Can we do that, the three of us?" I ask as brightly as I can. I still want to be the three happy travelers we've always been, at least for this day, this moment.

"We can do that, Mom," he answers, looking up to see his dad who has quietly come closer, and is now standing on the other side of the bed. I have the sense that Taggler nods his head in agreement before he wanders back to the front room.

"Proem, much of your life is still to come, and your dad and I will always be a part of you. This sad thing that has come over us must be the reason to continue on. This is the only way we can see what more will come to us. As long as you're alive, you have your own desires and decisions to live into. That's the way we grow stronger and wiser. The kindness we have for each other can lighten our way, and we can live with whatever may come. It is truly the reward for everyone, even though it may happen beyond this time of ours."

I know he's listening closely as he always does. There will be choices coming in the times beyond mine when he becomes the keeper of our shared memories.

"All right, Mom. I hear you. Just rest for now, and we can talk more later."

The remainder of the day, he wanders in and out of my room. At times when I know he is there I ask him to lie down beside me, sharing the only moments we have: these, today. Who knows if this day will be a marker of our lifetime?

Taggler also comes in and out of the room, unable to be still. He says the sun has finally worn down into dusk, so the house begins to stir with activity as I repeat my wish to be outside. We all move out the door, and into the soft evening air.

"Crysalline, you are even more beautiful today than ever," Taggler says as we start out. I am held on both sides by my men, our arms intertwined. I take his words to heart, knowing how he means every part of it.

"It feels lovely out here. I feel the air on my skin. Let's go down by the river. I want to hear it."

We get to the river's edge with Heth following a few steps behind. We find a comfortable grassy spot close to the water and sit. Both of them snuggle close, strong posts holding me up. The sound of the river is as always, carrying life on into other places and times. I can hear our boats gently tapping against each other as they sway, tied up, waiting.

"This is our river, isn't it?" I say softly.

Taggler has his arm around my shoulders and I begin to slip into another place. I'm not sure where. I find that little wooden animal in my pocket and rub it. I'm the little girl who found it in the woods and it's my mine to touch whenever I want. The sound of the water reminds me of somewhere else. I shiver as the wind burns my cheeks.

Hold me. I can see a man's face inside my closed eyes, and I hope he is my love. Where am I? I can't breathe. I'm afraid.

The world turns cold, and I'm gone. I don't know where I am. I can't feel anything.

# CHAPTER TWENTY-NINE
# A BRANCH OF LIFE

Taggler is screaming through a thick fog. "Crysalline, Crysalline! She's passed out. I think she's still breathing. Let's get her back to the house."

Strong arms hold me and I'm floating. The sound of the river disappears, fading off behind. It seems like a long time and then the breeze is no longer around me.

Maybe it's Heth's voice that says, "Get her into bed and I'll be right there as soon as I can with hot compresses. Start rubbing her arms and legs."

I feel my limp body floating onto the bed. Maybe I'm surrounded with leaves. I can't be sure.

"Hurry, please," he yells loudly. It hurts my ears.

"The fire has cooled. I'll be there as quick as I can."

It's Taggler next to me in bed, cradling me close. I know the feel of him. He starts rubbing my arm. I'm so cold. Someone is rubbing my feet. I must try to take one more breath.

"Please go for Gliffindish. Maybe he has something that can help," Taggler urges.

Heth's hurried breathing is close, then her footsteps fade away and the front door slams shut, a harsh noise.

It's good to feel Taggler's warmth. He is life. His hands are rubbing, rubbing mine. I can't find any way to help.

The door opens again and I can hear Gliffindish and Heth as they come back into the room. I hear sobbing. It's his assistant Lethoritha, I think. She must be here too.

"What can we do? We must do more. Tell me what should we do?" Taggler's frantic words cut painfully through the room.

"I have nothing else now, Taggler. It's out of our hands," Gliffindish says.

Silence falls. I feel Taggler, still here. *It's out of our hands*. The air stings but somehow I must breathe. Somewhere far away there is the sound of my heart beating.

Mama's sitting on the porch, looking out at the distance, waiting.

The silky carpet of trees flows all the way to the top of the hill where they reach up to touch the sun marbled sky. Sweetness is everywhere. The smell of warm flapjacks is in the air. I'm wearing my sweater and it shines in the sunlight, while Papa hums at the stove. I'm going home. I'm happy.

Then there's another voice, loud and close to me. "We must keep her body working, that's the thing to do. I'll get into bed on the other side so we can all massage her arms and legs to keep her feeling us here." It's Heth.

"Yes, go ahead. Please do anything you can." Taggler's voice carries desperation.

Now she's on the other side of me, her hands rubbing me hard. It hurts.

Jenna's softly stroking my face as only she can. I've been missing her. Her loving touch is so comforting. I hear Proem somewhere. My little boy. He's yelling, Mommy! Mommy! Where are you?

I'm so tired. Let me sleep.

There are branches above me and leaves all around me. The leaves are bright and show their shadowy shapes on a wall. In one more breath, they change from green to gold, then they're gone and the tree branches look sad and bare. The shadow of a bird appears right over me. The shadow turns into a leaf and drops away. *How can this be?*

The empty branches have little tightly wound buds that begin to unfold. They are sticky, bursting with juicy sap. The lacy thin beginnings of leaves swell and change shape in a breath of air.

A bird calls. The scent of flowers arrives and I smile as I feel it flow straight through me. I'm on the front porch with Mama and drops of rain begin to fall, hitting the loose dust just beyond me with a muffled splat. I'm amused, just like when I was small.

A vine is crawling towards me. I watch as it curls to call me out into the fresh rain. I rise and go out, and the raindrops fall on me. I turn back to the house where my younger sister Adele is playing with her dolls just inside the doorway. She looks at me, annoyed.

She becomes a doll herself and now Raspartan is sitting beside her.

"You are to be living in the future, not the past. You will know what to do. Trust that. You must go alone on your way forward. There is no other way that will give you your life." He looks directly into me, smiling.

For an eternity I drift on the dark night air, watching the stars as they wink only for me. This must be the eternal sky.

Taggler and Proem are somewhere but I can't see them. I can only feel them.

Taggler is worried. Proem, too, and I know he's wondering what the future will be.

There are words, spoken by someone. "We are doing all that we can, Crysalline dear. We will hang onto you. Thank goodness for Heth and Gliffindish. I don't know what we'd do without them."

"And for, Mom, too," Proem adds.

I think that might be me.

A moment is passing but it moves so slowly I wonder which moment it is.

Hands bathe me softly with soothing, clean water. I don't know how long this has been going on.

I feel Heth and Lethoritha come closer.

"Crysalline, it's time for the tonic that Lethoritha has brought."

It's Heth's voice.

Hands pull me to sit upright and Heth has her hand behind my head. Lethoritha spoons some of the tonic to my lips. It smells lovely and my body wants it, so my lips part to take it in. I can swallow. I'm so happy.

"Taggler! Proem! Come in here. She smiled."

The rumble of footsteps on the floorboards is all I hear before they both hit the sides of the narrow door frame and burst into the room together.

"What did you say?" Taggler asks.

"She smiled. She smiled! She was taking the tonic Lethoritha brought today."

Taggler bends down at the side of the bed, stroking my arm and talking to me. It feels good and his voice is soft and smooth, something I remember. A teardrop falls onto my arm and he rubs the wet spot. I feel the water moving under his fingertip.

Everything is new. I'm flooded with new feelings. A fire inside somewhere warms me. I can begin to tell the difference between the many thoughts and feelings that have been lying in a pile, tangled. I can tell the difference between Taggler, Proem, and Heth's touches. It all is flowing through me. I feel like a tree standing silent. The thought makes me smile. Maybe I will sprout leaves soon.

"I saw it! I saw it! She smiled!"

I can feel the joy as Proem reaches out to hug someone. It's Lethoritha, and she's crying. She's spent a lot of time helping to heal me.

Joy is flowing all around.

I sense rather than see Proem kisses the angel he holds in his arms.

"We must start rubbing her again. Everyone start with one of her arms or legs," Heth commands.

Proem moves to my side, and I can feel his tears on my arm.

I'm ready to sprout wings. I try to wiggle my toes a bit. Every muscle hurts, but I think I did move a toe. I do it again to see if I can.

"I saw that, she wiggled her toe," Taggler shouts.

The sound hurts, but at least I know that I have ears. I try opening one eye a little, but the light hurts too much.

"Oh, hooray, my dear," Taggler shouts.

"Now we must give her time to find out for herself what she can do," Heth cautions, emotion rippling through her voice.

I smile again.

This is a new beginning. For months I'm pampered by Lethoritha's visits and Gliffindish's herbs. Everyone gives me so much special attention. I can open both eyes when the room is darkened in the daytime, but taking in solid food is hard for a while. Slowly, I become a living body again. I have no idea what has really happened or is part of a dream.

That will have to wait. Taggler and Proem smile at me from both sides of the bed most of the day. It's hard to sleep because my body is still jittery.

"You're very lucky to be alive, so you must take things slowly," Gliffindish says with a stern yet playful tone.

There's some impatience floating around, but slowly is the only way I can do anything.

After another month, I'm able to stand, walk, and talk slowly. A wide brim hat keeps the sun from my eyes, and we walk at a snail's pace around the village to help me heal. Our conversations never vary:

"How are you doing today, Mom? Are you getting tired?"

"Yes, a little, so let's only go a little farther."

"All right. And you could stop and rest along the way," Taggler says.

This is my life for now, working to regain some sense of normal. It's bearable, but I'm sad that it happened.

We spend the next two months at Heth's while Gliffindish's herbs continue to help me gain strength. I'm grateful for the medicines that are working. All of it comes straight from the world around us. I wonder what other helpful medicines there are yet to be found out there. The mysterious workings of nature have been taking care of our world before we people discovered much about the wonders of a flower.

Every time Lethoritha has come with medicine, I see Proem at her side as she watches me drink as much as I can. I see them both linger in the front room, sharing moments of tenderness. It warms my heart to see them beginning to discover the joy that Taggler and I found.

This afternoon Proem is sitting with me as I drift through the day, impatient but recovering as best I can.

"Mom, I still feel how lucky we are that you're really recovering."

"Yes, it's wonderful to feel alive again, and to see what's beginning for you and Lethoritha."

"It feels good to be with her, even if it's just breathing in the air around her. I guessed you'd notice. Dad's been asking questions too. I'm glad you think well of her. That means a lot to me."

"I do. I know how great I feel with your dad. I'm glad that you have time to get to know her," I say with a smile that is beyond words. "But for now, I really want to take a nap. We can talk more later."

"Of course. Rest well, Mom."

As I close my eyes, I hear his footsteps as he leaves the room. It's easy to drift off to wherever I want. A slight breeze touches me after a time, and I feel the warmth of someone close by. It feels like Jenna. I open my eyes and see Proem with Lethoritha right behind him. The look on their faces says so much. They both are lovely. She has her hand on his shoulder, and his hand is on the bed beside mine.

"Hello, you two."

Hearing my voice, Taggler appears and sits at the foot of the bed. "While you've been resting these months, life has been blooming out here," he says with a twinkle in his eye.

I look up at her, and she is glowing.

"It seems like you are good medicine for both me and Proem," I say.

"If it weren't for you, we wouldn't have met. That's certainly a blessing for us all to share."

I take Proem's hand while he holds Lethoritha's, and the four of us all join hands, connected to each other. Lethoritha tips her head to rest on Proem's shoulder. Nothing more needs to be said.

***

My recovery continues as does the blossoming around me. Lethoritha and I have times to sit together, quietly exploring each other's world. She's explained to me how Gliffindish and Heth became her guardians when she was orphaned as a small child and how Heth has been a real mother for her.

Fortunately, no other travelers have stopped in distress since we arrived. We have become a big happy family. As I sit in the sun this morning, taking in the warmth, Lethoritha sits down with me.

"You look lovelier every day, Crysalline."

"Thank you. I *am* feeling more like my old self again."

"I'm so much in love with all of your family. I want to know that everything is perfect for all of us."

"Lethoritha, this is a blessing for all of us. With us together, I have grown fond of this place."

She turns her face towards a distant shade tree and then back to me. As soon as she does, Proem and Taggler come out of the shade to walk our way. I see her face filling with joy as they come close.

"There's going to be a big celebration to join these two," Taggler announces with pride.

And it is the best celebration possible, with everyone in the village happy for the blessing of the couple and my recovery. It is mid-summer and a home is built for them with everyone's help. Taggler and I will stay with Heth, adding on a bedroom for ourselves and helping now that she is slowing down. Taggler's handy at fixing things around the place and we enjoy our time together.

***

There is so much more to tell now that everything has settled down. I know that my days on the river are behind me. Taggler and I have been out in the boat, but the motions are hard on my body. I can't imagine leaving Heth and want to help out whenever other unfortunate travelers may come along. I know what this is like and know I can be a comfort to them. This is my way to continue to be part of everything, my part of All That Is.

We love it when others pass this way unharmed, enjoying time together as they come along. Several times a year a group from this village goes back to that place and shares what joy we have, hoping that they will awaken to a gentler way. Time will tell as we continue to work with any new ideas to do what we can.

It has been two years now since Lethoritha and Proem were joined. It is becoming clearer by the day that Proem has an itch to continue on, and since Lethoritha has heard so much about our travels, she, too, wants to move along into their own adventures. I fear they will want to go sooner than I will be ready to see them leave, but maybe that is just the way it is. It will be a sweet sorrow to see them finally leave. Now I know some of what Jenna might have been feeling when I left. But holding them here would be to deny them their own lives and dreams.

I certainly have been blessed by finding and following the flow of my life. The wonders of learning and loving along the way is a grand reward for those fortunate enough to be so blessed.

To those of you who will find and follow your own river, my heart soars for you.

## About the Author

W. Lee Baker writes about those qualities that open the way for life to be more deeply rewarding; that provide real well-being, deep happiness, and a sense of harmony. *My Feet Don't Touch the Ground* is inspired by his life path and the discoveries and wonder found along the way in that search.

He has lived long enough to know more about the ways life can unfold. A life-long creative with a career in professional photography, he has found the gateway to write and share this novel. After career training in professional photography, further education came courtesy of the US Army with duty stations in Florida, Taiwan, and Vietnam. Life after that provided the usual choices of mate, family, and career, also casting life into personal experiences he was not be prepared for. This led to personal questioning and opportunities to learn and move beyond the static of how life may seem to be, to become a more mature, well rounded adult. Continuing to learn from challenges has provided joy and rewards of character never previously imagined. The quest continues to expand his horizons to become more personally expressive. He has found a personal voice for the printed word, beyond his familiar world and continuing rewards through photography, beyond the commercial world and into this continuing adventure. He lives in the San Francisco Bay Area with his wife Rebecca. They have four grown children and four grandchildren, some close and others in the Midwest.

Through this novel, he aims to inspire others to reach out to find the wondrous horizons for their own fulfilling lives. It can be a wondrous ride.

Instagram: wleebakerauthor; Facebook: W. Lee Baker-Author; and my blog site: www.wleebaker.com

Made in the USA
Las Vegas, NV
01 September 2021

29412526R00098